# ROCK MY SOUL

## RISING WIND
### BOOK FIVE

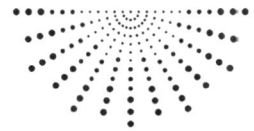

## DIANE OLSEN

# CONTENTS

*Rock-A My Soul* (also known as *Rock o' My Soul*) is an old-time spiritual based on Luke 16:19-31.

*Lyrics for 'Rock-A My Soul'*
*Rock-a my soul in the bosom of Abraham,*
*Rock-a my soul in the bosom of Abraham,*
*Rock-a my soul in the bosom of Abraham,*
*Oh, rock-a my soul!*

*I once was lost (I once was lost)*
*But now I'm found (But now I'm found)*
*And now my soul (And now my soul)*
*is Heaven bound! (Is Heaven bound!)*

*Rock-a my soul in the bosom of Abraham,*
*Rock-a my soul in the bosom of Abraham,*
*Rock-a my soul in the bosom of Abraham,*
*Oh, rock-a my soul!*

*So high you can't get over it,*
*So low you can't get under it,*
*So wide you can't get 'round it.*
*You gotta go in at the door.*
*Rock-a my soul in the bosom of Abraham,*

*Rock-a my soul in the bosom of Abraham,*
*Rock-a my soul in the bosom of Abraham,*
*Oh, rock-a my soul!*

*From the Making Music Fun Songbook

# ACKNOWLEDGMENTS

I couldn't have done this book without help from Valerie Inmee. Because of her consultation skills and editing experience, I was able to find a path to finish *Rock My Soul*. I also needed the help, encouragement, and expertise of three friends. Barbara Daniels Dena - my long-time buddy and author *For the Soul*, a collection of her life experiences. She brings humor and brightness to my life, which I treasure. Catherine Lyon is the author of *Addicted to Dimes* and is a Marketing Expert, but to me, she is a ray of sunlight, constantly picking me up, dusting me off, and making me laugh. J. Schlenker is also a prolific author and a constant source of knowledge and assistance. I am forever grateful for her assistance with formatting and uploading advice. Without these four women, my musings would never have taken shape. Thanks. You women are part of my "village" of literary best friends.

I'd like to thank three intelligent, knowledgeable, and courageous individuals for the parts they played in bringing this book to life. I am genuinely grateful to Mateo Arguello, an avid student of nature, for letting me use his outdoor experiences in the foothills and canyons surrounding Colorado Springs. His first-hand interaction with Sasquatches blows my mind. Glenn Norberg is a fountain of information for numerous Sasquatch sightings and contacts with other cryptid critters in the Florence and Canyon City areas of Colorado. You'll want to check out Mateo and Glenn's modernexplorer videos on YouTube. Finally, I'd like to acknowledge Heidi Cobblehof for her four eye-popping experiences. All three of these friends were so patient with my repeated questions. I hope they are pleased with the results.

Lastly, I'd like to acknowledge the photographic art Secora describes on Bill Hoffman's trailer walls. It is part of my collection of the works of William Munoz Photography, mostly taken around the Flathead valley.

# REFERENCE MATERIALS

* *The Advent of Asho Zarathushtra,*' Jamshed's story is told in Volume II, of The Saga of the Aryan Race

* *The Arctic Home in the Vedas*, 19 03 Bal Gangadhar Tilak, an Indian Journalist and educator, who lived from 1856-1920.

* The *Avestan* references to Yima are found in *Vendidad Fargard 2, Gatha 32.8, Yasna 9.4-5, and in several of the Yashts 5-19.*

*'*Baihu tongy,*' by Ban Gu of the Han Dynasty

*Gayomart/Q-mers *Gayomart, The Protoplast of Man*, (the translation of Tabari, Bal´amî, ed. Bahâr, p. 123)

*Glenn Norberg. Florence Colorado – Sasquatch investigator and collector of encounters.

"Those who are curious to find out more about these people can read the *Oxford*

**The Gods of the Egyptians* (1899) E. A. Wallis Budge

* History of the Prophets and Kings Tabari around 915 AD. "This is a universal history from the time of Qur'anic Creation, renowned for its detail and accuracy concerning Muslim and Middle Eastern history.

Tabari's work is one of the primary sources for historians, even today." http://en.wikipedia.org/wiki/Muhammad_ibn_Jarir_al-Tabari

* "The Heroic Age of Persia" - K. E. Eduljee, "In an effort to extract historical developments from the myths and legends, we will say that the Jamshidi age followed the age of Hooshang."

http://www.artarena.force9.co.uk/heroic1.htm)

*Introduction to Proto-Indo-European and the Proto-Indo-European World*, by Douglas Q. Adams and J. P. Mallory.

*The Legend of Haic*, a book about *Armenian Legends and Festivals,* written by Louis Boettiger in 1920.

* *Modern Explorer* - Mateo Arguello Modern Explorer mateo. arguello@modernexplorer.me

* *Myths from Mesopotamia: Creation, the Flood, Gilgamesh, and Others (Oxford World's Classics)* Stephanie Dalley, ed. and trans. New York: Oxford UP, Feb 15, 2009, Pg. 10 of 11; Pp. 25-26

* *The Peoples of Inner Asia*, Dr. Frank Bessac – My Professor at the University of Montana

*Primordial Creation* - From the *Avestan Yasnas* 9 through 17, Ferdowsi's epic poem the *Shahnameh* -and the *Bundahishn*, which is a collection of pre-Zoroastrian beliefs somewhat similar to Genesis in the Bible.

* *Prophet Ibrahim (Peace be upon Him)* This site is quite useful: Islam 101 –http://www.islam101.com/history/people/prophets/ibrahim.htm

* *The Saga of the Aryans*, by Porus Homi Havewala, 1995 A semi-fictional historical novel on the origins of the Aryan people, entitled

great Aryan tradition, deals with the lives of the ancient Indo-Europeans about twenty thousand years ago who proudly called themselves the Noble Ones.

*Saga of the Aryan Race: volume I of five books, Porus Homi Havewala - describes the Great Migration of the Aryan ancestors from their homeland in the Arctic Circle.

* *Tablets of Baha'u'llah*, p. 137 - The Tree of Life, the Holy Tree (Sadrat), is in a sense, 'a reference to the Manifestation of the One True God, exalted be He.'

* *Vendidad* - published in English 1898 ("Jamshid" http://en.wikipedia.org/wiki/Jamshid Quotations are from James Darmesteter's translation of the American Edition, of Max Mueller's *Sacred Books of the East*.

# LIST OF CHARACTERS

Alai Santiago - a sensitive and medium. Alas, last of her tribe due to a mudslide, Grandmother to Monta at request of her dead mother.

Aparu of Cliff City - Guero healer, married to Jane, father of their three children.

Bill Hoffmann - Grad student and cryptid photographer, son of Dan and Elena of Bonners Ferry.

Dr. Destiny Hawkins - New Dean of Social sciences.

Dr. Iris Snowden. Cultural Archaeologist, married to Kantun, has one child. Secora's sister.

Dr. Jane Roanhorse - PHD in anthropology and archaeology, Gideon's sister, mother of Kyah, married to Aparu, the have three younger children.

Dr. L.W. Dalton – Curator of South American Antiquities, wife of Sage, mother of Iris and Secora.

Dr. Sage Dalton – infamous anthropologist specializing in Human Religion. Father of Iris and

Secora – honorary Godfather of Jane Roanhorse.

Dr. Secora James – Paleontologist, teaches Paleontology and Archaeology classes at the university. Adoptive mother of Monta, married to Gideon.

Duendes - short on stature – long on courage

Garrett Mackay – canine search and rescue

Gideon Yellow Thunder: Lakota realtor at Treasuremont Realty. Has Thunderbird visions, some call him Heyoka.

Guanaco and Rocio - Kallawayas and dear friends of Alai, L.W., and Sage.

Jamal Hasan – Father of the loveable, Kamal Hasan, now deceased, and owner of the Resort property at West Glacier.

Jeannie Rutherford –most able secretary for Treasuremont Realty, a devoted and motherly friend of Gideon and Mitch.

Jimmy Lizardeye - Lakota Wichasha Wakan (holy man) Half Tewa (Pueblo). Gideon's mentor, and closest friend. Uncle and protector to an extended family. He served in Iraq.

Kantun of Cliff City - Guero herbal healer, married to Iris, father of their child.

Khiergan Sparks – Missoula County Deputy Sheriff. Works with Garret and Kyah in search and rescue.

Kyah Roanhorse - Jane's son, Gideon's nephew. Grad student working in Peru, Duendes friend.

Mitch Stevenson – Realtor, Assistant and close friend of Gideon, keeps him grounded and ever ready to help him out of trouble.

Monta James - Sensitive, Andean orphan, Secora's adopted daughter.

Raffique, Gullah, Sher Rahm and Manzoor Nadeem Agni of Termez their families. Kind, knowledgeable, and spiritual souls, proactive in water technology in the Afghan Karakum Desert.

Rocky Bernardillo - Excellent pilot of the Messerschmitt helicopter.

Tarkio Cyr – Best darn graduate student around. Husband of Anida and father of Frederick.

"Upon suffering beyond suffering; the Red Nation shall rise again and it shall be a blessing for a sick world. A world filled with broken promises, selfishness and separations. **A world longing for light again**. I see a time of seven generations when all the colors of mankind will gather under the sacred Tree of Life and the whole Earth will become one circle again. In that day there will be those among the Lakota who will carry knowledge and understanding of unity among all living things, and the young white ones will come to those of my people and ask for this wisdom. I salute the light within your eyes where the whole universe dwells. For when you are at that center within you and I am that place within me, we shall be as one."

Crazy Horse a colleague of Black Elk Quote: Source: https://quotepark.com/authors/crazy-horse/
The earliest publication of it dates back to 1980, by the Kahnawake Survival School in Quebec.

Birthdate: 1840 Date of death: September 1877 Crazy Horse, Ta Shunka Witco in Lakota, was a war leader of the Oglala band in the 19th century. He fought for the right to live on Sioux Nations territory, and deflect the encroachment of white settlers. He participated in several famous battles of the Black Hills War, on the northern Great Plains. The Fetterman Fight in 1866 in which he acted as a decoy, and the Battle of the Little Bighorn in 1876 in which he led a war party to victory, earned him great respect from both his enemies and his own people.

In September 1877, four months after surrendering to U.S. troops under General George Crook, Crazy Horse was fatally wounded by a bayonet-wielding military guard while allegedly resisting imprisonment at Camp Robinson in present-day Nebraska.

# SPIRIT BEASTS

Secora James ran from cave to cave on the Ennedi Plateau in Chad, thinking, *what am I doing here?* The formations which were part of the mesa she was racing across seemed surreal, like anthills or dung heaps. *How do I even know the water witcher is out here? I thought I heard a man scream, but maybe I just imagined it.* There was nobody in the first cave. Only the tracks of small rodents and the snakes that followed them. *Just two more to check.* Her mouth and throat were parched, and she prayed she wouldn't sprain an ankle as she ran through the difficult terrain.

Suddenly, she noticed she was not alone. *Where did these dogs come from? Why are they running with me like they know me?* They resembled thin pointers, or small greyhounds, with pale dun pinto spots on a mostly white background. Their eyes focused ahead as they ran between and around her legs. *I'm gonna trip for sure. Wonder what they eat or drink out here?*

Anthony, the tracker, had mentioned three caves near their job site. She cautiously approached the entrance to the second one, taking a moment to arm herself with a Maglite and a can of pepper spray from her belt. The dogs stopped in their tracks, listening. Then they moved forward wagging their tails in a playful manner. *That's a good sign.*

"Hello, anyone there? Mosa? Hello?"

She hoped she was in the right place, that this was the Shadow Cave, the lair of the strange cat that had been picking off calves and young camels from the flocks of the wandering Toubou nomads.

There was only silence, and shimmering heat. Secora rallied, and stepped inside the cave entrance playing the flashlight around, and illuminating the small room. There were large bones mixed with the cave dust, but they were not human – and they were not recent remains. She called again, "Mosa? Anyone in here?" She listened intently for a response. Could she hear the water witcher's faint voice? She shook her head and turned, and left to visit the third and final cave.

In the distance, a dust cloud drew her eyes. Squinting, through a sandstone arch, she thought she saw her husband, Gideon Yellow Thunder, and her grad student, Tarkio Cyr in a jeep headed toward the base of the formations of twisted rocks - many of which resembled mushroom caps, or cloaked stone-people on top of the mesa. She imagined it would take them several minutes to race up to her position.

What she *did not* expect was the humongous tiger materializing from behind bushes not ten feet directly in front of her. The cat was longer than the distance between them. She slowly replaced the Maglite on her belt. Its eyes were calculating her every move, waiting for Secora to flinch.

That wasn't going to happen. No chance for escape. Secora stepped forward lifting the camera from around her neck. She was fascinated by this beast, a relative of the great saber-toothed cats of the past. Its shape was more like that of a cave hyena, taller in the shoulders, a sloping back, shorter back legs and a stubby tail. Most notably, its canine teeth were flattened, and only protruded a few inches beneath the lower jaw. They weren't quite as long or round as the ones on Smilodon, or a bull walrus skull. This animal was extremely large, and had short reddish-brown fur with vertical white stripes. She couldn't see any black stripes like on a Bengal or Siberian tiger. Long fur surrounded its toes and padded the feet. She guessed it helped the animal to walk more easily across shifting sand, or to protect its toes from sharp rocks.

The phrase "scimitar toothed cat" popped into her mind as she snapped several photos.

The mechanical noise made by the automatic film advance caused the beast to blink, and the dogs, emboldened by that reaction and her advance, backed up Secora's legs with low growls and exposed teeth. They stepped toward the beast in a stalking manner. The unanticipated results were more than the cat could take. It wheeled and sprang down from a pinnacle, disappearing about thirty feet below their position.

"Secora, wait." The guys were catching up fast. The dogs whirled around and yelped a sharp warning.

Gideon pleaded, "Weah Witco," Crazy Woman, in Lakota. "What are you doing in that cave?"

"I think the water witcher is up here somewhere. I heard a voice, sounded like he was calling for help. I'm sure it was Mosa."

Anthony, the team tracker and translator, said, "Not likely, madam. Unless he is in the kingdom of the unseen. Only the voices of the dead are carried through these rocks by the caressing winds – You can hear them all around this area."

She sighed. "I can understand that, but Anthony, whose dogs are these? They can't live out here alone."

Everyone became quiet. Eventually, Gideon gently asked, "Dogs? What dogs...?"

Secora looked around with increasing concern, then seeing no dogs, fainted.

She roused back at camp thinking she'd had an awful dream. Gideon, Tarkio and Anthony anxiously surrounded her.

"What happened?" she asked.

Gideon responded gently, "You fainted, dear."

"Where is the water witcher? Is Mosa ckay?"

Anthony responded, "He must be around somewhere."

Secora said plaintively, "No, I heard his voice calling for help, very faint at first, but clearer as I closed in on the second of the three caves you told us about. There was nothing inside the first one except for the tracks of small rodents and snakes. At the second cave entrance I heard a faint voice, but saw only a few dried antelope bones. When I turned around to get to the last cave, a mountain tiger stepped from behind some shrubs and would have attacked me if it wasn't for those snarling dogs that were protecting my legs."

"The animals must have been in your imagination," Anthony smiled.

Secora felt his smile looked a bit patronizing. "I'm not sure exactly how large this cat was, but I took pictures – even though I won't be able to develop them until I am back in my lab. If it wasn't just a spirit beast, there should be a clear image of an ancient tiger that looked about eleven feet long, and it stood as tall as my chest."

"I believe there are tales of a legendary Ennedi Tiger. But it is a spirit beast. So don't be too surprised if nothing shows in the photo but rocks."

"Fine, but we still have to go back and check out that third cave."

Anthony cautioned, "Not interested. Those caves belong to the spirit cat."

Tarkio asked, "What are these dogs you're talking about?"

She didn't feel like answering that question - as concern for Mosa was her priority. "Has anybody heard from Mosa since I left for the caves?"

Tarkio said, "Not that I know, but maybe he left to go home since he had staked out all of the areas that were above subterranean aquifers."

Gideon agreed, "That makes sense. I doubt anyone would stay here after their part was done. Raffique even left for Afghanistan yesterday after he finished setting up the collectors at the wadi."

"But," Secora queried, "Can anyone confirm that Mosa went home?"

Her persistent concern prompted a trek with the others to the third cave. There they found Mosa's torn robes, and bones mostly cleaned of flesh, among the vestiges of camels and calf heads. Remembering the large cat, Secora felt forlorn, realizing she probably couldn't have saved his life even if she had made it to the third cave. Suddenly she flashed on the image of the comfort and joy of eating breakfast at a restaurant. It had been one of Mosa's favorite occasions, rare, and to be savored. The image made her smile, a comforting contrast to the way she felt inside while looking at what was left of her friend's mortal remains inside the cave. *Mosa? Is this you trying to keep me from being morbid?* She smiled. *It would be just like you. Safe passage, my friend, Go with God.*

On the way down the rocks carrying poor Mosa's remains, Anthony explained that although he'd always believed the Ennedi Tiger was a spirit beast, there *were* persistent legends of cave dwelling cats, mountain tigers in the Tibesti and Ennedi mountains. "It was supposedly larger than a lion, perhaps twelve feet long, with short reddish-brown fur marked with vertical white stripes."

Secora responded, "Well, they are more than spirits if they are stealing animals from the Toubou at the drinking wells, and are willing to attack people during the light of day."

Once back at camp, Gideon pleaded with Secora to rest, while he, Anthony, and Tarkio finished securing the self-contained turbines and net structures over the aquifers.

She agreed, and found the spot the team used for Wi-Fi connectivity. There she located an article which described the scimitar tiger having unusually long protruding upper fangs, quite visibly dropping below the lower jaw. Its short reddish fur was marked with white vertical stripes, stubby tail and long fur on the paws. It was big, running 425 – 993 pounds (200 – 450 kg), and strong enough to carry off large antelope. Encounters had been mostly nocturnal, although confrontations in broad daylight had been recorded. This description linked the animal to the prehistoric Sabretooth. *Tell me something I don't know.*

Reports mentioned two different species. One inhabited the mountains of Chad and the Central African Republic, also possibly Libya, Sudan, and Uganda. This beast was called by several names: Hadjel, Gassingram, the Vossoko or Vicago. The latter, according to regional folklore, was followed by clouds of butterflies. She paused, *Okay, that's new.*

The folklore of river people throughout the southern half of Africa spoke of a second, very fierce riparian species called Mourou N'gou,

Mamaimé, or Dilali. They came in three color patterns: red with white markings comparable to mountain tigers, leopard spots interconnected with the stripes, or plain brown. This water tiger was also larger than a lion (8–12 feet). Its teeth were compared to a bull walrus, and the tail was always long in the reports. The claws were also long. The tracks were much larger than those of a lion, and had a strange circle in the center. The southern varieties were described as amphibious, nocturnal, and living in caves along the river.

Western witnesses noted that they ate hippos, stole hunter's trophies, and capsized boats. *Almost sounds like a giant river otter.* She closed the laptop and got a bottle of water. *Any way you look at it, these animals and humans don't make good neighbors.*

*Toubou nomads congregate at the "Well of the Young Girls" in the Ennedi Mountains of northeastern Chad, Central Africa - David Stanley from Nanaimo, Canada Checked copyright icon.svg by D-Stanley at https://flickr.com/photos/79721788@N00/24117104102. and was confirmed to be licensed under the terms of the cc-by-2.0.*

## 2
## A CRY FOR WATER

Secora, Gideon, and Tarkio had flown into Africa to join this water project, inspired by Sher Rahm and his brother, Gullah, friends they met in Afghanistan, along with Raffique and Manzoor. These young men were kind, highly educated, and extremely spiritual souls – looking to expand water technology in the Karakum Wilderness. The crew from Montana was able to supply funds and equipment, and together, they successfully extracted water from the night air of the desert.

Sher Rahm and Gullah were currently planning to participate in an experiment sponsored by a major charity in Chad. The plan was to find out if larger amounts of water could be collected above underground streams, in an uninhabited area north of the town of Fada. The Afghani brothers had invited the Missoulians, because they had already worked well together in Afghanistan.

If successful, this project might benefit the refugees, nomads and flocks passing through the Ennedi Mountains and Plateau. It was a sub-Saharan sandscape decorated with sandstone peaks, cliff-sided mesas, and upright columnar formations that at times resembled shrouded humans, mushroom rocks, natural arches, or giant labyrinths. Until now, there had only been isolated water catchments – but many were shrinking or disappearing altogether.

Gideon and Secora, along with Tarkio, now found themselves in the BET (the Borkou, Ennedi, and Tibesti region), which occupied a full third of Chad's territory, but supported only 5.8 % of its population. Most of these people were refugees from Sudan and Libya, but there were also the nomadic Toubou or "rock people", composed of two tribes, the Teda mostly in the northwest, and Daza further south and east. The Daza area was home to a cruel president who took power in 1979 – a fact which immediately deterred half of the water project's applicants.

Gideon and Secora donned head coverings made for them by Noori, Manzoor's kind sister back in the Karakum Desert last summer. She had designed head coverings specifically for each of them. They sparkled and jingled with Raffique's glittering metal trinkets.

Secora glowed as she put on the beautiful red and cream-colored scarf and shook her head. She heard the tiny clinking of miniscule bells which had been sewn on. Gideon looked wonderful in his single tiered cap that had a dark taupe background with a black squiggle outline, a gold star design, and little pieces of mirror sewn in. Tarkio covered his head with a towel and a Montana Grizzly cap.

As they entered the arid Ennedi, they were lucky to spot a trio of rare, desert-adapted crocodiles lounging near a small pond. If there were any fish, Secora thought they couldn't be very big. She wondered if they were scanning for thirsty herds of regal, shaggy-legged aoudad, or Barbary sheep.

Unfortunately, the area had sustained excessive poaching and resource extraction by international interests, notably East Asian, which threatened the lifestyles of nearly 30,000 members of the nomadic tribes who had lived in the area for thousands of years.

Recently, several charities were attempting to protect them with strong community-based conservation management. Over 500 plant species clung to life here and there around upwelling underground rivers, or water catchments, but the current goal was to start sustainable, drip irrigated groves of olive trees, crops of corn, and melons.

Three types of environments had been selected for the water project. The first was a sandy wash between cliffs where sparse brush was already established. This was the place Raffique and Gullah had chosen to work. The second was in the weird hills which rose twelve feet above a hidden stream. This was where Tarkio, Secora and Gideon were working along with Anthony and Mosa. The third was a control station, set up by Sher Rahm, where no water had been detected underground. The areas were separated by several miles, so communication between sites was sparse. The work was difficult, and the temperature was hot – almost stultifying.

But now, since the death of Mosa, the water witcher, things naturally came to a halt. It was too late in the day to take his remains to Fada, so the crew sat to plan an impromptu funeral for this solemn man, an Islamic servant of God. Gideon called his friend and holy man, Jimmy Lizardeye, a Lakota Wichasha Wakan on the Satfon for his sacred contribution, while Anthony prepared to recite the Moslem funeral prayer, Salat al-Janazah. Secora carefully collected a few wildflowers, being careful not to damage future seed production. When they were ready, Tarkio encouraged them to arrange themselves around the deceased to begin the eulogy, and prayers. Secora praised their coworker and friend, then Anthony stepped forward and began to chant.

"Bismillah, O God, forgive our living and our dead, those
who are present among us and those who are absent, our
young and our old, our males and our females. O God,
whoever You keep alive, keep him alive in Islam, and
whoever You cause to die, cause him to die with faith. O God,
do not deprive us of the reward and do not cause us to go
astray after this. O God, forgive him and have mercy on him,
keep him safe and sound and forgive him, honor his rest and
ease his entrance; wash him with water and snow and hail,
and cleanse him of sin as a white garment is cleansed of dirt.
O God, give him a home better than his home and a family
better than his family. O God, admit him to Paradise and

protect him from the torment of the grave and the torment of Hell-fire; make his grave spacious and fill it with light.'
Asalamu 'Alaykum Warahmatullah, may the peace and mercy of God be unto you."

As he finished, Tarkio offered, "La ilaha ila Allāh". "There is no God but Allah".

Jimmy Lizardeye chanted a Lakota Prayer over speakerphone. Though no one else could see it, he slowly drew out the sacred pipe from its beautiful and intricately beaded bag, revealing the polished red stone bowl and two owl feathers hanging from a beaded suede strip that encircled the stem, then began:

"I offer the 'Between Worlds' prayer on behalf of my dearest friends. Hey-a-ho. First, I offer this pipe to Wakan Tanka, the Great Spirit who is One." He raised the pipe with both hands toward the sky. "Behold this sacred pipe. Behold us on this sacred earth. O Wakan Tanka, you are our Father, and Grandfather. You are everything. You have always been." Jimmy took a braid of sweet grass from a pouch, but did not light it. Its perfume, however, graced his room.

"Grandfather, this is your herb, its fragrance belongs to you. Behold the good young man before you. He suffers between worlds now. I beg of you to cause him to move toward you, as is your will. Be merciful. Help him."

He offered the pipe to the Earth. "Our Grandmother and Mother, you are sacred. Every step upon you should be taken as a prayer. It is from you that our bodies come. Help this brave man. He wishes to be one with all things. He serves the good of all your peoples, the four-leggeds, the two-leggeds, the green things, and the wings of the air. Help him."

Jimmy turned his feet to the west. "I now beseech the four directions to help this man. First to you, O winged Power from where the sun goes down. Send your servants, ancient and sacred. The Thunder Beings who come to us in the terrifying storm. Send us your two sacred red and blue days. Help him."

He then turned to the south, the east and the north, similarly beseeching aid for Mosa. Finally, Jimmy announced "Hetchetu aloh. It is finished."

Secora began the Baha'i Prayer for the Departed...

*"O my God! O Thou forgiver of sins, bestower of gifts,*
*dispeller of afflictions! Verily, I beseech Thee to forgive the sins*
*of such as have abandoned the physical garment and have*
*ascended to the spiritual world.*

*"O my Lord! Purify them from trespasses, dispel their sorrows,*
*and change their darkness into light. Cause them to enter the*
*garden of happiness, cleanse them with the most pure water,*
*and grant them to behold Thy splendors on the loftiest mount."*

Gideon placed the delicate flowers on the makeshift coffin. The entire funeral was videotaped by Tarkio to be sent along with the remains, which would be escorted by Anthony to Mosa's elderly relatives.

After the finishing touches on the water project were complete, the remaining crew including Secora, Gideon and Tarkio, stayed to help transplant the olive tree seedlings, and plant melons and corn. Perhaps the area would earn its nickname, "Eden of the Sahara".

Afterward, Tarkio lingered with the planting crew, while Gideon patiently took Secora on a side trip, to allow her the opportunity to check out some of the prehistory of the region. He doubted they would be back in the area any time soon. There were a few spectacular pictographs in the region, globally significant rock art, that contained contributions from as far back as 14,000 and as recently as 2,000 years ago. She wanted to study them in person while she had the chance.

They found a cliff displaying paintings made through time by various types of people. The images recorded several types of humans, horses, cattle, goats, deer, and camels. Artists from the different eras used distinctive "paints," and they didn't hesitate to cover earlier scenes. The oldest figures were ashy gray, probably made with charcoal. Others were tinted with red and brown ocher. There were more recent depictions of white camels which overlaid some of the other compositions. She noticed two or three possible catlike figures with long tails near the bottom, toward the right.

As she pored over the drawings, then photographed and sketched them, Gideon patiently sat in the shade of the jeep.

*He's probably thinking about going home.* Secora was keenly aware that Monta, their adopted daughter, and grandmotherly Alai, the last woman of her tribe, would be waiting for them. Kyah would still be working on his excavation in Peru. This was a trip he'd taken with other archeology students who had been selected from universities across the western states, to broaden their understanding of the Americas. While he was in South America, Kyah also wanted to share water capture techniques with friends in the settlement of Bosque Alto. Gideon had smiled with pride at the thought of Kyah's continued help and support for both the Duendes, whom he thought of as short in stature and long on courage. The little people lived on the cliff edge, and their regular sized neighbors lived on a hillside meadow below.

Recently, his friend and chopper pilot, Rocky Bernardillo, had sent Kyah ominous photos of a drought. The land around Bosque Alto was changing. It looked drier and more desolate than before. Rocky mentioned that very few of the chickens they'd dropped off as a gift at the end of their last visits had survived. And those few struggled daily to evade desperate predators. The people had applied for trees to plant a protective ring around the village, but it would take years to get them to flourish – and for that, they would need water. Kyah and Rocky had brought equipment to share Gideon's water capturing options with the big and little folk. He hoped to check in with them, and find out if their situation was improving.

Secora knew that Gideon longed to talk to his nephew. He missed knowing the boy was close by. At times his heart ached, and he wished he could call. Instead, he wrote extensive texts that the boy would receive when he reached a Wi-Fi location. What was she thinking? Kyah was no longer 'a boy,' he was now twenty years old, having had his birthday while he was away. He'd turned into a wonderful young man whose life held limitless potential, and was dearly missed during his first away trip. They couldn't wait to see him when he got back.

Secora approached her husband with a satisfied grin. "Thanks for bringing me." She reached for his hand and gently kissed his cheek. She could see that he'd just sent another text. When he looked up they agreed it was time to leave – they were finished here.

Manda Guéli Cave in the Ennedi Mountains, northeastern Chad. These prehistoric rock paintings are in Manda Guéli Cave in the Ennedi Mountains, Chad, Central Africa. Camels have been painted over earlier images of cattle, perhaps reflecting climatic changes.

*By David Stanley from Nanaimo, Canada - Prehistoric Rock Paintings, CC BY 2.0, https://commons.wikimedia.org/w/index.php?curid=51016097*

## 3

# A SINGING HEART

Kyah Roanhorse was thinking of his family and friends as he packed his few belongings and prepared to leave the Peruvian excavation site. This six-week dig had been a remarkable success, and Kyah had honed new skills, especially in regards to using ground penetrating radar. With its aid, they were able to locate houses and storage facilities in what at one time, had been a Pre-Incan habitation site.

His assignment to the dig crew also allowed him the opportunity to visit old friends in Bosque Alto. Kyah visited his buddy, Rocky, a capable ex-military chopper pilot he met on his first trip when his mom and Auntie Iris had hired Rocky to access the remote mountain region, in his vintage Messerschmitt, giving Kyah his first eagle-eye view during the flight over a beautiful highland patchwork, dotted with llamas and alpacas.

After his visits, he would eagerly return to the University of Montana to finish his studies. His plan was to follow the path of his mother, Dr. Jane Roanhorse, who had taken him to a dig she'd overseen a few years ago, while he was still a high school student.

During that excursion, she'd met and married Aparu, a wise Guero healer. He and his friends rescued Kyah, Jane, his Auntie Iris, and the other archaeology students who had been captured by a group of rene-

14

gade guerilla soldiers in the high jungle. The Gueros whisked them to the safety of their hidden Cliff City.

Now, Aparu, a kind and gentle man, was Kyah's stepfather, and the father of Kyah's three younger siblings. The entire family had bloomed since he'd joined them in South Dakota Thinking of the children, Kyah smiled, *in more ways than one.*

It was time to leave. He filled his lungs with the fresh cool air as he hopped on the transport that would take him and the other students to a small town where they could catch busses to continue their journeys. As the craggy road unfolded, Kyah secretly wished he never had to leave this gorgeous land. This part of the world was beginning to feel like home. So different from the semi-desert land he'd been familiar with as a child.

He did most of his growing up in rural Pine Ridge, South Dakota, with his mother, Jane, and his grandmother, Ursula. When he was twelve, his estranged father, Robbie, drank excessively and was physically abusive to his mother. One night he started swinging and knocked Jane completely off the porch, then he went to where she lay on the ground, and punched her unconscious. That was a breaking point, Kyah couldn't take it anymore. He tackled Robbie as the fierce man beat his mother. He was too small to help much, but he jumped on his father's back and tried to choke him off.

God bless their closest family friend, Jimmy Lizardeye, a troubled war veteran who had served in Iraq. He knew the struggle with the drunk wouldn't end well for the boy, so he pulled himself together and knocked Robbie out cold. That night Jimmy saved Kyah's little family. He firmly helped Jane up and into the house, while Kyah called 911. Grandma Ursula locked the door and they all waited for the police and an ambulance. That marriage was no more. Kyah fidgeted at the uncomfortable memory.

Jimmy was half Tewa and grew up in the gentle hill country of New Mexico with its small enchanted red and white sand canyons. He was spiritually gifted and would have become a healer there; but after his father passed away, Jimmy's mother chose to raise him on Pine

Ridge, where she grew up. He'd remained there until he was called to duty.

The transport hit a huge rut and the driver got out to make sure they hadn't popped a tire. Close call, and the vehicle would need an appointment for an alignment, *if they even had those here.*

When they were underway again, Kyah's mind drifted. It was hard to believe that he and his mom had found Jimmy, then a distraught wanderer, watching the buffalo over by Porcupine Creek. His eyes looked empty and cold after he returned from Desert Storm. He'd wandered around Pine Ridge for days, weeping constantly over two Kurdish villages that had been gassed. Humans, animals, and birds lying where they fell. It was an ugly death.

Kyah and his mom could see he was filled with a deep, unhealed sorrow. Jimmy was broken, he'd suffered humanitarian tragedies in Iraq he couldn't resolve. They didn't want to leave him alone in that state. He might do something crazy like maybe challenge the buffalo, thinking life wasn't worth continuing.

Jane and Kyah brought him back to the trailer to rest. That was one of the best things that ever happened to their family - finding Jimmy. They kind of adopted, and cared for him. That became an amazing turning point in all of their lives. Jimmy Lizardeye became an "uncle" and protector for an extended family. Now he was a noted Lakota Wichasha Wakan, one of the smartest and funniest holy men anyone had seen in a long time - once he broke out of his malaise.

After a rough start with Jane's brother, Gideon, Jimmy became his mentor and closest friend. Gideon had really stepped up as an uncle in recent years, even though he had been distant in Kyah's early life. The two had grown very close in the last few years, and Kyah adored his wife, Secora James, who taught classes in both paleontology and archaeology at the university. Together Gideon and Secora adopted Monta, an Andean orphan, as their daughter.

Until his life was changed by Jimmy, Gideon Yellow Thunder had stayed far from reservation life in Missoula, Montana, where he worked hard to build a real estate company.

After his shady partner at Treasuremont, was eaten by a thunderbird, the business morphed into a successful realty team. Besides him, it featured his two inseparable friends as equals. Jeannie Rutherford was a most able secretary, and devoted motherly friend of Gideon and Mitch. Mitch Stevenson was a fine realtor, assistant, and Gideon's close friend who kept him grounded. Mitch was always ready to help him out of trouble.

Mitch and Jeannie had stuck with Kyah's uncle through ups, downs, even deadly events that cropped up in his uncle's life since he realized his telepathic connection with Wakinyan Tonka, the great thunder being. Kyah had actually seen the thunderbird. After her death, he and his enlarged family circle had welcomed her daughter – White Feather, into their lives and hearts. *That was amazing!*

LATER THAT EVENING, Kyah left the transport vehicle with a few other students. He gratefully ate pupusas, at a home that had placed a picnic table out front to serve others. Afterward, he was lucky enough to catch a late bus to the ferry, where he could cross the lake for a brief visit to Isla del Sol in the morning. Before heading home, he would spend a day and a night visiting old family friends Rocio and Guanaco. They were Kallawayas, savvy angels ministering to the needs of many with calm and peace in their hearts. They had been lifetime friends of Guillermo, also a Kallawaya, until his passing, and they saw Alai, daily, until she left for Missoula, where she had recently moved with little Monta.

Forty years ago, Guanaco had befriended Sage Dalton, Secora's father, who also seemed like a grandfather figure to Kyah. The Kallawaya even went on a trip to India with Dalton and with another friend Eliot Stearns, a BBC correspondent. Their plan was to return a tiger's eye mala to the Dalai Lama after he fled Tibet. Rocio and Guanaco had since come to be known as the guardians of the ancient *Book of Hope*.

Now this wonderful couple and Sage and his wife, L. W., were getting up in years, and Kyah treasured each moment with them and with Jimmy. All of his other elderly relations had passed and he cherished the moments he spent in their presence.

DAWN over the lake had been serene as Kyah boarded the ferry from Isla del Sol to La Paz, Bolivia. He would miss the Kallawayas, and also hated to leave his buddy Rocky, and the people of Bosque Alto. His heart begged him to return to Peru and Bolivia as soon as he finished his degree. He was determined to make this region his home.

It wouldn't be long now before he would hug his Montana family, but on a whim, he decided to stop off in Jamaica for an exciting two-night stay. Who knew, maybe he might meet a pretty young woman there.

# 4

# DAZZLING VISITATIONS

The Missoula team was ready to fly home. It would be fifteen hours travel time, not counting a four-hour layover in Chicago, but to Secora felt like forever. During the layover, Tarkio and Gideon were already dozing and Secora's eyes were drooping, but suddenly they opened too wide as a cheerful older woman introduced herself as Heidi Cobblehof.

Not knowing what to do but smile when the lady sat in the open chair beside her, Secora turned her full attention on the woman who began to regale her with fascinating stories of UFO's, clones, and lizard men.

Heidi's eyes sparkled and her curly white hair glistened, as she opened with an account from years ago in Colorado Springs. "My friend and I were on our way to a 'goodbye dessert party' at Fort Carson Military Base, Saturday evening, November second, 1963. It was a social function to honor the GIs heading out to Vietnam. We drove from Peterson Air Force Base to the south end of the Springs, when we became lost. We'd looked for the proper dirt road exit to Fort Carson for about an hour, before we pulled over. The clock on the dashboard read 10 p.m.

"Our vehicle was parked facing west, across the street from the northeast corner of the base perimeter wall, near a railroad crossing. I asked my girlfriend to hand me the map, and snap on our flashlight. The whole interior of the car lit up and I remarked how strong that little light was - much stronger than I anticipated. She told me in a nervous voice that she hadn't turned it on.

"I looked up from the map. Across the road, at eye level, just in front of us, was an airborne triangular shaped vehicle hovering twenty yards away, even though it appeared to be much closer. The vehicle itself was around twenty-five feet long and eight or nine feet tall with a large window that covered most of that expanse.

"Three clones appeared to have identical East Asian facial features, bowl cut black hair with bangs, and brown-yellow skin. They were wearing dark gray Nehru jackets with short upturned collars, and were seated at control desks with panels, concentrating on their work, I supposed that they controlled the flying triangle. Now, they were looking out the windows of the cockpit at the center of the triangle – at us.

"Between the two clones on the left, stood a thin seven-and-a-half-foot tall individual with a praying mantis-like head, shaped like a slice of pizza from which the first third had been bitten off. He had brown hair, but I don't remember much of a mouth or nose. Long arms hung to his knees and he donned a doctor's white lab coat complete with a stethoscope. I got the impression he had a cold personality. No empathy.

"To the right of the 7 ½ foot bug, stood a six foot two-inch-tall man who appeared to display Nordic qualities – extremely pale skin and light blonde hair. He wore a light gray uniform that might have signi-fied an engineer or a commander, with a medallion hung around his neck. He seemed kinder. He then turned his head and talked to the bug man."

"Well, that's different," Secora managed. She could feel Gideon rousing beside her and noticed Tarkio was listening intently.

"That's nothing. Next, I felt that I was somehow mentally trans-ported to the vehicle, and a scan of all that I knew was taken.

"Later, I realized I was back in my vehicle and I looked at the dash clock, it read 10:18. I looked across, at the ship's window. The Nordic in the grey uniform waved and smiled in a friendly manner, I waved back and smiled. It seemed I knew him, had seen him before – not now, but at a different time - earlier that night. We had communicated before this - likely a mind probe. I knew this was goodbye.

"The tall bug individual bent over and looked out the window. I was not surprised that this praying mantis person had no feeling for me. I knew I wasn't of value. To him, I was worthless. There was no smile or wave. Then he stood up again and a large screen rolled up covering the entire window.

"The spotlight turned off, and they sped toward the entrance of the underground facility at Cheyenne Mountain, where they again turned on the light. The window rolled open as they paused to view or scan the thick metal doors of the North American Air Defense Command. The light illuminated a fifty-foot swath above the doors to the entrance and the surrounding concrete road. It felt as if my mind was still captured by the ship even though my body was still in the car. I saw the scene as if I was still in the craft.

"Next, I could see the silver-gray color of the triangular ship, distinguished from the surrounding mountain. Quickly, the vehicle closed its window and turned off the spotlight before rotating upward, then it shot westward. In a flash it disappeared over the top of Cheyenne Mountain. Gone in a split second - super fast!

"I lost connection with the ship as it shot over Cheyenne Mountain, and again found myself seated in the car. My car's engine was no longer running nor would it restart for some time. To say the least, my friend and I did not go on to the goodbye party. We were petrified and went home. She never said she was transported to the vehicle, only that she saw it. But she was so shaken by the events that she would not discuss her feelings with me. She did talk later with her stepfather who was a master sergeant in the Army. He counseled her never to speak of those events. And she never did as far as I know."

As an aside she added, "I checked later to see that I still was a virgin."

"And?"

"I was. I later heard on 'Coast to Coast', that a career Army officer stationed at Fort Carson saw triangle shaped vehicles flying around Fort Carson during the Vietnam War - with out of this world technology." She quickly offered to her audience that she had taken no drugs or alcohol, just the Coca Cola and chips they had in the car.

Gideon, who was now looking on sleepily, was skeptical. He said, "Wow, remind me to stay away from that place, Secora."

Heidi's eyes glistened again with excitement. "If you liked that, wait till you hear what happened to us in Arizona!"

Not waiting for much of a response, she began. "During spring break in April of 1984, my family and I were returning home to Scottsdale around midnight from a shopping trip to Tucson. Our five-year-old daughter, Cindy, and our three-year-old son, Tony, were sleeping in the back. We left Tucson about 6-6:30 that evening and headed north on a two-lane road, and noticed we were running out of gas south of Phoenix. We neared the southern end of the South Mountains, which were on our southeast side, as we travelled north. We wouldn't make it very much longer without stopping for fuel. In those days, it was nearly impossible to find an open station in the middle of nowhere - at midnight. At last, we spotted a gas station with its pump lights off, but dim lights still illuminated the inside of the store. We noticed as we pulled in, that six Humvees appeared to have recently filled their tanks at the pumps, so I went in to pay for some gas.

"The sales clerk was very nervous. He asked me why I was there. I told him we were out

of gas, and he could either let us fill our car tonight or tomorrow morning because we had coasted in on fumes.

"He took my twenty-dollar bill, turned on the pump, and told me to leave. When I turned around to do so, I saw six clones in a line - reptile men dressed in desert camo uniforms and wearing black wigs. Their oval shaped bodies looked like horny toads with three-foot-wide shoulders, and they stood five-foot-eight inches tall. Their hands and fingers were also similar to the claws of a horny toad and the arms were short. Their faces had tan skin, with 1 and a 1/2 inch wide by 2-inch-long dark brown overlapping rectangular scales that looked similar to horny toad belly scales, or the overlaid shingles on a roof. Their noses and mouths came to rounded points - like the head of an iguana, and the chins were bumps to the neck. No ears were visible, perhaps because the wigs covered them. They looked at me with dark brown eyes.

"I returned to the car where Philip was already pumping gas, and I took over that task. Giving him a dollar, I told him to go and buy some gum. He said he didn't need gum. I told him to go inside the store and pick out any gum then pay the clerk. Look at the people in line, and then come back.

"He was shaken when he returned - as shocked as I was. He described the same horny toad men I saw. One of the 'soldiers' came over to our car. He was drooling from his slit mouth when he looked at my son, Tony. I said, He is mine – not yours! 'He is not for you. Go away.' As he left, I added, 'Leave him alone!'

"After the lizard-man left, we pulled away from the pumps, then pulled over to the side of the road as if to switch drivers, and pretended to study a map. We waited while the Hummers drove in a convoy directly west, then followed as they chugged down a dirt path toward the SE corner of South Mountain. For our vehicle, that pathway was impassable, so we watched from a distance.

"When they arrived at the South Mountain, a type of garage door opened up in the mountainside and closed behind them.

"The next day, I drove back to the gas station by myself. It turned out that the primitive dirt road was just a cart trail – a path just wide enough for the Humvees, but not passable for cars. I couldn't see the 'door' even with my binoculars, but that wasn't the end of the story.

"About three days later, Tony came running into the master bedroom at night. He'd seen his first reptile man 'closet monster,' a problem that continued off and on from 1984, until June of 1993 when we moved.

"My son and daughter had loved to play with horny toads before the event. After the lizard man started visiting him at night in his room, Tony became terrified of horny toads. In fact, his fear spread to all living reptiles, even dinosaur skeletons, and mechanical dinos. He's still afraid of them as a grown man. I heard a similar story on Coast-to-

Coast radio that also took place at South Mountain four to five years ago."

Tarkio observed, "You're one gutsy lady."

"You have to stand up for what is yours. I'm hungry. Anyone want something from the vending machine?"

The others declined, and she stepped away. A few minutes later, everyone had taken a bathroom break or gotten a snack from a small café, before reconvening at the chairs. Secora noted there was still an hour left to wait if the plane was on time. She felt herself becoming drowsy with boredom.

Gideon returned looking all spruced up and gave her a kiss on the cheek as he sat down.

"Where's Heidi?"

"I don't know. She hasn't gotten back yet."

Almost as if she had heard them, she strolled up smiling, opening a package of cookies, eating them as she sat down. "One more story if you have the time."

"We do," acknowledged Secora.

Tarkio answered, "I was hoping there was more."

"It was a visit from a ghost grandmother." She winked. "I think you're going to like this one. We moved into our new house in Phoenix, Arizona on a Thursday, actually Halloween day 1982. Four nights later, Sunday November 4th, I was sleeping alone at our home since my husband was away on a trip. I woke up at 3:00 a.m., and put on a robe to go to the bathroom. As I returned to the bed, I saw a dark brown or black human-shaped shadow against the gray-black wall. I panicked and I asked out loud in a quivering voice, 'What do you want?'

"She mentally asked me 'Where is my family?'

"I responded, 'Houston.' Then she evaporated.

"The next morning my neighbor across the street was outside, so I went over and introduced myself and asked her if anyone had died in my house. She said yes, but she wasn't supposed to tell me. The previous family's grandmother had died peacefully in her sleep several years ago, but not in my bedroom, a different room.

"I told her I had seen and spoken with her, and sent her on to Houston. Her phone rang. After answering it, my neighbor handed it to me - it was the former owner. Apparently, Grandma had showed up at their house this morning.

"While the family still lived in Phoenix her ghost would come and go, and had been away for two weeks before they were transferred and had to move 'instantly' according to both the daughter and the neighbor. She must have been looking for them since then. But now that she had 'moved on' to Houston, I never saw grandmother again."

Gideon said, "Thanks, that was interesting. Made the time fly by."

"Sounds like she also made Grandma fly by. No small feat!'" laughed Tarkio.

## 5
# BACK HOME

I t took a few days for the travelers to readjust to a more routine schedule. Tarkio, the youngest, not surprisingly, bounced back first and went to the office the very next day. Gideon required a second day of rest before he returned to the Treasuremont Realty office in Missoula.

The next morning at the university, Secora groaned as she sat at her desk with a coffee in hand rather than her usual tea, and called Bill Hoffmann, one of her grad students, and now, a cryptid photographer. He had lived in Bonners Ferry with his parents, Dan and Elena, but recently moved to Missoula, and somehow acquired enough credits to graduate.

She asked him to stop by the office and pick up a roll of film, to develop the images from the desert. "Okay... see you in five."

The phone immediately rang again. It was Gideon, saying Jane called to let him know Kyah would be late returning from his summer work in Peru. She happily explained that by the time the job ended, he'd learned a great deal and excelled in many facets of the dig. He'd become skilled with the ground penetrating radar, and especially enjoyed the cultural research, artifact preservation, and recording and tracking the data. Jane boasted that she wouldn't be surprised if he *ran* the next project.

She'd also mentioned that the young man would take a mini vacation on the way home, beginning with visiting Guanaco and Rocio on Isla del Sol. After that stopover, he intended to visit some exotic beach since he'd managed to save a few hundred dollars from his work.

With joy, Gideon also told Secora that with an assist from his friend, Rocky and his chopper, Kyah had stopped at Bosque Alto to observe the differences that the water capture techniques had made in the lives of both the "Big" and "Little" folk. Since things were markedly improved, Rocky planned to deliver another twenty chickens and a few hundred pounds of scratch to enhance and nourish their flocks which were devastated by the drought, and the onslaught of desperate predators.

Although, it didn't hurt that a few seasonal rains had begun to green up the parched earth, the people welcomed the sustainable water project which was off to a good start. A vast combination of nets and turbines reliably produced 60 gallons of water per day, on the cliffs and in the village below. Kyah and Rocky had been ecstatic. Jane and Iris were thrilled by the news. The Bosque Alto folks took lots of photos and would share them with Gideon and Seamus McGill, who would be truly amazed by their accomplishments. Gideon promised to send them on to Secora.

She was still smiling from the news as she organized materials for her new Pliocene - Pleistocene megafauna class - animals that lived 4 million to 12,000 years ago.

A few hours later, Bill popped into the office bearing a handful of prints as if they were golden treasure. He handed them to her as she set aside her files. She slowly soaked in the images. The last few shots showed the two snarling dogs stepping toward the scimitar cat – plain as day!

Bill asked, "What's all *this* about? Did you pick up a few pets while you were in Africa?"

Tarkio bounced in and sidled up to peek over Bill's shoulder at the photos. "What... the heck is *that*!?"

Secora pushed her desk chair back and coughed, choking on a sip of coffee. "Kinda. Actually, it's a scimitar tiger. And two snarling spirit dogs."

Bill remarked, "Spirit dogs!" Looks like a fang flashing orgy. *Isn't that a gigantic sabretooth?"*

Tarkio shook his head slowly from side to side with his eyes wide and lower jaw sagging.

Secora calmly said, "I think the dogs may have been some sort of spirit guardians because until now, I thought I was the only one who saw them. No one else believed they were real."

Bill squeaked, "Where was this?"

"Near the second in a series of three taboo caves in the Ennedi Mountains. I'd thought I heard the water witcher cry out for help, and followed the faintest voice up that hillside to the place Anthony told us about."

Bill said admiringly, "You managed to get a tail shot as he left. That tiger was definitely a boy. How come you were taking pictures? Looks like that thing could have reached out and licked you to death."

"Maybe. Impossible to run – what would you do?"

Tarkio considered. "She's got a point, Bill. You'd have taken the pictures too."

"Guess that's true," Bill agreed. "Those brave dogs remind me of the old mama cat in the forest with the Amphicyons."

"Good one. Surprised she lived through that," Tarkio added, "It was also that way when we were with Mr. Sasquatch. Nowhere to go."

"But," Bill reminded, "He made it clear he didn't want us to take the pictures. Did you know I brought Mamma Cat with me when I moved?"

Tarkio shook his head. "No, that's great! Talking about Mr. Sasquatch jogs my memory... Dean Hawkins told me about this Marine vet, Mateo Arguello, from the Colorado Springs area. She wants me to do an interview because he has had several opportunities to interact or play with Sasquatches, mostly children. I'm going to give him a call at 9:00 this morning so we can set up a visit for an interview next week."

Secora thought that over and said, "I'll need to get an update on the amount of time that would take, for scheduling purposes."

"Done."

Bill queried, "Hey, I've got about half an hour before class. Secora, tell me more about the scimitar cat and what happened to that water witcher guy?"

"Maybe later. I have a lot to catch up on, how about a pop quiz? What can you find out about this animal in the next twenty minutes? Here - use my desk."

Bill looked stricken, but he sat down and immediately began to work. He found out that in 1824, Brent Hugelman first described it as possibly a *Homotherium*, a *machairodont* species – a scimitar cat which displayed flat, serrated upper canine teeth. Until then, any such creature was thought to be extinct having lived from the early to mid-Pleistocene until 12,000 years ago in North America, Eurasia and Africa. Tribesmen described the beast to western explorers as *Gassingram*, a ghost-like cat that hunted in their district.

In 1937, one was spotted at night carrying prey off to a mountain cave. Western scientists identified it at the time as a *Machairodus* sabretooth.

Rumors persisted of a similar cat, the *Hadjel*, which was referred to as "fairly harmless." It grabbed up smaller prey because its teeth hurt when it had to open its mouth. *Sounds like one of a kind,* he thought.

In 1969, Christian le Noel, a cryptozoologist working with an elderly tracker, heard the powerful roar of an unknown animal in a deep mountain cavern. The tracker claimed it was a mountain tiger and refused to approach. Apparently, it carried off prey like antelopes, and lived in dry mountain caves.

Le Noel showed color pictures of cats to the villagers, and they immediately picked the "machairodont." Describing what we would call an "extinct" animal, a sabretooth known as Smilodon. They claimed it was bigger than any lion or regular tiger. They told of an incident which took place thirty years before that involved one of the trackers who was hunting with his father. A mountain tiger stole a 150-pound antelope which they had just killed - in broad daylight! It emerged from bushes just in front of them, and forced them to return to the village, empty handed.

*Illustration of the Ennedi tiger by Carnby on Wikipedia, inspired by the drawing of Tim Morris.*

Aside from accounts preserved by Yolo peoples in Chad, Kenya, Sudan, and the Central African Republic; there were also reports of scimitar cats sometimes referred to as "water lions" in tales further to the south. A second, very fierce species called *Mourou N'gou*, *Mamaimé,* or *Dilali,* was threaded throughout the folklore of peoples along river complexes in Angola, the Congo, and Zimbabwe. Witnesses described the beast as amphibious and nocturnal. It lived in river caves, but some said the *Morungu,* or *Dilali* actually lived in dry mountain caves, but hunted the rivers. One walrus-like creature with a long tail was said to have appeared to witnesses inside a South African cave.

Tribes reported three color patterns: red with white markings comparable to mountain tigers, others had leopard spots interconnected with the stripes, and some had no stripes - or spots. The water tiger was also larger than a lion, 8–12 feet long and 420 pounds, and was described as being waist to chest height on man. This cat was maned, and the tail was always long in the southern reports.

Though sightings have dwindled, they continued sporadically in the 1940s, 1950s, and even into the 1980s. In 1991, Lucien Blenko was told of a boat carrying French soldiers that was overturned and the crewmen were dragged under, by a *Mourou N'gou* or "Moruroungo." Nineteen years later, Blenko witnessed the ferocity of these beasts for himself. He shot a hippo at night, then saw a large animal come out of the water and drag the hippo carcass off to its hiding place.

Secora stepped in and stood beside her desk. "Time's up Bill, what have you got?"

He looked up and stared with his mouth open. Then summarized what he had just read about the two varieties of scimitar cats that had been sighted in Africa within the last century.

"Good job." Secora's grin widened then she asked, "So, what's been happening up in Bonners Ferry, these days?"

# 6

# HOLLAND PRAIRIE

Gideon needed to list a property on the Swan Valley hoping it would be a good fit for Jane, Aparu and the children who had been commuting between Missoula and the Lakota Reservation in South Dakota. They had been thinking of picking up a place to be closer to relatives and leaving the family trailer back home, for Jimmy Lizardeye and his girlfriend, Destiny.

After traveling through Bonner and up the Blackfoot on Highway 200, they turned left onto Highway 83 at Clearwater Junction. Monta was thrilled because they would picnic in an area beside Holland Lake on the way.

Secora, Monta and dear Alai, who was the last survivor of her Peruvian tribe, and a grandma to Monta, came with him to enjoy an outing. Sitting at a picnic table they enjoyed their simple lunch of sandwiches and water, and listened to a group of people who were gathered along the shore telling a story. Secora thought perhaps they were taking part in a ceremony, a memorial for the Swan Valley Massacre which had involved a native hunting party in 1908. By this time, Gideon and Alai were also intently listening. Monta was happily playing with some pinecones.

The story was about a group of Pend d 'Oreille hunters, who

following tribal traditions had left the reservation in September 1908, to procure enough meat for the winter months. Clarice Paul had been six months pregnant with John Peter-Paul, when she joined her husband, Camille, and another family, Antoine S-tseh-wee, and his wife Mary Tah-pahl and their children, thirteen-year-old Pelassoweh and Little Mary. There was also an elderly couple in the group, Martin Yellow Mountain and his wife Sahp-shin-mah.

Even though the Hellgate Treaty of 1855 guaranteed the tribe's right to hunt in aboriginal territories, due to recent changes they now needed all sorts of permits to hunt. To that end, they purchased the required licenses and Mr. Yellow Mountain had gotten written permission from the Agency Superintendent to accompany the group on the off-reservation hunt.

Even so, they were harassed by an edgy game warden named Peyton who pestered them three days in a row, October 16th, 17th, and early on the morning of the 18th as they were nearly finished packing up to leave and return to the Flathead Reservation - just beyond the mountains.

Peyton brought a deputized citizen with him that morning, and they charged into the camp with attitude. Harsh words were exchanged, and then Peyton shot and killed the three adult males, Camille, Antoine, and Martin Yellow Mountain. Clarice Paul reached under her dead husband's body to pull out his hunting rifle, while the distraught teen, Pelassoweh shot and injured Peyton, who fell from his horse while reloading to kill the women and children. The boy was then shot in the back and killed by the civilian deputy, Herman Rudolf. Clarice pulled up the rifle and killed Peyton before the females could be wiped out. Herman Rudolf took off and never looked back before leaving the state.

After the massacre, people were definitely nervous about going out to hunt. Pressure had been building because non-Indians were homesteading on the reservation with assistance from the allotment acts, and white settlers were complaining about hunting parties crossing their lands. They harassed, and told the hunters off. Eventually, the Confederated Salish and Kootenai Tribes worked it out in the courts with the

Montana Fish, Wildlife and Parks department and things are a little smoother now. Mutual understanding and respect are prevailing over harsh words and rifles.

After some final prayers, the people were returning to their cars as the memorial dedication had ended.

"Thank God things are improving!" Secora felt crushed. "Oh, my gosh, what a tragedy."

Gideon rubbed her back and reassured her. "*We* are here. We still can change things for the better."

She knew it was true, and looked at her kind husband, who was known to be a heyoka because he had befriended the now deceased thunderbird, Wakinyan Tanka. She snuggled into his shoulder.

Once the picnickers finished eating, they each joined a round of prayers for the departed in their native tongue and way, and especially for the healing of the tormented souls of the disturbed murderers.

"On the way back let's stop at the highway marker."

"Maybe, but I'm thinking we'll be pretty tired unless we spend the night at Hasan's place."

They traversed the Swan, and drove up the valley on highway 83 from Clearwater to Bigfork, on to Columbia Falls and then joined Highway 2 to West Glacier. Along the road, they saw all kinds of deer, and a band of elk through the sun-spotted trees, which greatly pleased Alai and Monta as they rambled up toward Glacier. They were on the way over to the Hasan Resort to take in a rendering of the fading story of Abraham, as presented by Secora's father and resident spiritual pre-historian, Sage Dalton. This relatively short talk came at the personal request of Jamal Hasan. Alai would take Monta out for occasional trips into the yard to burn off energy on the swings, and to run the flowered paths.

# 7

# A FIERY YOUTH

O n the way to West Glacier, Secora's sister, Iris called, eager for their arrival. Iris had been in her early twenties when she completed her Master's Degree in Archaeology. She cherished and eagerly anticipated their father's talks on the prehistory of human religion, and became his regular assistant for the talks at the Hasan venue.

Jamal had taken to calling him "the Sage" and was very eager to hear what he had to say about Ibrahim or Abraham, and had been encouraging him for some time to share this piece of religious history. Today, the banner hung across the top of the stage read:

***"La ilaha ila Allāh. There is no God but Allah."***

When Sage climbed the stairs, he looked up at the streamer, then hooked up his mike and sat in his signature stump chair. People were already standing and applauding, which made him chuckle.

"Good afternoon. In response to a request earlier in the summer, from my wonderful friend, Jamal Hasan, I was scheduled to speak about the Abrahamic faiths, or those derived from his three wives."

The audience signaled their joy with a jumble of cheers and kind words.

"Let's talk about Abraham. Who was He and what was His faith?"

Eager hands shot up. He pointed to a few men and women.

"First off, we know he was Jewish."

Another woman said, "His people were the wandering tribes of Moses, right?"

An old man added, "I think he wandered the desert like Moses did, but before. Yeah, that sounds right." Several others had similar ideas.

After a pause, Sage asked, "Would it surprise anyone to find out Abraham wasn't Jewish? He was born a Babylonian Hindu."

The audience was utterly silent.

"As with any layer of God's ancient Faith, there is a beginning, a zenith, a decline, and an end. This is the truer meaning of "the end of the world". Then there is a renewal – a "dawning of a new day, or age". So it was that Abram, meaning from *Brahman*, picked through the cinders of His father's Hindu religion, and shook its very core as He renewed the primordial, the eternal Faith of God.

"Abram, or later known as Abraham, came from the lineage of Noah, probably a tenth-generation descendant through Shem. He is widely acknowledged as the father of all of the *newer* revealed religions, such as Judaism, Zoroastrianism, Buddhism, Christianity, Islam and the Babi and Baha'i Faiths. These Prophets were all blood relations, as well as being joined by the Holy Spirit.

"Much has been written about the three wives of Abraham, and the fact that the newer Messengers literally came from them. I'll explain. Sarah's line included Isaac, Moses and Jesus. Hagar's line produced Ishmael, Muhammad and the Bab. Keturah engendered Joksham, Zoroaster and Baha'u'llah; also, through Shoah came Gautama Buddha. But, in truth all Messengers of God are related, both before and after Abraham, by lineage, and by the Unity of the Holy Spirit which they bear."

A man with a puzzled look on his face raised a hand. Sage called on him. "Yes, go ahead."

"But I don't understand why your banner for today looks Islamic?"

"Very insightful, my friend. I think we'll know the answer by the end of our talk. If not, please call me on it." The man nodded agreement and sat to listen.

"The following story of the early life of Abraham can be found in several religious traditions, most notably the Qur'an." He looked at the man with the question and added, "But that isn't the reason for the banner."

The man nodded.

"This favored Being was born about 4000 years ago outside the city of Ur, along the Euphrates River in Mesopotamia – now Iraq. The king, possibly Nimrod, feared destruction from one to be born in his land, so Abraham's mother fled to a field to give birth and avoid the dictated slaughter of all children. We know this fearful destruction was repeated at Moses' birth, but Krishna's virgin mother as well as Mary, were also forced to flee to save her unborn sons.

"Abraham's father, Terah, a follower of the now decadent Brahmanic Faith, named his child "Abram, meaning 'of God.' Each Prophet or Manifestation of God's Word is born from the preceding spiritual tradition. Through Him or Her comes the regeneration of the ancient Faith. Each of these Bearers of the Holy Spirit lovingly affirms and praises the Message of the One Who came before Him. They also make mention of the One who will follow, and of a Great One, who will arise at the 'end' to begin the new cycle or age. There is never a disagreement among Them. They are united in spirit and Message." Sage flipped to a page, in a notebook he fished from his shirt pocket and read:

*O Agni, Holy Fire! Purifying fire! You who sleep in the wood, and ascend in shining flames on the altar, you are the heart of sacrifice, the fearless wings of prayer, the divine spark hidden in everything, and the glorious soul of the sun!*

— VEDIC HYMN ATTRIBUTED TO RAMA

"But now, Terah and his people were worshippers of idols. Followers of the distant pre-flood Prophets became idol worshippers.

Forgetful of Ahura Mazda, their loving Creator, some now worshipped Mitra or Mithra as a god. Over time, humans tailored Rama and Sri Krishna's Messages to suit their tastes, thus corrupting the noble Faith. The purity was laid low by the trappings and pomp, of goddesses, gods, and icons. The old conviction had faded into visible distractions. So it was that the priests rejected Abraham, because they were afraid of losing their statues, wealth, and power. They didn't like the thought of serving the miserable and poor, with justice and kindliness." Again he read:

> *I am retiring to the mountains of Airyana-Vaeja. From there I shall watch over you. Guard the sacred fire! The symbol of the divine unity of all things. If it should happen to die out, (and you fail to worship the One Creator) I shall reappear among you as a judge and terrible avenger!*
>
> — VENDIDAD

"Those words about a judge and terrible avenger absolutely befitted Abraham! Sensing trouble, the people had tried to kill him as a young child. He was placed by a corral of hungry cattle, then the gate was opened and the cattle were stampeded over him. By the grace of God, He remained untouched.

"In Ur, the giant king called Nimrod, and his consort were themselves acknowledged as gods. Their priests rejected Abraham and His teachings, because they were afraid of losing their powerful positions and lucrative temples. According to two passages from the Qur'an we have this story of young Abram.

> *They prayed to idols which they brought with them from India. Once He asked His father, Terah, 'Do you take these idols for gods? If you do, then you and your people are wrong.'*
>
> *This did not sit well, because the priests of the area were wealthy, powerful and they demanded respect. 'Our fathers worshipped them,' Terah responded*

38

*'You and your fathers clearly have been wrong,' said Abraham.*

*When he said to his father and his people: 'What are these images to which you are so devoted?'*

*They replied, 'We found our fathers worshipping them'.*

*Abram said, 'Then you as well as your fathers have indeed, been in manifest error.'*

*They answered, 'Is it really the* **truth** *that you have brought for us or are you jesting?'*

*He replied, 'Nay, your Lord is the Lord of the heavens and the earth. He brought them into existence and I am of those who bear witness to this, and by Allah, I will certainly plan against your idols after you have gone away and turned your backs.'*

*True to His word, when the people were gone one day, He broke all their idols and images to pieces, except for the very biggest one which was thought to speak and listen.*

*When the villagers returned, they were very angry, and remembering His admonitions about idolatry, they sought out Abraham. When they found Him, they asked 'Did you do this to our gods?'*

*He answered, 'No, it was the biggest one of them, who did it. Why don't you ask him, he can tell you; if it is really true that he can speak properly?'*

*Some of them felt ashamed and said 'You know they cannot speak.'*

*He said 'Do you worship things that can neither be of any good to you nor do you any harm?'*

— QUR'AN (21: 53-58)

"Nimrod asked him, 'What can your God do that I cannot?'

Abraham answered, 'My Lord is He who gives life and death.'

Nimrod assured him he also had the power to kill people.

Then Abraham said, "God makes the sun rise from the East. Can you make it rise from the West?'

"Nimrod had been beaten at his own game, and was embarrassed in front of his nation. Angrier than ever, the people pitched Abraham into a fire pit to incinerate Him, but God cooled the flames and He escaped permanent harm. Nimrod and his priests - and even the common people He protected, were more than willing to burn Abraham to death. Disgusted by their unchangeable stubbornness He left the king and the rest of the idolaters and fled Babylon.

"He left Terah's household in Mesopotamia where they had tried to kill Him at least three times, and journeyed north to live among the Harranians of Turkey. They lived in beehive shaped mud structures, and studied astronomy and astrology, a type of divination that interpreted the influence of the fixed stars, sun, moon, and planets on earthly affairs and human destinies. They felt it gave them power over forecasting earthly and human events.

"For at least a thousand years before Abraham was born, astrology was inseparable from astronomy. Practitioners believed it allowed them to both predict, and affect the destinies of individuals, groups, and nations. Though regarded as a science throughout history, astrology today is widely considered to be worthless compared to the theories of modern Western science.

"In Harran, Abraham thought the perfection of the stars, moon and sun was divine. One day, He understood they were only creations, *shadows* of God's grandeur, and He too, had been guilty of worshipping stellar idols like other people.

"In obedience to God, He left Harran and ventured towards Canaan near the west coast. The fact is, Abraham lived his life as a nomad constantly traveling from one place to another. Along the way, He rid the people of the Arabian Peninsula, including Canaan, of their idols, becoming known as the Father of Many Nations. The only land he ever owned was a burial plot He purchased from the Hittites to bury Sarah when she died.

"The sun, moon, and stars could not give people anything to eat. Abraham submitted to the Lord of the Universe. The Creator made all things, including the interplanetary objects, and the earth so people could have a home. Abraham proclaimed He would no longer worship any god but the Master of the worlds and freed himself from joining partners with Him. Or, as the Moslems still acknowledge – He pointed to the banner *La ilaha ila Allāh. There is no God but God.* He shared this with everyone that they might turn away from all sorts of false gods - to worship and serve Allah alone. Sage took the little notebook from his pocket and read:

*Verily, my Lord hath guided me to a way that is straight, a religion of right, the path (trod) by Abraham the true in Faith, and he (certainly) joined not gods with Allah.*

— QURAN 6:161

"In case you wondered about Abraham's followers, you might look to the Sabians of Harran - a monotheistic Abrahamic group mentioned three times as 'people of the Book' in the Quran - similar to the Jews and Christians. Their further identity is still a matter of discussion and complex investigation by scholars, who have identified groups with similar names, Sabeans, Sabines - but differing histories."

"According to some Moslem authors, these Sabians followed the fourth book of

Abrahamic tradition, the *Zaboor,* which had been given to the Prophet David of Israel, and is identified by many modern scholars as the book of Psalms in the Old Testament. However, the timeline for Abraham's people would have begun nearly *1,000 years earlier.* But it is likely they recognized the truth of these Psalms as soon as they were received. Interestingly, Seth was said to have received perhaps fifty psalms *way* before David. Maybe the Sabians knew of those psalms.

Abraham would have relied, like Rama and Krishna before him, on pure hearted seers to preserve his teachings. I know of no written record of Abrahamic scripture at that time.

"Their beliefs resembled those of Jews and Christians, yet they were neither. In their view, all of the Great Prophets brought the Word of God. There was no one specific route to salvation. They believed that the universe had a Creator and Sustainer, wise and above any resemblance to created beings. The Sabians of Harran said, 'We are unable to reach the Creator without intermediaries, so we have to approach Him through the mediation of spiritual, pure, and holy Beings who are above place and time.' It seems certain that Sabians were wise enough to acknowledge Bearers of God's Word which came both *before* and *after* the Great Patriarch, Abraham.

"Many practices in use today can be traced back to Abraham's teachings. Fasting is a decree basic to all modern religions. The fast of Ramadan was practiced by the Sabians, including the Harranians, before it was observed by today's Moslems. Abraham began the concept of pilgrimage, also practiced by all faiths. His Sabians practiced initiation through submersion in water, in remembrance of the deluge of the world during the time of Noah, which temporarily cleansed man's sinful nature from the face of the earth. Today's practice of baptism is also widespread.

"Interestingly, Harranian Sabians, similar to the Essenes, acknowledged Hermes (Enoch) as a Prophet from the time before the flood They considered the Corpus Hermeticum, a dialog between Hermes and His disciples, as sacred text. Harran became a center of intellectual and religious activity that evolved into a philosophic tradition based on Hermes Trismegistus. Validation of Enoch, or Hermes, is known as the Prophet Idris in the Qur'an (19.57 and 21.85).

"Ablution before prayers is practiced by people of all living Faiths. It was a rite of the Mehr religion, which is still being practiced by Sabians in Iraq. Sabians, as well the Essenes, may have influenced Christ. They washed themselves with water, wore long hair, and white robes. They had a monotheistic faith, acknowledged the Zaboor and the teachings of the other Great Prophets.

"Muhammad and his companions were often considered to have been *Sabians*, because they uttered the Sabian phrase *'La ilaha ila Allāh. There is no God but Allah.'*

Sage turned to Jamal and asked him, "Could you please put up the map image?" Jamal complied, the Sage continued, "This map of ancient Mesopotamia, shows the areas and towns of Abraham's journey. From Ur at the bottom right, to Harran in the north, then southwest towards Canaan. The only property he ever owned was purchased from the Hittites in the north. Thanks, Jamal."

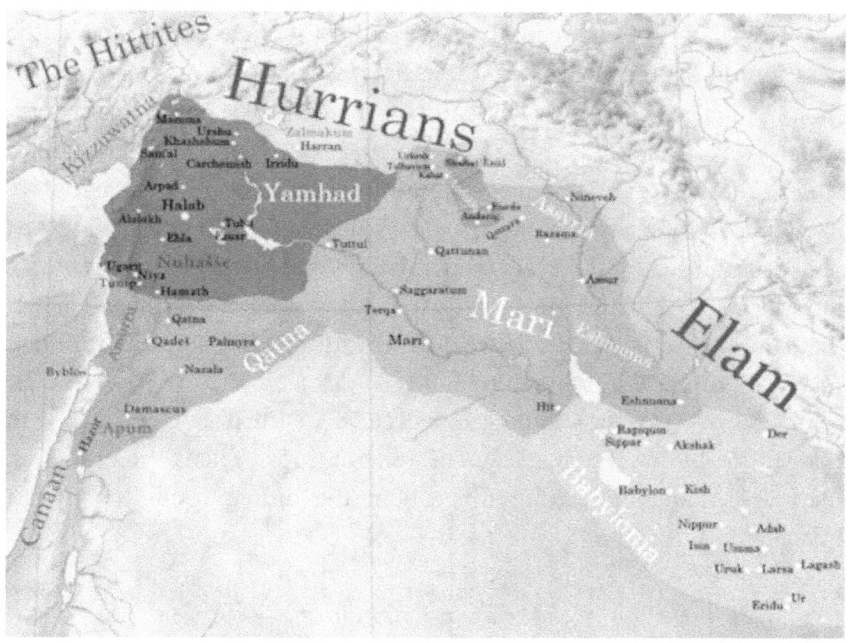

"LATER IN LIFE, Abraham was told by an angel to sacrifice Isaac, His only son at the time. He knew that if it was God's will He must do it, but first He asked His son. The son was good and pious, and he consoled his father. 'Dear father,' he said calmly, 'if Allah has ordered it, then you must obey, so sacrifice me. Do not fear: With the help of God, I shall be brave.' As Abraham sorrowfully prepared to kill His son, he heard a voice. 'You have shown your good intentions. This is sufficient. You have already fulfilled God's will.' They were so relieved and thankful! They slaughtered a ram instead, as they were bidden.

"Abraham's other son, Ishmael, later built the Ka'ba in Mecca toward which Muslims all over the world turn to pray.

"So even the faintest threads of faith continue to connect us to only one God. Abraham renewed the very ancient Faith, which some might call Mehr, (Mitra) "Light", or Mithraism, by recalling the original purity of its light - bright shining as the sun."

"Constantine the Great who along with Licinius, put an end to the persecution of Christians with the Edict of Milan in 313, convened the first Council of Nicaea to decide upon the official date for Christmas, which was standardized as December 25 - Roman celebration of Mithra the sun god. However, that holy day had been set eons before by Rama and Zoroaster, or who knows, even before that. This date was chosen specifically to protect the Christians and be more inclusive with the followers of Mithra, in a brilliant move. As an interesting side note, the Three Wise Men who journeyed to find the newborn Savior were followers of the Mithraic religion."

Sage rose from the stump and stretched, "I'd like to leave you to ponder this PowerPoint image of relationships. Thank you. I think there is a banquet waiting for you in the dining room if I'm not mistaken."

## *Abrahamic Religions*

Initial source: Table of Abrahamic Religions

Adam, Seth, Enoch (Edris or Hermes), Qinan, Mahalalel, Jared (Yard), Methuselah, Lamech,

Noah (Nuh), Shem, and Araphaxad.

Krishna (Vasudeva), Hud (Eber), Salih (Sila), Peleg, Reu, Serug, Nahor, Terah, Abraham (Ibrahim) Ishmael, Isaac, Jacob, Joseph, Lot, Job Ayyub, Jethro (Shoaib), Aaron, Miriam.

Moses or Musa,

Zoroaster

Buddha, ca 2500 years ago, India

Christ, ca 2022 years ago, Jerusalem

Mohammad, 610 AD, Mecca, and Medina

Bab, 1844 AD, Iran

Baha'u'llah, 1863 AD, Iran

THE AUDIENCE WAS ready to applaud Sage's compelling discourse when a young woman lifted her voice to ask, "What about the Tower of Babel?"

"Perhaps later, just for fun, we could pick up this thread and several other global memories either later today or tomorrow if Mr. Hasan can schedule us in.

Jamal Hasan stood up and announced, "How about after dinner?"

# 8

# RELATED GLOBAL MEMORIES

When the audience had reassembled after their meal, Sage came across the stage to where his questioner sat. "The Tower of Babel. Interesting question. Babylonians built a tower big enough to reach heaven, perhaps in the land of Shinar, according to Genesis 11:1-9. This human creation is remembered by people from all over the planet, and is often associated with giants, and tales of the Great Flood.

"The Akkadians referred to a structure, probably a ziggurat, calling it 'Bab-ilim,' the 'Gate of God,' built around 3500-3000 years ago. In Sumer, they spoke of Enmerkar of Uruk, a building, a massive ziggurat in Eridu. The wealthy demanded tributes for its construction.

"Romans told of the battle fought between the Giants and the Olympian gods for supremacy of the cosmos. The Greeks let us know that Giants attempted to reach the gods in heaven, by stacking mountains, thus rendering the heights of heaven no safer than the earth. They said giants attempted to take control of the Celestial kingdom, piling mountains up to the distant stars, but they were repelled by Jupiter's thunderbolts.

"In Central America, the Great Pyramid of Cholula is linked with the Tower of Babel. Shortly after the conquest of Mexico in the 1500s, a Dominican friar recorded a story related by a hundred-year-old priest who was taught that when the light of the sun first appeared upon the land, giants appeared and set off in search of the sun. Not finding it, they built a tower to reach the sky. This angered God in the Heavens and He called upon the inhabitants of the sky, who destroyed the tower and scattered its peoples.

"About that same time the Toltecs remembered that men had multiplied following a great deluge. They erected a tall *zacuali* or tower, to preserve themselves in the event of a second flood. Rather than preserve culture, their languages were confounded and they went to separate parts of the earth.

"In the USA, the Tohono O'odham people who live in the wide Sonoran Desert of Mexico and Arizona, said Montezuma escaped a great flood, became wicked, and built a house reaching to heaven - but it was destroyed by the Great Spirit. A similar construction has been noted in a version of the Cherokee origin story. This account says the top of the structure, which was built with the hope of storing food and surviving a second deluge, was destroyed on several occasions by divine intervention. When they attempted to repair the damage for a third time, they found that the language of the tribes was confused or destroyed.

"In Africa, Dr. David Livingstone reported he met people living in Botswana who mentioned the builders' heads were cracked open by the fall of the scaffold. Other lore mentioned wicked men built a tower to pursue the Creator-God, Nyambe, in heaven. The men were destroyed when the masts collapsed. Apparently, the Ashanti tale substitutes porridge pestles for the masts. People of the Congo and Tanzania tell of men stacking poles or trees in a failed attempt to reach the moon.

"In East Asia several tribes in Assam have a similar story. Inhabitants of the Admiralty Islands tell of human languages becoming confused after a failed attempt to build houses reaching upward to heaven. Also, the Karen of Myanmar say their ancestors separated from the Karenni and migrated, after abandoning a great pagoda in the land of the Karenni, when their languages were confused thirty generations after Adam. Traces of the legend have even been found in Northern India.

"To sum things up, the Jews felt the tower had been constructed as a defiance against God, ordered by a giant - the arrogant Babylonian tyrant, Nimrod - no stranger to the sin of pride. This ultimately caused disunity and many people left the area. Right or wrong, the exodus both before and after the fall of the tower, became an explanation for cultural and linguistic distinctions."

A hand shot up in the front row. "Another question if you have time?"

"Sure, go ahead."

"You mentioned some guy named *Hayk* in a previous talk. Could you elaborate?"

"Yes, that was sometimes spelled with a 'yk' – other times with an 'ic' He was descended from Noah through Japheth, and like his forbearers, he was a loyal believer in the ancient faith. Some of us may remember from last summer's talk, the Armenian story that refers to the Spiritual hero and descendant of Noah, named Hayk, and his arch enemy, Bel, who was also called Nimrod, were both giants of that time."

"My daughter, Secora, and son-in-law, Gideon, introduced me to a lovely Armenian story teller Maja Turandokht who elucidated that she and her husband were descendants of *Hayk,* and called their country *Haiastan* in his honor, rather than Armenia. She had explained that the Great Progenitor - Hayk, son of Togarmah, had been living in the plain of Shinar where he busily directed the construction of the tower of Babel. This hero among men was not merely a saint but also a mighty giant, as beautiful as a god – maybe a type of ancient human - perhaps Denisovan? He was also a warrior in times of need, and his greatest strength was in the throwing of spears.

"Almost 4,500 years ago, Hayk and his people stood firmly against Bel, also called Nimrod or Nemrud. When Bel's devotees became more prevalent, Hayk fled, taking his sons, daughters, and extended family that numbered about three hundred, along with their herds of sheep and cattle, etc. They journeyed north until they came to the land of Ararat, in the shadow of the great mountains of the Caucasus where the climate was harsh. Friends, it's interesting that this is in the same vicinity as Abraham's Harran.

"Bel, or Nimrod, in other sources, had established himself as the patron god of Babylon. But Hayk refused to submit. He and his people stood firm in their faith in one God and maintained independence from all idol worshippers. Bel felt cheated when they left." Sage read:

*'Thou hast departed and hast settled in a chill and frosty region, urged the Assyrian god. Soften thy hard pride, change thy coldness to geniality; be my subject and come and live a life of ease in my domain.'*

— FROM, THE LEGEND OF HAIC,"
FROM *ARMENIAN LEGENDS AND FESTIVALS* BY
LOUIS BOETTIGER, 1920.

"Hayk knew Bel was a liar, and refused the cordial invitation. This so angered Bel that he marched his troops to Mount Ararat to *persuade* Hayk to come back from the land of golden jackals and white-tailed eagles near Lake Van, and worship him.

"Hayk was fearless when he fought Bel in front of the army he brought, to force the hero into submission. In the end, Hayk slew Bel with an arrow from his bow and the tyrant was buried in a place called Kerezman. Armenians still sing songs and tell stories of Hayk's great beauty and valor. He died, around 2028 B.C. at the age of four hundred having stood strong. He was not a great Prophet, like Abraham, but he kept the Aryan Faith intact."

The man who asked the question stood and said, "So, Hayk was a true epic hero? Sounds like there are quite a few similarities with Abraham."

"Indeed, there are. Armenians are still fiercely protective of their monotheistic faith. Except now, they serve God through the Lord Jesus the Christ."

Mr. Hasan came to the stage, clapping. "That was amazing! Thanks for taking the extra time. And thanks to all of you in the audience for coming. May you further be blessed by Allah. Good night."

## 9
# NEARLY EXTINGUISHED

Though classes wouldn't start for almost another week, word of the scimitar cat sighting had somehow gotten out, and many students, and even instructors who saw 'something,' seemed to be sending emails or knocking at Secora's office door hoping to find a sympathetic ear for their cryptid stories. She was secretly delighted, and even though it was, admittedly, a distant side theme to her job at the university, she found herself scanning possible sightings which she, Tarkio, or Bill might check into. While she scrolled, Tarkio came in and looked over her shoulder as he often did when he caught her researching.

An encounter with a Bigfoot caught his eye, and he reminded Secora that he and Bill could travel to Colorado for a couple of days, before classes really got off the ground, to interview Glenn Norberg and Mateo Arguello about their experiences with Sasquatch.

"That's right. I guess I forgot." She told him to write up and submit requests for time off and funding. "Get them to the department secretary as soon as possible."

Tarkio agreed, and said he would find a way to make the interviews work - even if he paid for the trip himself.

Secora already had a sizeable list of intriguing emails she wanted to follow up on during her weekends, but the daydreams were squished when she was asked by Destiny to recheck the dates from a small cave in Wyoming, where intermingled human and megafauna tracks were apparently etched into bedrock. The proposed radiocarbon date was 40,000 years ago, + or - 500 years. The University of Montana was asked to recheck the strata, and validate the exclusivity of the carbon base used for extracting those dates. Secora wondered momentarily, why the call didn't go to the University of Wyoming. Destiny suggested they might have a more urgent engagement.

Secora reflected that his date was much older than the 22,000 years for the skeleton interred at Billy Riggins' Mammoth site that had caused such an uproar not long ago. Billy and she had been physically attacked for proposing such a preposterous date, and Billy had nearly been killed - twice!

She sighed and agreed to leave early tomorrow after class, and return Monday before her noon lab. Destiny offered to take the lab if the schedule was too tight.


IT TOOK a little over seven hours to drive through Yellowstone to the Wapiti area. Secora's mind wandered to her family, especially Little Monta who was so happy to go with her class, on a field trip to a bakery this morning. Sage would pick her up after school, and she would visit with Alai, and L. W., and him - her grandparents, until Gideon could pick her up. She already missed her husband. They were almost never apart more than the length of a work shift. This time she would be gone at least one night. She needed to think of something else.

Sage's talks popped into her head. Her dad had been a vigorous global adventurer in his youth, but most of his adult life was spent giving seminars and lectures on early human religion in venues around the world. He always seemed to come up with surprises which generally were a shock to complacent and traditional audiences. She found it reassuring that the basis for even the Revelations was a solid pillar of faith: a loving Creator encouraging humanity to increase its potential.

Sage came up with some pretty amazing concepts. One of his favorites being the point that many of the early Prophets weren't 'modern' humans. She let her thoughts drift with images of the various hominin possibilities, until she had to brake for a leisurely herd of elk that chose to dominate the road.

She had always loved how inclusive his themes were. How we are all inherently tribal; African, Eurasian, East Asian, and Native American. He liked to point out that the divine Messages revealed by Prophets shared a glowing oneness, and that was love. Unfortunately, over time, empowering prophetic statements were often replaced by wisps of nothingness, leading to isolation and cultural disintegration. 'Written on the subway walls.' Secora chuckled thinking of the song.

Before she realized it, the trip was over and she'd almost passed her turnoff to the vacant trail head parking lot. From there, it was a short climb to the little cave. Once inside, she could barely make out any details until she hung a lamp from a root dangling from the cavern roof. After her eyes adjusted, she began to clean up a vertical wall from which she could collect samples, photographs and records.

The suggestion that this was an extremely early settlement did not surprise her. She had no doubt that humans came to the Americas far sooner than many of her colleagues considered plausible. Sites as old as 32,000 years old had caught her eye as a student years ago. Even though those dates had summarily been discredited, tossed aside as being outlandish - right or wrong. But there was a new trend in Archaeology. Dates much earlier than previously acknowledged were proposed – even a couple of claims of over 100,000 years.

She was here simply to verify or question the results of the previous dating, not to judge the result. It was all the same to her. No prejudice. She knew radiocarbon dates were only accurate if the carbon source was reliable. *Was the carbon-based material in the dated sample exclusive to that layer with tracks, and not part of a continuum of dates which might muddy the outcome? Or, did the camels and sloth survive past their "best by date" and intermingle with humans at that site later than previously thought?* She recalled recent reports of several megafauna species which survived until relatively recently –

she'd even had a few experiences with supposedly "extinct' beasts herself.

She was just finishing the work, when the immediate question became, ***who turned out the lights, and why?*** She instinctively crouched, and quietly backed further into the recess she'd been exploring, her ears straining to hear even the tiniest sound. After an intense moment, she began inching forward, the whole time wondering, *could that new bulb have somehow burned out? Was this paranormal? What's going on?* She felt the presence of at least one person, and waited for them to take the next step until it occurred to her, she might get blocked inside the darkness, like Gideon and Billy in the Montana ice cave – sealed in with dynamite, a terrifying thought.

She skirted the wall sensing more than one enemy in the cave. *Who would do this? Did someone lure me here for dangerous reasons? Was the plan to harm or kill me?*

Did she imagine she heard them sniffing the air for her scent? The mental image gave her chills because she was chewing cinnamon gum, and was afraid they might smell it. She edged sideways in a crouched position towards the entrance with her back to the wall, thinking an intruder would likely be armed in some fashion, and would try to take up all the space in the middle to corner their prey. As she crawled almost worm-like for another three feet, she heard mouth breathing opposite her position, and ducked even lower down until the hunter passed. She might have crawled; except she had recently put on a couple of pounds making that awkward. Then moving as quickly as she dared into the blinding midday light, she clung to the outside of the cavern until her eyes adjusted, then took off running for her car when she heard people whispering inside.

An older white pickup with blue beauty lines streaking its sides was parked near her vehicle. Before leaving she decided to flip open the lid and pull off the battery cables to slow down their pursuit. There was no visible license plate but there was a big dent in the tailgate she would remember.

She backed, turned, and then sped down the dirt road in her trusty old Dodge Dart. Questions churned in her head. One rose to the fore.

"Who did I tick off this time?" Maybe someone didn't want her to look too closely at the strata which encased the prints. "Quien sabe? Could be anything – or nothing at all. She wasn't staying to ask.

AS SHE CURVED onto the freeway, she suddenly found herself in the midst of a two-lane convoy of RVs, dodging in and around the normal traffic, in a hurry to who knew where. *Reminds me of a group of thirsty sauropods stampeding to water.* She determined she would pull off the road at the first opportunity. As they drove into a valley bottom, they were socked in with a thick layer of fog. Just as she was wondering what would happen if...? One of the rigs turned sideways across both lanes. Screeching brakes couldn't save everyone from becoming a giant RV sandwich. She had turned her wheels to the edge of the road to take her chances in the grass and nearby fence, when the trusty Dodge was hit from behind. The rear end of the vehicle had been crushed but the front end was virtually untouched. Still her head had hit the driver's side window and she was blissfully unaware of everything except occasional loud sounds and uncomfortable jostling.

At one point she wondered if the rock cave had come down, and she was trapped in the rubble. Her head hurt and she missed Gideon terribly. There was one time she thought she could hear Monta's voice and she tried to open her eyes. Everything was dark, but after a while she could hear voices other than Monta's. *Ooh my head hurts.* She tried to move around and found that she could. *Perhaps I'm dead or out of the rocks at least.* It was still dark, but not pitch black. She didn't feel well so she just drifted off to sleep again.

GIDEON'S VOICE was calling her. She groaned in response and tried to open her eyes. This time she saw fuzzy figures in a dim light and tried to sit up. "Ow."

"Just stay down for now," someone said. "Can you see anything?"

"A little, but it's fuzzy. Are we in the cave?"

Gideon's voice was asking, "In Africa?"

"I meant the one where Destiny sent me today."

"No Secora, you're in a hospital in Jackson Hole." After pausing, he added, "Honey, that was three days ago. You've been kept asleep to let the swelling in your brain diminish, and allow the skull fracture to start to mend before you start moving around."

Secora heard Monta's voice saying, "Guess what Mom, I'm going to have a baby brother."

Gideon's voice countered, "She's been telling me that all morning. We don't know the gender yet, but if Monta says it's a boy... Well, I guess we will have a boy."

Secora didn't respond, she'd closed her eyes and looked as though she was thinking.

"Mom, did you hear us?"

She winced, "I did dear. That's wonderful, but it's a little more than I can handle at this moment."

Monta said, "He likes the name, *Steve* in case you are wondering."

Secora did a double take, focusing in on what Monta was saying. "You mean I'm *pregnant*? Seriously?" Her eyes leaked tears and she reached out for a family hug.

It seemed like no time at all before the doctor arrived to check her vision, and remove the bandage where bits of parietal bone had broken the skin. He said, "Looks like things are beginning to mend. The swelling is down. I expect you'll make a full recovery, but it may take months or even years. In a side-impact collision, a driver doesn't get any protection from an airbag, often resulting in a skull fracture."

"What airbag? No airbag in my old Dart. Is this about a car accident? Ow."

The doctor paused. "I see. When the head strikes the window or frame of the car, the bone is damaged at the impact site, but brain tissue can also be pulled away from the other side of the skull, causing an increased risk of a contrecoup injury - when the brain "ricochets" from the trauma site to the opposite side."

"Great, like Jell-O?"

"In your case, the scans indicate damage was mostly limited to the impact site."

"Thanks. When will the throbbing stop?"

"Not sure. Oh, and get rid of that car without an airbag. On second thought, I think you've already managed that. I'll check in with you tomorrow, Ms. James."

As the physician left, he signaled the visitors to leave. Gideon and Monta gave her another hug and Gideon said, "Goodbye love, we'll check on you this afternoon."

"Love you both." Secora groaned. She could hardly think past the throbbing in her head.

"Goodbye Momma and *Steve*." Monta waved as she walked out.

After they left, Secora dozed off thinking *I lost my trusty old Dodge, and a baby boy has found me.*


SHE REMAINED in the hospital for a couple more days, but finally, her discharge date arrived. While she waited for Gideon to pick her up, she dozed off and began thinking of Wakinyan Tanka. She almost felt a connection with the ancient, but now departed guide. Secora realized how much she missed the thought of the old bird being around to help her husband. She focused on his name "Gideon" and suddenly she was aware of fuzzy action around her and she opened her eyes wide to see if she might be in danger. Her eyes focused on the man himself and she smiled. He had her hand in both of his and leaned over to kiss her forehead.

"Ouch."

"I'm here to take you home, Kimimila."

She smiled at his special name for her, "butterfly" which she'd earned by darting off here and there, on various projects. "Thank you."

He helped her sit on the side of the bed to get her bearings, then as she was dressing, he said, "I hear from Destiny, that you will be amazed when you see the article the boys sent you."

"The boys?"

"Bill and his 'big brother' Tarkio."

"On what?"

"You'll see. They're finishing up their visit in Colorado with a trip into the Rockies to look for Bigfoot."

"That should be interesting... can't wait to hear how their interviews went."

As they slowly walked from the wheelchair to the car, Secora asked, "How's Kyah? Shouldn't he be finished with his work in Peru and heading home soon?"

Gideon closed her car door and went over to the drivers' side before answering. "He is making a couple of stops along the way back. He'll be catching a flight to Jamaica after he leaves his visit with Rocio and Guanaco. He calls it his mini vacation."

"I swear those two are angels – still serving as Kallawayas – giving their best to everyone."

"Jane hasn't gotten any updates since he left Isla del Sol a couple of days ago, so we don't know much more than that."

"Do you ever remember being that young and carefree, Gideon?"

"Not really. No money for that."

"Guess my big *vacation* was being in a university."

WHEN THEY WERE ALMOST to Missoula, Gideon took Secora to their cherished vista above the Blackfoot River. It was good to feel the warm breeze near the cliff's edge. With her elbows on her knees, she rested her head in her cupped hands.

They talked about Steve, their new son, who should be arriving in two months, and how that would impact their lives. It seemed like a lot to cope with - even though they'd looked forward to having a child of their own, and had prayed for such a blessing for years. Then they smiled at each other, realizing that together they could handle anything.

# 10

# BIGFOOT CULTURE

After a good night's rest, Secora ate a small breakfast and decided to open her laptop at home, since Destiny was taking her classes for the week. She was looking for the Bigfoot paper from Tarkio and Bill. She heard Gideon's phone ring, and was halfway listening while she was searching her many emails.

Her attention shifted to the phone call as she realized he was talking to his sister, Jane, about Kyah. When he finished his conversation, he joined her in the living room.

"That was Jane. She still hasn't heard from Kyah but she expects that he will contact her soon. His plans were to go from El Alto in Bolivia, to Bogota, then on to Kingston, Jamaica. Stop for two nights, then on to Miami, then to Missoula, which would take another 15 hours. Should take him a little over three days to get here."

"Ah it'll be nice to have him back." Then her eyes returned to her screen. "I am getting ready to read Tarkio and Bill's report."

"Good. I'll leave you to it. Got to get to work. Love you." He kissed her, and then left with his coat and briefcase. She smiled fondly as he left, then began reading.

## A Strong Pattern of Observation as a Prelude to Interaction

Tarkio Cyr and William Hoffman - with lots of help from Mateo Arguello, Glenn Norberg, and Heidi Cobblehof.
Mateo's video links for some of the incidents can be found at the end.


"UNLESS YOU TELESCOPE IN and listen with both ears and mind you might not notice anything. There might be a soft 'woo,' almost a sigh, then you start to wonder if this could be something strange. You wait to see if there's a pattern, or an increase in the intensity or types of sounds. Maybe there's a growing sense that you aren't alone. How small and vulnerable you feel when you realize something much bigger and potentially far more dangerous than you is hiding just a few feet, or inches away watching your every move."

Mateo continues, "In so many ways we limit our view of the world. When we think of predators it's easy for us to see only the aggressive side, as when it attacks or eats something. We scope in and focus on fearful things and interpret all intense situations as horrible or aggressive. We slant things to the dark side, for some reason we crave scarier things. Fear sells.

"Are they dangerous? There *are* accounts of Bigfoots, or red-haired giants, or trolls eating humans. Perhaps it is a few incidents, but the stories are passed all around the lore of the planet. If humans are willing to eat each other in different cultures – then it's a possibility. I think it's important to recognize they can definitely be very dangerous to humans but there's a good indication that they're not inherently aggressive – unless someone has threatened them with a gun, shot at them, or harmed a family member.

"It's more difficult to see all of a creature's other behaviors, but nature gives us plenty of examples of peaceful interactions between species, and evidence of one type of animal helping another in distress. It's not just us. We see interspecies cooperation play out not only with humans or other primates, but there are occasions where a jaguar that normally eats baby deer is taking care of one instead. There are a number of accounts of Sasquatches helping humans and also asking humans for help. It's universal and it may be more common than we think.

"Before my encounters I didn't feel the need to carry any weapon except a hunting knife on my excursions. Of course, I thought it would be cool if these hominids existed, but like many others I thought they would run from us. Even bears or mountain lions will eventually run away, but it would be a fallacy to think all animals are afraid of us. Sure, most animals are afraid of humans because we hunt them. Squirrels are an exception. They aren't afraid of me at all - even after I show them a pellet gun, or I eat one of them. The others are still not afraid of me. But squirrels quit chattering and are quiet around Sasquatch.

"My first interactive encounter with Sasquatches was really scary because I expected that they would stay away from people like chimpanzees and mountain gorillas do. I figured they would distance themselves far from contact – maybe somewhere in the wilds of the Pacific Northwest or the Himalayas - to avoid humans at all costs. So, I always had this impression they wouldn't be anywhere near the area in which I lived and worked. Certainly, they did not live and travel where I hiked, ran, and played near the canyons and parks adjacent to the city of Colorado Springs. I was wrong. Right there!"

"I used to be terrified of Bigfoot like squirrels are, but now I've done a 180-degree reversal in my thinking. I seek their company." Mateo mused, "Maybe Sasquatch looks at us as pets and they're trying to domesticate us," he laughs. "Sometimes they'd play with me like I'd play with a kitten. Ironically, now that I know them and understand them better, this group which I'm more familiar with, I'm speaking of the ones that live in and near the canyons on the west side of Colorado Springs, I feel *safer* when I know they're around." He laughs. "Because all animals - even large predators - vacate the area.

"But nothing prepared me for Sasquatches conducting experiments on humans; *observing us*, politely trying to get our attention to see if we want to play on their terms - literally a quarter mile from the first houses in town." Mateo's first suspicion came when he noticed three extraordinary bears.

"My friend, Austin, and I had been hiking all day exploring the south side of Pikes Peak. It was getting dark and he relied on me to navigate us back to the Jeep safely. Normally, it was easy for me to remember reference points, even by moonlight. However, it was getting pitch dark and there was no moon to be seen. We were over 12,000 feet, 500 feet above timberline when the entire landscape became formless and I realized I couldn't make out anything - even with my headlamp fully illuminated. It was like looking into the void of space. Everything was so far away, nothing reflected in the distance. In that moment I was unable to tell where I was on the mountain. For the first time I understood how people could get lost and die on a cold night like this high above the trees in what seemed like an endless void, a black abyss that absorbed all light. I was chilled with fear, not only for me but for my dear friend who came with me on these crazy escapades because he trusted my judgement and experience.

"In the inky darkness the valleys were gone, indiscernible, and my head lamp only illuminated sixty feet ahead of us before evaporating into darkness. I pushed fear to the side and brought my confidence back to the surface. No point in being scared, I needed to guess which valley to take down, and see where it led.

"The problem was that from our mountain top vantage we were looking for the *genesis* of a swale that would become a large valley farther down. No easy feat as many of them started as small depressions in the ground about a foot deep, before rushing down 2,000 feet into streams that carved out valleys and canyons further down the slope. Even worse, different valleys could begin as small dips which might only begin a few feet from one another, very confusing.

"With as much confidence as I could muster, I let Austin know we would have to pick the start of a valley and just hope it was the right one to take us back. He seemed to take it well since I showed no fear or doubt.

"In the dark it's hard to gauge distances. For what seemed like two endless black miles, we pushed our way down into the valley we thought we had come up. After hiking down about 1,000 feet we thought lady luck was on our side because we ran into a road we'd used briefly, earlier that day on the way up. It was either a new cattle road, or one that had recently had a lot of maintenance done. This gave us more confidence and improved our morale. Now, we at least had a road and trees that our lights could illuminate, giving us the illusion that we could see and that this world wasn't so vacant.

"Our walk continued but it soon became clear that even though we had a path to follow, we had chosen the wrong valley and it had placed us hours farther from home. Our morale dropped to nothing. We were cold, hungry and sleepy. It was edging close to midnight, but we had no choice but to keep going. After a few more hours passed a strange sensation overcame me. The way I'd feel when I was in a kill zone in Afghanistan. You knew you were vulnerable; something was watching you! This feeling lingered for about a mile, then we finally pushed out of the trees to one of the reservoirs where this valley ended.

"I shook the dread off thinking it had been my imagination, and felt emboldened because Austin was with me. Additionally, we'd both brought side arms in our packs which gave us some perception of safety. But the feeling of being watched did not cease, and because of this, I was prompted to look to my right as soon as we cleared the tree line where the slope ended. A flat space emerged that was covered in tall grass and giant willow bushes near a reservoir, and to my surprise, I saw three massive black figures leaving the tree line and barreling down the last of the small open slope. They walloped on all fours through the tall grass and silently jutted, or dodged behind a huge willow bush about 45 ft. feet away. Their eye shine varied between yellow and green as my light caught them at different angles. My first thought was that these had to be three *massive* black bears. Yet my personal experience with countless bears raised red flags about their behavior. These things did not move like bears, but like apes. They were bounding with incredible speed and agility. Their movements reminded me of hyenas bounding in African documentaries as they entered into a feeding frenzy.

"That was just the beginning. What happened shortly afterwards was even more perplexing. Sasquatch was not on my mind at the time, and I was struggling to categorize these three as adult bears. Adults were unlikely to peacefully share the same space. All we could see were these massive outlines and large reflective eyes looking back at us from just outside the reach of our lights. Simultaneously, they started peeking their heads out from behind this giant bush. When we would shine the light to focus on one head it would quickly hide behind the bush and the other two would jut their heads out - just like 'whack-a-mole.'

"If that wasn't enough, the one directly behind the tree was peeking over a bush that had to be over eight feet tall. I couldn't comprehend how fast and fluid this bear must be in order to look over the bush then duck its head. I had always seen bears as having to struggle to balance while standing, slowly rising, then falling to get off two feet. This bear was faster and more agile *than I was.* As soon as the light was directed at it, it shot down - just to shoot up as soon as we shined the light at the new head popping out on the side. I remember at the time I did not get any threatening indication from them and was not afraid.

"Austin suggested we should take out our firearms. Recognizing he was afraid, I agreed that indeed taking out our pistols was probably the best course of action to make sure we were protected. As soon as I drew out my 1911 WWII .45, the three giant bears galloped away from us on all fours so fast that they were out of sight within seconds. Unfortunately, that was no benefit to us since they went into the trees in the direction we planned to go, making it impossible for us to keep an eye on them. We just stood there, not sure what to do because we felt uneasy moving in the direction all these "bears" had fled.

"I commented to Austin that it was unusual to see three adult bears together, and how strange their movements were. The behaviors we saw didn't make sense; they were not the behaviors of bears. I told him I could not understand how they maneuvered with such agility and how they instantly knew we had drawn our pistols and fled the scene in haste. I may have understood a fear of rifles, but not pistols. Austin didn't have much to say since there was a lot to contemplate. As for me, I was highly suspicious of what we had just seen and could not get it out of my head. The way they moved, the interest they showed in us, the way they had been following us from up the slope in the trees in order to meet us in the open. If I had not looked to my right they would have just moved to that bush and neither one of us would have been the wiser.

"We probably waited about twenty minutes before deciding to push forward. Both of us were obviously perplexed and unsure if we were safe or not. So, we continued with our lights on and our hand guns drawn for about a mile and a half, until we ran into a forest service road and felt safe enough to put the guns away. However, our heads were still on swivels looking for any eye-shine that might indicate these things were still following us. It took another couple of hours to reach the Jeep and another two hours to get home. So, it was close to daybreak at 5 a.m., by the time this adventure was over."

"AFTER WORKING a shift at Seven Falls, around 11 p.m. my girlfriend Kaitlyn and I heard something moving through the brush across the road from where we were sitting on a picnic table in South Cheyenne Canyon. There was more than one sound signature, a group of something was moving and making crunching noises in the bushes. Kaitlyn asked, 'Do you hear that? What is it?'

"I easily dismissed the sounds and told her they were deer. I was familiar with the area and pretty confident that I knew what was going on. We had a huge population of "mulies" right up against our bustling city. She was frustrated, because for her this pattern had been building up for days. For me this was the first occasion, and I insisted that I heard noises like this all the time and it had always ended up just being deer. I was willing to let it go, but obviously it was bothering her.

"An hour later, we were still sitting in the dark on the picnic table chatting when I realized the sound signatures of the group of things that were moving through the deep brush and wooded area across the street had never stopped, they had continued for an hour and a half. Now I became curious, *what was going on?* There was a deer trail back in there, which is why I first assumed they were deer. But deer wouldn't chill, making noises in the brush. It was a dangerous place for them. They could get ambushed, right? They would simply pass through.

"I wanted to know what or who this was so I went across the road to investigate. I wasn't planning to go into the brush, just walk along the pavement and try to figure out the source of the noise. Kaitlyn had bad feelings, like something strange was up. She didn't want me to leave, and her intuition turned out to be right - something *was* off.

"Looking back, I can remember several times that women picked up on the Sasquatch vibe way before I did. I listen better now - I think. Before that, if I heard something fall near me, I'd dismiss it as the wind or an acorn dropping. All whistles sounded like human whistles, and the woos were almost imperceptibly quiet. It took several exposures before I learned to hear them. It was so easy to miss the signals because they *weren't for me* – their signals were for each other.

"Equipped *only* with my I-phone flashlight because I had no weapon, I went anyway, not expecting trouble. I closed in on the first of what I thought were three separate creature signatures maybe fifteen to twenty feet off the road. But the brush was too thick to see anything. When I stood directly in front of the spot where the first sound was generated, I heard the creature making noise. Then as I stepped toward it, it froze but I still couldn't see anything. It dawned on me that this wasn't a small animal, a deer, or any predator I was used to because they would have turned and run away by now.

"There had been three distinct signatures, maybe three to five meters apart. The other two creatures were still making noise so I continued to walk down the road about twenty feet to the second spot to see what or whoever was in there, but it also stopped making noise. I heard something hit the ground behind me. When I twisted around, I saw a small rock bouncing on the ground. I brought my eyes up to look across the street, and noticed Kaitlyn was getting into her car. I thought *okay maybe she threw it at me as a sign.* Then I realized that she was too far away to toss a small pebble like that, maybe a bigger rock with some weight behind it, but not a little pebble. I brushed it off and walked over to the third signature - and it stopped making noise too. It didn't leave, or panic, it stayed right in front of me – unseen. I couldn't figure out what was going on, so I thought *whatever,* and turned to start walking back toward the picnic table. After three or four steps I saw a little pebble come out of the brush and hit right in front of me. I actually saw it come out of the brush and smack the pavement; it even bounced a little bit. I thought, *okay those aren't deer. It wasn't Kaitlyn, what is going on?* No animal I knew could throw in that way. At this point, I don't know if I contemplated it was Sasquatches, but I was becoming suspicious about the behaviors, and the only other possibility was that it must have been people, but I couldn't think of anybody who would be willing to spend an hour and a half hiding just to prank someone by making little noises in the woods - much less *three* people being so patient. I was perplexed by such unusual behavior. Even I, a born prankster, wouldn't have done that.

"Deciding to be on the safe side, I went over to see Kaitlyn to ask her if she threw a rock – even though I saw the last one come directly out of the brush. I was in denial and I needed to think critically, it was my defense mechanism because the situation was too weird for me to take in. In my world view this had to be people, even though they had an unusual amount of persistence and the way they were trying to scare us was very odd. Realistically, what else could it be?

"When I explained this to Kaitlyn, she thought I was trying to mess with her. In frustration she said, 'Are you serious?' She was freaking out thinking something had been trying to get our attention. When we spoke about this night years later, she said that wasn't the only time pebbles had been thrown at us. The same thing had happened on several occasions. Little rocks would hit around us and our vehicles. So, it bothered her when I ignored the obvious signs. Somebody had been trying to get our attention for several weeks.

"Now, I was intrigued. I was going in to find out who this was, thinking it must be teenagers messing with us since that was what I had done up there when I was a teen - scaring other kids who were drunk or high, and I had gotten a kick out of it. Ironically that might have been what brought in the real 'monsters,' me pretending to be one.

"I'll explain, I knew the area well. I'd hiked and run all over that place since high school. Besides, I'd been through the Marine Corps and had a lot of strategic experience. I knew there was a 'social trail' that went up to the mesa that was nestled between the North and South Cheyenne canyons, and it came very near to our current location. From the social trail I would take the deer trail which ran alongside the road, only thirty feet away from where our cars were parked.

"My girlfriend didn't want me to go but I insisted, so she said, 'Fine, I'm not staying here. I'm going with you.'

"Because this was not a secluded area in the deep forest, I assured her these *had* to be people. We were on the edge of a big city and there were tons of visitors and hikers around day and night, particularly when it was warm. People were everywhere, *especially* in the summertime.

"All we had was the lights on our phones and they couldn't penetrate the brush very far. We walked cautiously along the trail to a little berm where the noises and throws came from, directly across from our cars. I didn't see anything but felt no urge to go in deeper. I felt vulnerable because the things I'd expected to find weren't adding up. There was no evidence of people in those places where I thought they would be. If they had moved or run, I would have heard them moving away in the brush, and there were no other manufactured light sources. We did find smaller marked trails in the brush that crisscrossed the normal human and deer paths. These weren't for large individuals, maybe the size a teen would make. Once again, I couldn't explain the situation, so I decided to dismiss it. 'Alright let's just head back. I can't see anything.'

"I returned to the paved road all the while denying the pebbles and other incidents when we heard people come and park in a nearby picnic site, located a little farther up the hill, and on the other side of the creek. So, what came to mind at that moment? I wanted to prank *them*. To scare them away for laughs. It was fun, what can I say?

"I started making loud scary screams, yells, and other noises. My efforts had the desired effect and they all ran to their vehicles, slammed their car doors, and bugged out. At some point Kaitlyn must have thought I was nuts.

"After five minutes of being impressed with myself, we started to walk across the pavement toward our cars, and when we were only thirty feet from the spot the noises and pebbles had come from fifteen minutes before - suddenly, *all hell* broke loose! The brush became an explosion of action and noise! We heard crashing and banging, large sticks and huge rocks were thrown all around us. When the scrub oak had started to tremble and shake, I knew these weren't humans. Normally these trees don't get very big – but these were *especially large*, maybe five inches in diameter – they'd been around for a long time.

"My whole world of denial was shattered that night. These beings were unmistakably Sasquatches. This knowledge affected me worse than war, which was also a shattering experience - but not like this – at least in war I knew my enemy.

"Then, it got worse. They had waited to rush us until we were on the road heading back to the vehicles, then we heard the *bluff charge*. Something sounding like a freight-train came right behind us - just like in 'Jurassic Park.' The rush of the charge tore through the shuddering oaks and came right up to the edge of the road - within inches of us. We stared ahead, like deer in the headlights – too afraid to look.

"These massive individuals had rushed right up to us - so fast! Everything became chaotic; they could have been on top of us in seconds, yet they stopped. It was clear even in that moment that they weren't trying to hit us, but they certainly managed to terrify us. Some of them were moving around in the tall scrub oaks, rattling them menacingly - a very clear sign for us to 'get the heck out.'

*"This* time I wasn't going to stick around to confirm their identity. Now I believed Sasquatches were very real, and a group of them, adults and younger ones, had been only a couple of branches away from our faces. Right in front of us! It was very clear that they were not happy and wanted us to leave – immediately. So chaotic!

"I felt my life was in danger. We raced for the cars, scared for our lives. If my nerves had allowed it, I could have possibly looked up into the Sasquatches' eyes. But at that moment the thought was simply too frightening. Instead, I quickly escorted Kaitlyn to her car, saying, 'Meet me at the gas station on Eighth Street.' Then I jumped into my

Honda Civic and we got out of there as fast as we could. I actually tried to put the lights of the Honda on them but the beams were set too low to see them.

"We met up at the gas station and I had her repeat everything that happened. I told her what I had experienced. We weren't crazy. It was all there, we'd both witnessed, felt, and experienced the exact same events. I didn't want to believe there were monstrous hominids in my backyard - because that changed everything. Until that night I'd felt comfortable in this part of the mountains. I used to feel safe moving around in the brush, on the trails, hiking and running around at night. Now I felt that assurance of safety and control had been taken from me.

"Kaitlyn and I drove back the following day and again parked across the road from our encounter which had banished my denial for good. We wanted to see if there was any physical confirmation of what we'd experienced and we found copious evidence of the destruction. Signs of the aftermath were everywhere. The adult Sasquatches broke several trees and they snapped off many branches to be pitched at us. Other limbs were broken when their rushing bodies crashed down a path to chase us away. We didn't find the specific rocks they threw because it was a rocky area, but such a destructive force was let loose!

"Unimaginably large foot impressions were crushed into the leaf carpeted earth right up to the pavement. One print measured sixteen inches; another was eighteen inches in length. These were not the juveniles from before, these protectors were huge! I tried to step into the leaf litter which concealed the red soil with my boots to recreate the deep impressions which were mind boggling. I couldn't even make a dent. The thick topping of leaves wouldn't stay down even when I continued to jump in the soil right beside the huge impressions; I didn't have the weight or strength. I'd smash my boots into the ground to make my prints stay - the leaves would crinkle but then they would crinkle back up. I said, 'Wow this must have been something big and heavy.' The tiny little suggestion in my head that we'd gotten hoaxed, ran away screaming. There was no alternative explanation for the conclusion we drew when things went crazy the previous night. And with that the hoax idea was finally obliterated.

"We came back again the very next night and I brought chem-lights, or glow sticks which were less powerful than phone flashlights but we also used headlamps which were brighter to do some tests. My mind couldn't eradicate the events, so I needed to control them with experiments. Kaitlyn couldn't see me twenty to twenty-five feet inside the brush with her phone light and headlamp. With the glow sticks I could see only five feet in, or maybe fifteen feet at certain angles, but nothing beyond that because the shrubbery was too dense. I'd like to reach out to her again now, for more of an interview.

"All at once, I realized that all the weird stuff I'd seen, or events I'd heard about in the canyon and up at Seven Falls over the years was true. The accounts my friends had given about creatures they'd encountered at night were valid. Before this experience I disregarded such stories, deciding those people were either mentally unstable or had experienced something paranormal in nature. I never thought it was actually something alive and physically operating in the vicinity where I lived and worked. Then I remembered finding weird deer kills that I couldn't explain along the side of the road. Some people said it was the work of satanists. I didn't agree, but I had no other explanation at the time.

"It occurs to me now, that they were probably watching us do our reconnaissance - the whole time. In retrospect, I realize that my actions elicited the adult Sasquatches' response. I went in there screaming, outranking this group. I think they reacted to my aggressive behavior. I feel pretty confident about that now.

"When introducing yourself to any new culture you don't want to approach someone in a bold scary manner. You should be gentler, more patient – not tense, on guard, or too eager – They might let you know they are interested if you are placid. Wait for them to come to you. But that's not likely to happen if you're scary.

"We must consider that we are very dangerous. They have to be gentle - careful when approaching us too. It's a two-way street no matter what species you're dealing with. Humans need to be more tactful in their approaches - to build that rapport. That's how Sasquatch approaches us and that's how we need to approach them.

"Even their pebble throws are a gentle sign of inquiry - a kind of experiment to get your attention and let you know they're there waiting to see what you do next. Sometimes the intensity increases if they don't get a reaction.

"Pebble throwing is a universal primate behavior. It's like when a boy throws a pebble at a girl's window. We do it, they do it, gorillas and chimps do it to get someone's attention. They want you to know they're interested in interacting with you. It's a behavior to protect themselves yet let you know they are interested without freaking you out. If they came right out and said, 'Hey what's up, my name's Bob,' we'd be terrified, that's just too aggressive. This group in the canyon has been around so long that they've built up an understanding – a way to interact in an effective manner. They know how to open up communication channels with those of us who are perceptive. At first glance I didn't understand this behavior. It took me years to realize this wasn't aggression, I was making it too complex. The simpler, obvious answer was the right one."

"AFTER MY VERY PERSONAL introduction to Sasquatch, I was still nervous about going alone into South Cheyenne Canyon after dark. It would be two years before I went out after dark alone. I guess I wasn't technically alone, I was with Tom and occasionally other friends in the Glen Erie area, a location slightly northwest of the Garden of the Gods.

"For some reason I thought we'd be far enough away from the Cheyenne Canyons on the other side of Ute Pass, that Sasquatches couldn't find me. It gave me a false sense of security. I was certain I'd be safe in the area of Glen Erie, an English Tudor Castle built in 1871 by General William Jackson Palmer, an early resident of Colorado Springs who took interest in the arcane inventions of Nicola Tesla who built his Tesla Experimental Station in 1899. Tesla had found a way to harness lightning, but the outcome was not necessarily popular with the inhabitants of the region. Even though he was an extraordinary scientist and made theoretical physics functional, most of his inventions were patented by others.

"The adjacent property was the celebrated Flying W Ranch, famous for their 'chuck wagon dinners' served on rolled metal plates like the cowboys used. Guests were entertained by what some called 'tumbleweed' music played by the Flying W Wranglers, a cowboy band.

"There was a wash or gully between these two iconic properties where Tom and I would run miles through the wilderness at night. Using cunning and stealth, we'd chase and hunt each other in glorified games of moonlight tag, or rather hide and seek among the conifers, scrub oak, and upright sandstone ridges and pinnacles. We went to the same spot almost every night around twilight to play. It became a ritual for us and it helped us become really strong. We tested different strategies and tactics trying to escape from one another.

"I was the first to arrive one night in November, at 11p.m., at a spot between the borders of the two properties. Tom always ran late. It was a Tom thing - late every single time. It felt like winter and there were little patches of snow on the ground. Not too much, but it was cold. While waiting, I decided to rock climb up a sheer sandstone ridge to keep warm and get the lay of the land. Perhaps I could get the drop on Tom after he arrived and started to look for me. It was really exciting to find a route to the crest in the middle of the night. I stayed up top checking things out before dropping over to the other side to explore, and continue waiting for Tom to come. Finally, I heard him a quarter-mile away doing howls. We would howl really loud to let the other person know our location or keep in touch with one another. If one of us hid too well, and the other person couldn't find them, the game got stagnant and it was easy to become demotivated and bored. A howl would keep the game going. Although howls could indicate our direction, sometimes we'd fake the distance with softer calls.

"As I listened carefully, I heard his howls getting closer. It sounded like he was pretty close to me now – 200 or maybe 250 yards away, but then his screams became quieter again. I thought he was faking me out. Sometimes I'd turn away and make my howl quieter so it sounded like

I was in a different spot, and it would be harder for whoever was chasing to discover me. I just assumed that was what he was doing, but it turned out that his howls *weren't* close to me. They were sounding farther away - strange because I thought he must be really close now. I was listening, paying attention, and I heard a noise – it couldn't have been very far away - within thirty-five feet. I assumed he was just out of sight around a bend. It sounded like he came onto the trail then scurried back up at an angle. I heard him crunching his way up the side of this gravel hill above me, *smash, smash, smash,* coming right over me to a small cluster of brush encircling a tree. I couldn't see him but I heard him, he's a big guy. You could tell he was trying to be very quiet, but because he was walking in gravel on a steep slope *crunch, crunch, smash.* He stopped right above me, behind the brush at the tree. At this point he was probably ten feet away – right there, I heard him. I'd been paying attention, listening, waiting for him to come and get me – then nothing.

"I'd heard him come right up to me but instead of rushing me he wasn't doing anything. Very uncharacteristic of Tom. The moment he saw you, he'd go right after you without stopping. That is his advantage because he's fast. Waiting in stealth was a weird behavior for him.

"Now he was just chilling. I waited thirty seconds, well, I'd already been waiting for him for an hour, so I said, "Dude, Tom, come and get me." And as soon as I finished the sentence, I heard Tom's howl in the distance. *Shit! Oh, my gosh. That's not Tom.*

"Because of the experience I'd had a year or two before in South Cheyenne Canyon I started panicking. Somehow in my head I thought the Rampart Range would be different. *Sasquatches were not going to be there.* That's why I let myself play out here at night instead of the canyons down south. I started panicking because there was a 98% chance that what sneaked up above to observe me, was a Sasquatch. It took the high ground; the key terrain – things that a regular person wouldn't do. It was right above me. Tom would consider it because we'd discussed military tactics and strategies, then we'd practice them. It came naturally to us. One of the essentials was to get *key* terrain and high ground.

"Now I was freaking out, but I wanted to be sure I was right. Getting really critical has always been my safety net, I thought *maybe that is Tom,* so I pulled out my phone and called him right then and there. 'Bro, where are you?'"

Then he said, 'I must be a quarter of a mile away from you.'

"Oh my gosh, please, please, *please* come over here as fast as you can. *Please.*" Then I hung up the phone. I had my headlamp, and I could have easily turned it on at this point – a sign of distress for Tom to see, and I could have used it to look right into the face of whoever was standing over me, but I wasn't ready at that time. I didn't want another frightening experience. I couldn't look into the features of a creature I knew nothing about.

"It was the middle of the night in the middle of nowhere, and I didn't have an easy escape route. If I went out the way I wanted, into rugged country, it would have been okay if Tom was the one chasing me - but not okay if a North American Hominid was chasing me, I'd have no advantage. My best option, even though the riskiest, was to run back down the trail. If this thing wanted to cut me off it would be so easy for it to come in at an angle as I ran. It wasn't the best bet, but I didn't know what else to do. In desperation I began screaming and running, trying to look as big and intimidating as possible. I sprinted with all my might, descending the trail as fast as I could down to the open mining scar, and on down to where I could look across the valley for Tom, but I stopped before the path dropped into the draw that separated the Flying W Ranch and the Glen Eyrie properties. I was terrified, but I was safe – so far.

"On the opposite side there was another hill where I saw Tom's silhouette on the slope which inclined up towards other Garden of the Gods type rocks. I couldn't imagine why he would be so far away. Something was off. He was *still* a quarter-mile away.

"I howled to get him to come down, and I saw him running into the valley towards me. But when he got close to the bottom, he turned around and started running all the way back up that slope. *What was going on!* I turned on my light at this point, a sign for *Dude, get over here!*

Tom saw my light and finally came all the way across the valley and up to where I met him. I still didn't feel comfortable even with him there because we were surrounded by trees and scrub oak, so we ran all the way back up the trail to the scar, which is a desolate hill that had been shaved off - mined for gypsum to help build the Air Force Academy. It was a large open space and we could easily see anything trying to sneak up on us.

"After we met, I told him what happened, that I was certain I'd been approached by a Sasquatch. He was a little skeptical, but he also had something weird to report. He explained the reason he'd turned around was because as he came closer and had almost reached the valley floor, he heard something behind and above him. He looked back and saw the silhouettes of two individuals following quietly, one behind the other on the path he'd just come down. He was able to make out their outlines because there was adequate light from the stars, the city, and the moon. Now he thought I'd tricked him, brought unannounced friends, which we did at times to make the game more interesting. He also said that when he came down into the bushes at the bottom of the gully, he briefly saw another figure creeping through brush, but it quickly left his view. He guessed that silhouette had been me – that I had double crossed him. He thought I'd made the phone call as a prank to draw him in. As far as he could tell, we were setting up a proper ambush - trying to catch him in the middle - so he took off to evade the trap. That's when his howls became more distant, because in his mind I was now chasing him. That is until he saw my light illuminate across the valley. That's when he knew I was serious and headed back down to join me.

"I assured him I had been there well over an hour, and there were no other humans. I told him about the chill feeling that came over me when I realized it wasn't him behind me. *Oh, oh m gosh that's not Tom. That's something else.* The only thing I could think of was Sasquatch.

But my intuition told me it didn't want to cause me harm. It was there because it wanted to play what we were playing. I was still scared because it was an uncontrollable element, an unknown variable. I thought, *I don't know anything about you. Right now, you're kind of a monster.*

"I was certain it was a North American hominid who wanted to play. I didn't get any threatening intent, similar to the way I felt scared, but not *endangered* during the first encounter - until I became aggressive.

"My thoughts were reinforced when Tom told his story of another pair of individuals just following him around, and perhaps another one observing him in the valley bottom. Apparently, we had intermeshed with a group of youngsters. My immediate thought was they had seen us play here night after night, and wanted to be included. They could associate with what we're doing because they almost certainly played tag and chase when we weren't there. One thing Tom said, and it's hard to know for sure, was that one of the vocalized howls wasn't him, and he didn't think it was from me either. He thought it was strange. I didn't hear anything like that but I also wasn't paying much attention. I thought it was Tom the whole time, but the closer calls coming up to me might not have been him.

"The realization of what we'd experienced was so frightening, like out of a scary movie or book. *You've gotta be kidding me.* I've run into bears and mountain lions at night and I did not feel scared. It wasn't that they weren't dangerous, but I knew what to do. That night I had been interacting with creatures that weren't even supposed to exist. I didn't know how to operate. What would happen if the situation became violent or aggressive? How could I avoid them? You can't just go around them like you would a mountain lion or bear if you needed to. That was one of the scariest pieces at the time. I decided not to go out anywhere at night without a gun.

"In retrospect, it was the perfect setting for a group of young Sasquatch to conduct a controlled interactive experiment with humans. There was lots of cover for concealment and they had a myriad of safe approach routes to get close, to observe, and interact with us. They had the advantage and knew the trails. Curiosity and interaction were the main points of their visits. We were playing games out there so we weren't focused on them, we focused on each other – right up until they let us know they were around!

"They were interested in what we were doing because they could identify with the games. I stand by that assessment. That was something they did – they saw us doing it and they wanted to join in. That's why they got so close, just trying to follow us, playing around – presumably hoping we might be open to the experience."


"SIX YEARS AFTER MY FIRST, scary encounter I was now hoping to *interact* with Sasquatch. I chose that space right up against the city at the start of the plains. I settled on a deer trail next to a spring, a prime spot for most animals to come through. I'd park in such a way that a dense patch of tall scrub oak would assure the hominids a safe approach to my vehicle if they decided to visit. Before, they had observed – then tried to interact with me. Now it was my turn to observe *them* and seek interactions. For three enjoyable months my then girlfriend and I spent our nights hanging out in this same spot. She thought it was something fun to do, a weird hobby I had. Nothing out of the ordinary happened and we became complacent. Even though we were respectful and careful, it took three months for the interactions to start, but suddenly there were very clear noises that didn't sound like birds, rodents, or mule deer in the scrub oak and underbrush. We'd wait up listening carefully every single night and at times our sleep was disturbed by sounds of someone approaching our vehicle.

"The day after the first noises, we saw evidence of broken brush, very subtle, small snaps on willow branches, just enough to expose the white bark so they could mark a pathway in the dark. They were about chest height so a person could easily have made them. Mainly willows were marked, but when there were no willows, they would break the scrub oak. I slid back into the thought it might be teens sneaking around, maybe building a shelter in there for themselves. The breaks crisscrossed the normal human trails and deer ruts. I followed them until they just stopped, and there was nothing. I tried to dismiss the Sasquatch intuition. I wanted it to be teens or loners. For some reason any other thought would have been terrifying. But if they were kids, it was odd that they would brave the really thick brush between major paths for no apparent reason. Following their trail was annoyingly inconvenient and my only reward from the endeavor was that I scratched myself up crisscrossing the original trails through the brushy undergrowth. This system could help observers stay clear of people and the main trails, as they ran through the area on hidden paths, which I found later on led to huge nest-sites where I collected hair samples.

"A couple of days later just as the budding leaves began to open, sure enough; we started getting the pebble throws. It was dark, there was no moon. My girlfriend noticed it first. 'Do you hear that? It sounds like someone is throwing rocks or pebbles at the Jeep.' Then, I started hearing them too, and said, 'You're right. If it is them, let's just wait because they'll just keep doing it. In the meantime, let's eliminate any other things it might be, like the Jeep engine making little popping noises as it cooled down.' We checked the engine and the wind. Nope, we couldn't locate any other explanation for the noises. In my mind, I denied the pebbles and other incidents, because the marked trails weren't made for large individuals like giant Sasquatch, and they were crisscrossing the normal paths.

"The rocks were tossed from the trees alongside our Jeep and we soon realized that they were specifically used because someone was trying to get our attention. That first night they were hitting the jeep from multiple angles. Sometimes two would hit at the same time. We were certain there was more than one being, probably two or three. My stomach knotted; I was internally freaking out but I didn't show it outwardly. My girlfriend stammered, 'Oh my God... oh my God you were right!'

"It was overwhelming for both of us. The pebble throws became pretty intense. I had wanted stability to learn more about them, but now I felt scared, surrounded. Imagine trying to face and contain your fear. For several nights in a row the pebble throws became even more intense. It was clear that several individuals were concealed and were tossing pebbles from a variety of directions while we tried to sleep inside the vehicle. We'd hear multiple pings as stones hit the Jeep simultaneously smacking the front, hitting from the sides, the windows, and the doors. By this point, the Sasquatches, probably juveniles, were making their intentions to interact unmistakably clear. You know how your stomach feels when you're really freaking out? I don't know how to describe it, there were knots in my stomach *and* my throat. I tried not to show my girlfriend, so I said, 'Oh my gosh the waiting experiment worked.' Although I was scared, I was also excited about the success. When the behavior became really obvious my girlfriend kept repeating, 'Oh, my God, they exist, oh my God you were right.' That felt good even though I was afraid. 'I told you they did, I told you so.' And that was the beginning of a ridiculous month and a half of interactions and evidence collection. We experienced constant pebble smacking, and faces peeking in the windows. We found track impressions and fresh branch breaks in the willows up against the hills, right at the edge of Colorado Springs.

"Their trail network began to expand. Our visitors trampled sticks and brush to form these huge nest sites deep in the brush. This was where I collected hair samples which you can see in my documentary. These large hidden areas with several body impressions appeared to change locations every few days, confirming for me that these were not teens or kids. They had to be a group of these hominids. There were other new features. At one point a bunch of branches had been broken almost parallel to the jeep, into a formation similar to a hedge row. At first, I thought it was a boundary marker - like don't go beyond this point! But I reconsidered, and now I think it was a blind – a safe place for them to observe us. The branches had been broken right in line with the jeep to break up their profiles while they looked at us from that position.

"Now my focus was centered on two-way interactive experiments, where I placed various things out for them to take like the fuzzy wires used for crafts and decorations. I tried several things but there were a lot of experiments where it didn't look like anything was touched. After two weeks of getting pebbles thrown every night, I offered food gifts to see what would happen. Everyone tries snacks to see if the Sasquatch takes them and to see what behaviors the gifts might elicit.

"The apples most definitely got noticed. I decided to leave out four apples for our guests and I brought bulk apples in a little net. I left four inside the netting, taking a bite out of one of them to assure our guests the food was safe to eat. Then I strung the net up next to a big tree on the path where they had made the blind. I used a branch that was seven or eight feet high and I left a foot and a half lead on the rope to make sure squirrels or raccoons couldn't get into it. It was high enough that deer couldn't get it either. We continued to hear the rocks hitting the jeep but even after three days they hadn't touched the fruit even though they came through that area and looked at them every single night. Each morning we could see the grass was freshly pressed down, I thought maybe they didn't know what apples were, or maybe they were scared, thinking they were ours. I didn't know.

"Finally, on the fourth day I checked the whole perimeter to see if there were any subtle changes in the environment. Two of the apples were gone! They took the one I bit into and the one on the top and left the other two in the net. I was excited when I noticed they were taken from the top. The whole net was intact, no tears or marks on it as if someone tried to rip or bite through it. They went in through the top without damaging the net and they only took two which is pretty unusual for most animals. Raccoons have been known to leave some, then come back later for the rest. But there was no evidence that other known animals had taken any, and it was unlikely other creatures were around because we were still getting pebbles thrown. So, I got the impression they were being polite – sharing the offering with us. I was excited about the fact they left the two apples because it might indicate that they understood sharing and counting – perhaps they were just trying to divide the food equally – was that evidence of calculation and math? Maybe they left two for the two humans.

"The next night when the pebbles started hitting the Jeep, I came outside and I took one of the apples and made gestures for about five minutes to assure them they were welcome to all of the apples, I returned to the Jeep, and the pebbles stopped. This time they obliged, understanding they could have them all.

"Fifteen minutes later, we heard a 'yahoo,' a yip of excitement -

and then heard a curt 'Woo!' in a much deeper voice - everything got quiet as if a parent was cautioning a juvenile. I entertained the idea, but I could be wrong, that what transpired was that one of the juveniles, who was interacting with us, took the apples up to mom and let out that "yahoo," then mom told her or him to be quiet with that short 'woo.' Like, 'Shut up!'

"The next day when I checked, of course, the other two apples were gone and the net was still there. That was the only time I used the apples, because I didn't want the food to become a focal point, and I didn't want to run the risk of developing aggressive behavior from a sustained expectation of food. I felt they already experienced enough interaction from us with the pebble throws, because the pebble throws were a game. When we stopped doing it in response, they got more dramatic to get our attention. That was already working well enough I didn't want to add another factor with food and potentially have escalating negative side effects.

"We tried to catch them watching us with a thermal camera, but my girlfriend was traumatized to see a figure walking beside me to my left on the thermal. The worst part is that I forgot to tell her how to snap images with the camera so we had no visible proof of the experience, just her mental anguish from what she'd observed.

"In the end, I realized that I had to relax in order for them to try interactive activities. I had no experiences when I was tense or on guard, in my PTSD mode, looking over my shoulder with a defensive posture – nothing. It wasn't until I had this friendly demeanor, let my guard down, and wasn't paying attention to external factors that interactions started to happen. Now I'm allowing myself to be available to the creatures, but it takes time and patience to politely wait for them – as one might with a hunter gatherer group. It is the best way to do it. Waiting can be very difficult but it works. People have been successful when they waited in a spot and built a rapport, like they would with any wild creature. Of course, it only works when the Sasquatches use manners – and we use manners – signs of mutual respect.

"I used to feel terrified, now I feel safer when they're around. I don't have to worry about predators – or squirrels. This summer I plan to really get out there. I'm in good shape and I know where to look. Hopefully this will be the year there will be more close interactions and engagement. It's time to get to know them better - get to know them like they apparently know us."

## HEIDI'S EXPERIENCE

Tarkio met this woman, Heidi, at the Chicago airport who gave another example of how a quiet friendly demeanor allows Sasquatch to feel more comfortable interacting with humans.

"When my son was grown and in his early twenties, and out of college for the summer, we went camping near Weaverville, California, about a hundred miles from the coast, to do some rock hounding. The two of us chose a site at what was left of Trinity Lake. The Forest Service campground was totally empty because the lake was virtually gone, so there was no boating or fishing. We set up a tent on the south-west side of the lake near the trickle of a creek that flowed in from the mountains. After Tony finished setting up our tent, which was big enough for a family reunion, we dammed up the stream to have a little place in which to bathe. I felt like someone was watching our progress, but we checked around again – there were no other travelers. After cooking dinner, we ate at the nearby picnic table then cleaned up the site to make it bear safe. Tony monitored the campfire embers to make sure the embers went completely out while I went to bed. He felt watched. Our camp area was about six foot higher than the stream we had dammed up for bathing. There was a little island, maybe five or six feet long and ten feet wide. Tony looked across the mini-island toward the other side of the stream, and watched as a male Bigfoot came to get a drink. He looked Tony eye to eye as he was sitting on the top of the picnic table, with feet on the bench. That would mean that this fellow was at least eight and a half to nine feet tall – and he was only standing about fifteen feet away. His hair was red brown.

"As I said, Tony got the impression it was male, but it was too dark to see clearly. Tony walked around with a flashlight, to see if he could see more. It must not have frightened my son, because he didn't call out or wake me up while I was sleeping in the tent, unaware anything unusual had occurred.

"Next morning, I was preparing breakfast before my son woke up. I cut up a honeydew melon and threw the rinds out on the island, and began to cook sausage and eggs. While I was preparing coffee, I heard rustling and looked up. On the Island, I noticed a three-foot-tall Bigfoot child and its mother gathering the honey dew melon rinds. When they saw me looking at them, they turned away and disappeared into the forest. I felt no ill intent."

## GLENN

Glenn Norberg, who works and lives down in Florence, Colorado, a town with a population of 4,000, explains that if he climbed up on the roof of his house, he could turn around an imaginary compass and tell accounts of Bigfoot sightings from all the directional points in the vicinity; one or more stories from each direction from every canyon and even across the plains towards Pueblo.

"I used to dismiss local accounts of Sasquatches at first, still under the assumption they try to avoid people. It seemed unbelievable; after all, our small town is in the high desert. I thought *no way*. Although it is adjacent to the Arkansas River it is 10 miles from the nearest mountains, and nowhere near the Pacific Northwest where I believed Bigfoot lived - if it existed. I have since had my world-view altered radically in regards to the reality and presence of Bigfoot in and around Florence.

"That was before I knew how close they were to urban environments, but if you look into it, you find there's a lot of cover for concealment. They seem rather unafraid of people but they prefer to remain obscured. Like a mountain lion is probably not afraid of you, but it chooses to be behind you. That's the way it operates. That's where it feels like it has the advantage. If that mountain lion wanted to, it could face you and take you out but it prefers not to. That's not the way it feels comfortable. It's an ambush predator. I think these hominids have a similar mindset.

"I've found a number of accounts - ranging from one in the 1960s, three during the 80s, another in the 90s, and maybe a dozen more recently that describe hairy men though some called them Bigfoot. Most accounts center around the drainage ditch we call the "wash" that goes directly through town, leading from the Wet Mountains and issuing into the Arkansas River at the Northern edge. It passes under highway 115 which is the main street, through a twenty-foot-deep dirt culvert, lined with vegetation.

"They might even move through larger populated areas, but at least for now, we know about several small towns. When they come into Florence, they could be observing us as they pass through, yet, I almost think we're incidental. This group doesn't seem to have a problem just walking through streets the way other animals like bears, raccoons, and coyotes do, but it can be traumatizing for the poor souls who look out their windows and happen to see them under the street lamps or the light of day. Sometimes these folks will hold their story inside until someone like me comes along and asks them in a non-judgmental way what they saw.

"I think they observe us in the mountains. If they're around when we're camping, I think they'll check us out. I'm sure they are aware of guns, so they might show caution or alarm. But they are not reluctant to come into town. Primarily at night, but surprisingly, even during the day. They act nonchalant during observations in public spaces where they could easily avoid us, but they don't seem to care one way or the other.

"A good example was when a lady who was driving at night noticed a pair of Sasquatch casually standing beside the road, like hitchhikers a couple of hundred feet from the bridge over the Arkansas River. As she drove by, they just watched her, not attempting to hide.

"Mateo and I have located structures in trees and brush along the river which we have documented in videos – that were possibly used for spotting game - but also for watching canoes, hikers and fishermen, and bridge activity. Still, most encounters occur near the wash within fifty feet of what used to be a popular donut shop that sat kitty corner from the drainage.

"WHAT GOT me started asking around and gathering Bigfoot reports was a sighting from 1987 that became the subject of a **BFRO (Bigfoot Research Org.)** taping in 1991. Three witnesses encountered something strange. Two employees at the donut shop saw an eight-foot tall, hairy figure walking down the street at 3:00 a.m. About that same time, a paper delivery truck driver heard something scary behind the building where he deposited the stacks of newspapers set for distribution. A cop stopped by the shop while on patrol, and he was told of the strange occurrence. Reportedly, the policeman returned to the donut shop after searching behind the building and asked the boys at the shop what they had seen. The employees told him and asked what *he* found. He said, *'Didn't see nothin, nothin at all.'* They told the BFRO that the cop wouldn't say anything, however, he was so traumatized and shaky, and he spilled his coffee. Here is the link for the BFRO video. http://bfro.net/GDB/show_report.asp?id=3185

WHILE SEARCHING for the original witnesses one autumn in the mid 1980's, Glenn stopped in the local hardware store. He asked the guy, a long-time resident, about the BFRO story. Glenn was shocked by the response. *"I was there."* The witness described the event. In the mid 1980's one of his jobs was to put coal in the basement of the junior high in the early morning to heat the school. As was his habit, on the way home he would stop at the donut shop for coffee and a doughnut. That morning he looked out the window and saw the figure of a hairy man walking down the street.

"I asked him, *'Why do you say that it was a man?'*

*'What else could it be? The guy probably came from a party at the bar, and left in a gorilla suit.'*

Glenn queried, *"This is a small town. Was anyone crazy enough to do that here in the 1980s? He said, 'No.'* But his worldview wouldn't allow for alternative explanations.

Worldview dictates how we perceive or interpret the things we experience. Another example of worldview denial came from the local gun shop owner. I asked if he'd ever noticed anything weird in the area. He denied seeing or hearing anything strange, yet he remembered one odd occurrence. He would go hunting in the mountains with family and friends. They camped in campers, and one night this man noticed rocks being thrown and hitting his camper.

'I just figured it was my nephew.'

I asked him, 'Was it your nephew?'

'Well, he denied it.'

'Is your nephew prone to doing things like that, then denying them?' He responded, 'No'

"So, rather than believe it could have been Bigfoot, he blamed his nephew. Bigfoot wasn't a part of his worldview.

"In contrast, we have this openly descriptive account from the mid-1980s involving one of my neighbors, Shannon Proud. Usually, after Florence's annual Pioneer Day parade in September, everyone gathered at the city park which abuts the large drainage ditch we often call the 'wash,' for a follow up barbecue. However, Shannon decided to walk home just after 12:00 noon instead of attending the picnic. As he crossed over the wash something caught his eye. Twenty feet below him a very large, dark hairy figure was walking up the ditch from the river and heading out of town – at midday, just three blocks from the barbeque in the park!

"The creature didn't seem perturbed by the man's presence or even take notice of the observer. Shannon watched the figure continue to progress for a full minute until it walked out of sight around a bend in the ravine. He later exclaimed, 'Thank God, it never looked back at me!'"

"SOMETIMES THEY DO LOOK BACK. Coal Creek is an old part of Florence, an unincorporated mining town, more like a collection of buildings. Mateo and I recently heard of a woman who was traumatized when one dark night in November, 2021, she was shocked to look out her front window in time to see a Sasquatch strolling down the middle of the street lit up by a street lamp -barely thirty yards from her living room. When she spotted the figure, it looked directly back at her as it continued to walk, not run, into the darkness, moving toward the wash. That experience really got to her.

"The last thing you would expect is something like that just brazenly walking freely through town in the middle of the night. I think this is similar to South African elephants who are dealing with the encroachment of cities. The herd breaks into parts and silently moves through the town. Most of the time their passage goes completely unnoticed. Documentaries show them silently walking through the streets with no one noticing them even though they pass vehicles and people. They are quiet, and they find the avenues that have fewer vehicles and they are barely noticed even going through a city of hundreds of thousands of people. If a massive elephant can do it, a clever Sasquatch can get away with it - no problem. It's amazing, you wouldn't expect that.

"The distraught woman's brother, now sixty years old, has believed in Sasquatch for twenty years. But his sister never believed him. For years, since they were kids, she'd made fun of him and called his ideas stupid. The guy is an adventurer who pokes around looking for weird things, or signs in the mountains. He has seen Bigfoot and took us to the wash where he had his experiences. His sister happens to live near the wash but until that night the lady's position was, 'There's no way these hominids exist.'

"Her incident validated that these beings have no fear of people. I think they do it because they get away with it without any altercations - even if people see them from time to time. Most dogs don't realize they are around because they're not looking, they're not sniffing. A lot of dogs are complacent just like their owners. If they did sniff a Sasquatch, they're not going to know what it is. The place you find dogs going crazy is when something weird starts coming up to the house or sometimes hunting dogs will notice because of their skill sets and training. Most dogs are clueless. Their instincts are not developed. People also have instincts that are not developed. You have to practice to be aware. It's testable. Many times, my friend Mateo has experimented in the woods around tons of dogs and people. He'd just stand motionless off to the side of the trail, not making any noise. Neither dogs nor people saw him - even out in the open."

"DAKOTA A BOW HUNTER had watched as a Sasquatch burst out of some trees below his position. He was very surprised to see it was not an elk, but a biped running down the side of the ridge to the campground below. It continued to cross the Phantom Canyon Road and climbed the opposite side of the canyon, up the mountain and over the ridge which was covered in sparse south facing scrub. He observed that the individual was dark and hairy, and Dakota had no trouble identifying it as a Bigfoot. This event took place over a span of several minutes.

"Yet sometimes, they are simply observing *US*, as he later learned when he and a girl went up to park near a large boulder aptly called Party Rock in Oil Well Flats - a popular place for kids to go to drink and hang out. They built a fire in a pullout camping spot and were drinking and dancing to the music blaring from the truck radio, when all of a sudden Dakota looked over his shoulder, his eyes widened and he ran back to the truck.

"When he'd turned around, he'd seen a nine-and-a-half-foot tall gray or white Sasquatch only thirty feet away – peeking over a bushy juniper tree fifteen to twenty feet across. He even saw its fingernails glistening in the beam of his flashlight, because it positioned its hands on the top fronds, like it was looking over a tall fence. The image scared the crap out of him. He and the girl loaded into the truck and tore off.

"In the middle of 2020, Dakota, now twenty-five, took me to the spot. It was decorated with scattered junipers, all about twenty to thirty feet across and ten feet tall. I'd been skeptical but he pointed out the bush which actually *was* only thirty feet away from where we parked. I still tried to disprove the account with my measuring tape and a ladder. We walked over to take a look at the tree. I was surprised to find a two-foot-wide gap had been tunneled into the back side. Some of the juniper's central branches were broken out creating a hollow that ran all the way to the top. Presumably, the creature had cleared out a hiding booth from which to observe human shenanigans from the inside - perhaps for years - looking out through branches splayed apart with the tips of its fingers.

"Oh, *heck* no! I leaned the ladder against a measly two-inch branch and unsteadily climbed up. Sure enough, I could spread the branches and look out to see the truck and the party area. I measured the height from the ground to the top with my tape measure - nine and a half feet exactly. *That* really brought it home for me. We made a video."

"BUT THAT WASN'T the only time I had reports of Bigfoot trying to interact with and observe humans. Near the Canyon City area, a long-term RV couple had experienced pebble and stone tosses, and seen imprints around their campfire. But one day when the woman walked along the fence line of the campground, she looked over the edge and down the hill. She was surprised when this Sasquatch popped out from its observation post beneath an innocuous pile of dead leaves at the edge of the hill. After the jig was up, it stood and turned, and quickly moved away in the direction of the nearby river."

"SOMETIMES THEY WATCH us from above, but one woman explained in a 'Modern Explorer' video that she heard something heavy running along her roof, much heavier than a squirrel or a cat. She went outside to find out what it was. As she came out of the door she looked up to the roof. She described seeing a 'gargoyle,' a three-foot-tall ugly creature sitting on its haunches looking down at her from above her doorway. Could the gargoyle have perhaps been a Sasquatch baby with a parent lurking nearby? Watch the video, see what you think."

"THOSE INDIVIDUALS DIDN'T SOUND TOO PERTURBED by their odd neighbor's surprising antics, but there are plenty of stories to the contrary. Glenn tells us that, "Before Dakota and I left the Flats that day, we drove through other campsites up one of the area's dirt roads and found a retired guy who was living in a caravan. In June or July of 2020, he was asleep in his van at another location. It was darkening, and within ten to fifteen minutes good-sized rocks began landing all around his vehicle. He said, 'I tried to look, but my flashlight quit. I *threatened to shoot anyone* throwing rocks. Whoever was pitching them left so they must have understood my intent.'

"A NEIGHBOR down the street had a different solution. In the wee hours, he was working on his car to avoid the heat. He thought he heard something that 'sounded bipedal' walking up to the backyard wooden fence and growling behind it. Although it was within ten feet of him, he couldn't see the source of the growl because the fence blocked his view. He ran into the house to grab his guns, and that night decided to quit working outside in the dark, no matter how hot it was. Within a couple of weeks, he heard small stones hitting against his fence. When he investigated to see if he could find any evidence, he noticed one small stone had landed on one of the bags of topsoil he had piled up behind the back fence. He didn't see it as a peaceful inquiry and has since moved out."

EVEN THOUGH THEY may have seemed frightening, or annoying, no one in his regional accounts has described them as overtly aggressive. Glenn's own experience was that he felt someone watching him as he hiked up Newlin Creek trail after crossing a sturdy bridge twenty feet long and four feet wide. It was very stable, built with 2 x 12s set in secured joist hangers on cement footings. The bridge was raised on 4x4 up rights and bounded by two handrails.

"On the other side, I continued to feel watched as I walked in the woods. It made me feel uncomfortable but I couldn't see anything and eventually left. I returned a few days later to find that the stout bridge had been dented by something very heavy hitting it. The entrance had been shifted five feet downstream causing the exit to twist at a 30-

degree angle, and though all of the 2 x12s were split along their full lengths, the bridge was still attached at the upstream connections. The other ends were *down in the water*. Since there were no oil tankers on the little creek, I took it for a sign – 'PRIVATE PROPERTY - KEEP OUT!'

OUR TAKEAWAYS from these interviews are that these beings are emphatic but not aggressive. There are undoubtedly exceptions – for instance, I can imagine that if an individual had been shot, or a family member was injured or killed by a human it could sometimes lead to trouble. Maybe they have cranky SOBs like we do. But these particular reports never included physical harm to humans.

Still, some people assume any movement, even tossed rocks and pebbles, or peeking from behind a tree warrants a death sentence. Sometimes Sasquatches let us know we are not welcome to stay on their turf, but it would be nice if people with dangerous attitudes would stay home or at least not shoot first and wonder later if it was really necessary.

One man, feeling surrounded by multiple Sasquatch while waiting for a friend, shot one with a big 303 British rifle which produced a massive exit wound. He hit it in the right pectoral / shoulder region. It spun around, dropped down behind a rock, then turned back and looked at him as if wondering why, then it walked away. Another individual shot with a turkey load – continued to walk over a mountain. If they died, it would have been on their terms. You see these stories played up all the time. What a waste. It is sad when everything they do is interpreted as aggressive - worthy of shooting and dismembering them. Is this how we treat a 'newly' discovered culture in the twenty-first century?

IT TAKES an immense amount of courage to calm one's internal terror in such moments, but thankfully, there are accounts of people who have either tried to learn how to interact like Mateo or take a hint and leave the area as bidden like Glenn. In this age of greater degrees of harmony, can we not respect a culture which has interacted with several types of hominids – including modern humans, for countless millennia? In these accounts they may have displayed curiosity and a desire to play, and perhaps values such as sharing, and the ability to count as when the young one took only two of the apples until it was absolutely certain they could have the other two. There are a number of stories of Sasquatch befriending and helping humans. Who knows what revelations further interactions will bring?

It would seem that Sasquatch has found many peaceful ways to observe us, to see if we are ready to interact. From rooftops, to leaf piles, to moonlight tag or hide and seek, they make quiet inquiries, sometimes with pebble or stone throws to entice us. Secora check these out when you have time, there are some great new experiences.

"Thank God, it never looked back at me" Video: https://youtu.be/XCatOc5jDKw
"Snow white sasquatch encounter": https://youtu.be/1yfGfLsQkWU
Beaver creek sas p1: https://youtu.be/seXyWmV7cLc
P2: https://youtu.be/5B74cSB4Uf0
Gargoyle: https://youtu.be/AgOcw50gyc4

Secora sat back, blown away by the detailed report. This was going to make a great article. She could hardly wait to share the videos with Destiny and Gideon – and really everyone.

## 11

# BURIED

The dawn over the lake had been serene as Kyah boarded the ferry to La Paz, Bolivia. He filled his lungs with the fresh cool air, secretly wishing he never had to leave this gorgeous land.

When the ferry neared the shore, he stood to watch the approaching dock. There was still a part of him that would be glad to go home and see his family - not to mention the joy of spending two nights in Jamaica.

His thoughts were broken by the sound of a klaxon blaring, a warning of natural disaster.

The captain announced that there was a major earthquake southwest of La Paz and a number of strong aftershocks were expected. His message went on to make a plea for those who were capable to help pull survivors from the rubble of two towns in the vicinity.

Immediately Kyah thought of Alai, who had lost her community – her entire nation to sliding rock, and he knew he must take action. Busses were taking people to the area, and he did not hesitate to grab his bags, and hop on the first available bus the moment he disembarked. He thought about contacting the airport to let them know of his change of plans, but communication with El Alta seemed impossible.

KYAH WIPED filthy sweat from his brow. He'd just found what was left of a flock of sheep. Four looked like they would survive. They would be valuable resources to the surviving villagers in the coming weeks. The crew had found only a few surviving people, fifteen of three thousand – so far. Kyah wished he had access to the ground penetrating radar equipment – anything to increase the numbers before the air ran out.

A helicopter landed and dropped off two canines and their handlers. *Thank God*, Kyah thought. As luck would have it, he saw another dog pawing at some rocks to his left, so he immediately went over to lift rocks, yelling hello, anyone there? Alguien esta aqui? It sounded like he heard a faint muffled groan and the dog yipped. Kyah redoubled his efforts, forgetting everything else. He removed a huge chunk of rock, so heavy the muscles in his arms were quivering and a hand pushed through. Rolling that rock aside, he pitched others away from a family of three wedged in the rocks. With extreme effort, he pulled out the man who was closest to the surface, and with his help, they pulled out a young girl with a broken arm and a bloody face who was crying.

As they moved down another layer in the rock, Kyah noticed his cell phone had wiggled free from his pocket and rattled its way down through the rock slag - far beyond reach. He couldn't let that distract him for long, and at last, he and the other man were able to free a thin woman who seemed almost lifeless from the rocks, and a cat that shot out and away.

Kyah tried to recapture his breath and seek medical attention for the woman who was in bad shape. Somewhere a heartbroken man began to wail, but Kyah hardly noticed since he was able to get the attention of a medic to help the woman and the girl. He found a cooler and drank much needed water. The dog had remained at his side, as he pressed on, turning rocks near the family which had just emerged from the rubble of some sort of building. The man said there had been two other families in the area. He'd heard one woman moaning, and thought some of them might have survived. Shortly afterward, he and his family were taken to a hospital. Day turned to dusk. Kyah and a couple of volunteers had only uncovered two bodies at that site. They figured there were at least six as yet unaccounted for. Kyah was able to secure a lantern to continue his search, with only the dog at his side, through the night. He was now hungry to the point of feeling weak. He smelled a pot of hot food and took another break.

New people were arriving throughout the night and into the next morning to assist with the rescue and salvage efforts - recovering surviving people and livestock from several aftershocks. They made makeshift camps and offered crisis services.

Kyah's strength was renewed after eating, and after he shared the remains of the meal with the dog, he returned to the same family housing complex he'd been searching. He thought he might have heard a faint sound and worked swiftly, hoping to recover some being from the area in front of a partially standing wall. There it was, another muffled sound and Kyah at last uncovered a woman with a child that appeared to be gone. He called for medical assistance and as she was taken away, Kyah went back to work and found another dog in a bad way. He called again for help and as the creature was removed, the boy tried his luck again by the wall.

Just after dawn, there was a major aftershock. Kyah's world went black, and after the roar of the moving earth, things became eerily quiet. When he opened his eyes, he was covered by rock which had partially crushed his right arm and leg. He sadly realized he wouldn't be going anywhere anytime soon.

Sometime later, Kyah awoke to the sound of heavy equipment nearby and he tried to yell. He wasn't completely covered by the rocks, but it was hard to take in a large enough breath to produce an audible sound. He tried off and on to holler and noticed as he breathed in that the smell of decomposition was becoming overwhelming. He waited and hoped, calling out when he could. He had no idea how long he'd been asleep, but he figured at least a day.

At last, he heard the sharp barking of a dog, then it snuffled as it came to his face. He heard voices, blessed voices.

JANE AND APARU were worried and had spoken with Gideon, who was getting nervous since there had been no word from Kyah for three days. On the one hand, this was not surprising since his phone would have been on airplane mode much of the time, but he should have found time to touch base by now. Gideon planned to back trace the young man's journey, hoping to find out when or where he may have left his route. For that he would need the help of his old friend Clive Bull Bear, chief of the Pine Ridge Tribal Police, who began back tracing the plane manifests beginning with Missoula, Montana. Kyah was not listed on the flight to Miami from Jamaica. Further research found he'd never even arrived in Jamaica. He was, however, scheduled from El Alto, but he'd apparently never boarded the plane.

Gideon was able to figure out that his nephew had to be in the La Paz area. Through further investigation they learned the flight was postponed due a disruption of activities in the area because of an earthquake. A heavily populated valley southwest of town took most of the damage, but the entire region was affected.

Gideon sought out news as he quickly packed a few items and prepared to leave. Jimmy and Aparu insisted on accompanying him.

Jane, Destiny, and Secora anxiously saw them off at the airport. Secora handed them an envelope of cash in case it could somehow help. Then the worried women returned to their children or jobs with heavy hearts.


ON THE FLIGHT, Gideon and the others tried to stifle the worry that stubbornly refused to leave. The trip was taking too long. They used the time to discuss a plan, and decide where to start their search. Knowing Kyah, he would likely have gone to the source of the damage in the outlying towns to help. That is where they would begin.

By the time the men traveled to the damaged towns, rescue and cleanup crews were beginning to pack up and leave. Heavy equipment was busy leveling any dangerous standing rubble. Gideon was lucky to find one person still packing his gear – a cook who seemed to remember that a young man was pulled from the rubble yesterday. He was in bad shape and may have laid there for at least two days before he was taken to one of the hospitals. In fact, he was the last person the cook had seen removed alive. Kyah's relatives thanked him for the news, and out of gratitude and compassion they offered prayers for the cook, the towns, and for Kyah, from the Lakota and Guero Cliff City traditions.

They traveled back to La Paz with heavy hearts and set out to find which hospitals had been receiving earthquake victims.

By evening time, they stood at Kyah's bedside. He was awake. Alert would be saying too much. He seemed solemn, at best, care worn, like the joy had trickled away from his world. Remembering the joyful child they last saw, the men were saddened to see his current physical and mental state. He dozed off shortly after greeting his relatives.

A nurse came in some time later for a vitals check. Gideon followed her into the hall and asked about Kyah's physical injuries. She told him the boy had a badly broken right arm, his right leg was broken in two places and several ribs were cracked. He was also severely dehydrated from lying in the rubble for two days. Gideon thanked her and returned to the room to update the others.

At a loss for words, they pulled up chairs and sat respectfully beside the shaken young man. Their prayers were silent that night, until they were kicked out and returned to their motel.

## 1 2

# TRANSITION

The next morning, Gideon and the others found Kyah more alert. They gave him chocolates which they had brought, in hopes of cheering the boy up. When he opened the box, he sniffed them and smiled, which brought relief to everyone. After they had sampled a few, Kyah revealed that he had a constant urge to look for the dog that had helped him save a few lives – including, in the end, his own. He hesitated to ask, so Gideon just said it. "You want us to go see if we can find it?"

With moist eyes, Kyah responded, "Yes, please."

That afternoon while Kyah slept, the men went back to the rubble site and were able to find a scrap of a dog lying on top of the rocks. It fit Kyah's description of the white dog with burnished spots on her face. They couldn't be sure if it was the right one but they put it in a carrying cage since the dog was unresponsive. They took her to a vet in the city, who gave her IV fluids and a checkup.

As the vet shook his head, he said, "Are you sure she is worth saving? I mean, she is pretty far gone. We have a lot of homeless dogs in better shape than this."

Gideon let out a sigh and said, "I hear you, but she means a lot to a young man in the hospital, because she helped save him and several others after the earthquake."

"A hero, huh. We'd better give her a chance, no?" The vet told them she would need to stay at the clinic about a week – less if she could stand on her own and eat before then. As they left, Aparu and Jimmy weren't convinced they would ever see her again, so Gideon snapped a picture with his cell phone to show Kyah, hoping he would confirm it was the right dog. The joy on his face was validation enough. The boy decided to call her Penny due to the coppery blotches on her head and shoulders.

KYAH WAS TOLD that his rehab and recovery would entail a year-long therapy. When he took that in, he knew his life was changing. It might take a month just to get him stabilized enough to fly back to Montana, where he could continue to heal with his family.

He probably would not be finishing school this year. If he was lucky, he might be able to take incompletes rather than fails; and the trip to Jamaica remained only a dream. He would need to find housing close to appointments, and make a new set of plans.

Aparu insisted on staying at his stepson's bedside until he could accompany him back home. Although Kyah would spend another week in the hospital, Gideon and Jimmy rented a ground floor apartment for them, until he was strong enough to make the transcontinental flight. Then it was time for Gideon to get back to Secora and to his work at the office. Jimmy said he was also feeling the need to get back home to Destiny, who had surprised him with the announcement that she, like Secora, was pregnant.

Gideon grinned, "You're going to be a dad! That's crazy, buddy."

"Back atcha, Bro. Can't wait to see if your kid will be a baby realtor or a junior heyoka?"

At first Kyah, along with everyone else, was a bit stunned by Jimmy's news, but when he got a grip, his congratulations were effusive. This was an occasion for each of them to offer prayers for the unborn children, and the mothers – and fathers. The next morning,

Jimmy and Gideon said their goodbyes and headed for the airport. Gideon arrived back home in time to accompany Secora to her initial prenatal visit the next afternoon. Things went wonderfully and they got their first visual introduction to "Steve" during a sonogram. Of course, they took Monta along so she could say "hi" to the brother she had informed them was coming. It made Gideon smile, but he was nervous, wondering how a baby would affect their lives. They sent sonogram photos of "Steve" back to Aparu and Kyah.

A FEW DAYS later Kyah and Aparu were settled into the apartment, where Kyah spent much of the time in a state of boredom. Penny's health had improved markedly, but she was not ready to leave the clinic, which was for the best. It would take Kyah and Aparu a while to get used to having a "pet". No, they reminded themselves, she was a service dog.

And to that end, when she did arrive, Kyah struggled to teach simple commands to Penny. It was a totally foreign concept for her to interact with humans at their request. At best, she probably understood "get out of here", or "get away from that food." Just getting her to come towards him on command eluded her. She came over when she wanted to, usually to beg for food or water. Other than that, she didn't get the drift. He really couldn't get her to sit or lie down or stay, if she wasn't close enough for him to touch.

Aparu concluded, "You know what they say about old dogs?"

Kyah wasn't fond of stereotypes and patiently continued the lessons. It gave him something to strive for, and a goal worth achieving. Patiently, he tried every day. When he started using food as a reward, she began to respond. By the third and fourth week, there was some progress – not always reliable, but that would eventually change.

Partly to stave off boredom, Aparu taught the boy the healing ways of the Gueros. This inspired Kyah who was already spiritually inclined. He wanted nothing more than to help people, and found himself thinking about taking a new path in life. Maybe he wouldn't follow his mom's footsteps and become an archaeologist. He liked the idea of becoming a first responder, with a focus on search and rescue. Spiritual and emotional assistance could be offered to distressed clients, or their friends and families. It made sense. He could easily see that he and the dog could have a strong future. Hadn't he, and his buddy, Rocky, recovered the torn bodies of the Duendes at the base of their cliff, after they had been attacked by two young thunderbirds? *I have a knack for this,* he thought. It seemed like he was meant to continue this journey.

Maybe he and Penny would join a search and rescue team in Montana. They could travel to disaster locations where the dog would help him sniff out victims, or find missing people in the forest. He was eager to share the news with his mom and Aparu. They in turn, shared the idea with Gideon, Jimmy and the rest of the family, who were thrilled with his life choice. It made sense. He came from a family of holy men, helpers, seers, and healers from various parts of the world.

BACK HOME JANE and Iris removed Kyah from the student rosters in all his fall classes. His teachers wondered if he would finish his degree later this year. The two women had no answers.

They also found a local physician who could recommend a physical therapist to continue to guide his progress. The first appointment would be in eight long weeks.

NOW THERE WAS A TIMETABLE. Kyah had an appointment set for therapy. He must get the dog used to the crate Gideon had bought. Penny already had a raft of vaccinations including: leptospirosis, rabies, kennel cough, and Parvo Virus from her stay at the clinic. But they would need to file for an import permit for her to enter the US. All of a sudden it seemed like they went from blank staring boredom, to cramming for the upcoming journey. He and Aparu ached to be home in Montana, but Aparu also needed to visit his home in the Cliff City. While Kyah continued with the training and preparation efforts, Aparu left for two weeks to visit the land of his birth in the high canyons.

Kyah really missed his company, in fact, he missed everyone. Thank God Penny was there. His loneliness almost took on a life of its own.

Finally, the day came when Kyah was taken by cab to the airport with Penny beside him in a cage and Aparu in the front passenger seat. He made do with crutches until they checked in, at which time he was placed in a wheelchair for the flight. Then Penny was taken away, and the look of loss on her face almost broke his heart. A knot formed in his stomach and throat. He couldn't even speak. Aparu had been given a regular seat while Kyah was strapped into the back. There was that loneliness again – until the engines powered up to take off, and the floor began to vibrate. This became exciting!

## 1 3

# SECORA'S DILEMMA

B ack in her office, Secora was still struggling with an insistent
headache and nausea from the accident. In addition, she was
keenly aware of the drama which must be unfolding in South America.
The anguish generated by both of these torments became too much to
bear alone at home. It was time to get to work, and she wondered, not
for the first time, what the motivation was for the two intruders in the
Wyoming cave. Was it personal? Were they looking for something, or
hiding a problem? Did they want to destroy a remnant of controversial
evidence, or me? More importantly, who did they represent, what was
the payoff for frightening her, and how far were they willing to go?

Blinking back from the fog of her thoughts, she looked at the little
analog desk clock and realized it was time to leave for her fall intro-
ductory megafauna class. She began packing up her materials and left
the building, strolling across campus to meet the new students.

Secora wrote her name and the class number on the white board.
There were maybe a hundred faces before her this time. Once everyone
was settled, she ascertained that everyone intended to be there, before
handing each one a syllabus. She had printed only 90 copies and was
sixteen copies short in the end. She told them where her office was and
that she would have the extra copies available there. In the meantime,

those without a copy could look on with someone else. She began covering the key points they would need to know, before taking a field trip to an active dig site toward the end of the quarter.

About three minutes in, she was interrupted by an older female student, whose challenging tone surprised her.

"I heard you claim to have actually seen cryptid creatures... which I think is a poorly veiled stunt to get more people into your classes. In fact, you *claim* to have a photograph of one of them. I'm sure it is every bit as manufactured as are your random tales." The woman's dark hair framed her scowl, and her right hand fidgeted with the buttons on her long-sleeved plaid shirt. "You do have your own photo lab, don't you?"

At first, Secora felt her blood boil at the accusation. While she paused, other students were looking back and forth between the challenger and the charismatic professor.

Then, she smiled, "My friend, your statement is misguided - on so many levels. We could discuss this further after class if you'd like, but we aren't wasting class time on *whatever* this is."

"So, now you're afraid to show us the picture? I figured as much."

Secora shook her head and drew in a breath. "It's a series of photos, and I didn't develop them if that's what you're insinuating. You should see me after class."

Other members of the class voiced that they would also like to see the photos.

Secora sighed, "Let's see a show of hands."

It was virtually unanimous. "Well, there are too many of you to fit in my office – or even in the hallway for that matter. So, I'll bring them here if you want to wait."

That brought widespread approval from the group.

"I'll come with you to see you don't do anything underhanded."

"*Underhanded* - is definitely not my style. I will take three students – not you – to accompany me and get the photos. Is that acceptable to the majority?"

It was, so Secora and the three randomly selected representatives left the room. When they returned to class, it seemed to Secora, that surprisingly most of the students had remained, and were attempting to crowd around the front desk as she spread out the sequence of photos taken of the scimitar cat on the Ennedi Plateau.

"For the record, these aren't the only images I have of animals once considered to be extinct, but this particular cat is suspected of killing and eating my friend, the water witcher who helped us with our project in Chad. Sadly, his remains were found in the third of three caves, just a little beyond the place I first met him." She had to take a few steps back as students crowded the desk.

"Give everyone a chance to see, please."

"What is it?"

"One of the locals said this was the 'Ennedi Tiger', also known as *Gassingram*. Any questions?"

Another student suggested, "Isn't it a Smilodon?"

Yet another countered, "No, it's different."

"Okay then, that will be your first assignment. By Wednesday, you should send me an email, with your name and the various names of this creature, how you identified it, and a little bit about where it lives." She wrote Ennedi Tiger and her email address on the white board at the side of her desk.

"Now that we have that out of the way, could we proceed with our class schedule? We really ought to plan our field trip for the end of the quarter." The remainder of the class went smoothly, and Secora couldn't tell if the woman who accused her was still in the room.

As she returned to her office, she couldn't help but notice someone had spray painted across the door, KEEP AWAY FROM CAVES.

It seemed a bit unnerving. Secora sighed and took a seat at her desk, about the same time as her phone rang. She was relieved to find it was Destiny, who asked her to come down to the office.

Secora took a seat opposite her boss, who solemnly began, "I've been getting threatening phone calls loaded with defamatory remarks about you - which I would find ludicrous if it wasn't so disturbing. Any idea about the source of these threats?"

Secora was thoughtful as she answered. "No."

"And it appears someone spray-painted a message across your office door this morning.

Who *did* you piss off?"

"Tough to imagine. I've been pretty quiet lately." After a moment she offered, "Seems like I remember something was off when I went to recheck the dates on the Wyoming cave."

"What do you mean?"

"Whoa, guess I didn't tell you yet – what with the accident."

"Should I ask at this point, if it *was* an accident?"

Secora became broody, and offered. "I believe it was. A fleet of RVs crowded the highway. Then the road dipped into a fog bank and one of the drivers must have made a bad choice. I got a cracked skull in a huge pile up of RVs and cars, and was in the hospital for a few days. Then Gideon took me home and I rested for a week. Still have the nausea and headaches."

"Gideon told me you had sustained injuries – just didn't know the details. Sorry Secora, that must have been terrible?"

Secora shrugged.

"So, let's assume there is no way you personally angered anyone. If you had been able to follow through on those dates, what would have been your conclusion?"

"That's a great question. Not that I wouldn't love to be able to verify those dates with unimpeachable proof, but I would check to see if the vegetative matter that was used as a basis for those dates, was isolated to only one level. If it was scattered throughout the strata –it might invalidate, or at least call into question, the date of 40,000 years ago. The lab is now running the samples I collected from several levels, for dates. It will be a while before I hear back."

"So, what happened?"

"I was working far enough back in the shelter, actually, it turned out to be a cavern, that it was hard to make out details, so I hung a lantern from a root in the middle of the ceiling, so I could carefully define a uniform edge to take the clean samples, then the lamp went out. I crouched down and looked cautiously around. Things seemed pitch black and there were noises. I looked past where the lamp was hung, and noticed it was already dark outside. Then I figured I must have been there for several hours.

It seemed like I heard two individuals adjusting some gear. I crawled past them to get to the entrance. I could even hear them mouth-breathing. So, I practically crept along the bottom of the cave wall, and exited before they turned on their headlamps. In the parking lot, I disabled their truck by pulling off the battery cables, and drove off without looking back.

I experienced no further problems, until I entered the freeway and got involved in that pile up."

"Anything else?"

"Well, Destiny, there was a minor disturbance in class this morning." She proceeded to explain the accusatory comments of the student in class. "I have no idea who the student was, because it was the first day of class, but I could narrow it down by marking off the students I recognize from other classes from the roll sheet."

"Don't waste your time, she might not have been a student at all. Who would benefit from discrediting or intimidating you?"

"Not sure. I can't pull the pieces together yet. Well, when I think about it, I've been in a number of caves and rock shelters through the years – and most of those experiences were less than pleasant."

"This time it is a bummer for both of us. Both you and the department have been charged with trespassing."

"You're kidding, we were *asked* to corroborate or challenge the 40,000-year-old dates."

"Right, our lawyers are following the paper trail. Now, about the office door..."

"I'm not sure how to remove the paint."

"Don't worry, maintenance should be here..." She checked the time. "In an hour."

"Destiny, would you mind if I left for the day? I'm not feeling great and I have no other classes."

"Maybe I should drive you?"

"I'll be okay, oops, don't have a car at the moment, so I'll catch a cab."

"The heck with that! Give me a minute, I'll grab my keys."

Oddly, when they exited the building and moved to the parking lot, they noticed a cab idling at the curb. "That's strange." noted Destiny. "I'll just ask who they are waiting for. You go over and stay by my car."

When Destiny unlocked the doors and slid in, and said, "The driver said he was paid to wait for a female client, then he gave your name. Someone seems to want to intimidate you. Makes me wonder if you'll be safe at home."

"Maybe they want to scare me, throw me off my game. They needn't have bothered, I'm already pretty shaky."

"To be clear, Wyoming was the only project you're currently working on, right? You mentioned other tempting email enquiries, right?"

"Right. I left as soon as you asked me to go. I had been preparing for my classes and hadn't taken any other side projects at the time – at any rate it's the only cave I've inspected since the term started. Never was charged before, but now that I think about it, caves and rock shelters have presented various dangers to me and my friends over the years. Two assassins came after me and Monta for looking at the rock shelter near Custer, Washington, and we had to flee from another thug, to the Whatcom County Sheriff's Department for safety."

Destiny asked, "Could those criminals be back for more?"

"Not in this world. One was slashed by a terror bird and bled to death as she fought them beside me and Monta. The other was Robert Greenwood, a greedy miner and artifact trafficker, partnered with our previous Dean, Dr. Donald Chastain. They bought the land with the rock shelter and were selling questionably obtained artifacts on the black market to collectors with fat wallets – Donald was arrested for conspiracy to commit murder. Greenwood, the assassin, died from mysterious causes at the base of the Cliff City.

"Quite a pair."

"The burly assailant after me and Monta was arrested and went to prison – far as I know. In fact, only two men who attacked us over the years actually survived, and both went to prison."

"Well then, maybe this is something entirely new. Better watch your back."

"Thanks, you too. I think it's important for me to come to work – even though I'm now *pregnant*. Something else I found out in the hospital."

"You're kidding! Me too. I didn't think this was the right time to mention it, but yeah! I just let Jimmy know. I'd like to have seen the look on his face if he hadn't been in Bolivia. Maybe *pregnancy* is part of the reason you've been dealing with nausea. I had it bad for a couple of weeks."

"Sharing it with a friend puts a brighter cast on being pregnant at forty for the first time. This is amazing! Our babies will grow up as friends. Congrats to us both."

"Yes, we'll go through all of the happiness and doubts together. We'll need to watch each other's backs though. You'll move your desk and chair to my office temporarily. Or I could just give you your old office back, and kick out the oil shale grad Chastain put in there – but we do have a surplus of grad students and teaching assistants this year. Better we share this office. It's more than big enough. That should spare Tarkio any disturbing fallout from your new stalker."

"Good idea. He and Bill must be home from Colorado. We should see them any time now."


IT WAS a bit of a squeeze to get a second desk into the dean's office, but before long it was a natural and comfortable work station for both women. Secora made adjustments, by leaving the office for any conferences Destiny had scheduled, and Destiny hired a new female security cop, who became a standard presence in the anteroom. She had a small desk, a dresser really, where she sat when she wasn't patrolling the halls. Secora would work there if it was vacant, while Destiny was in conference.

Secora also began to arrive later in the mornings, taking time to prepare Monta for school, and making her lunches. Alai, who enjoyed sleeping in, would be home to receive her after school was over.

Monta, herself, was pleased as punch now that she was a student – *but not for long.* She managed to tell all her classmates who would listen, that soon she would be a professor like her mom.

The rest of the week passed without incident at the university. Secora was thrilled with her classes and new accommodations. She walked into the office with a cup of tea for herself and a cup of Destiny's favorite coffee.

"Good morning, thanks for the coffee." In return, the dean handed Secora a folder and a spiral record book. "One of our instructors had an accident crossing a stream on mossy rocks. His leg was broken and he will be out for two weeks. Since you are accredited, I wonder if you would mind picking up his two archaeology classes and a bone lab?"

"I might be able to work them in. What's the schedule?"

"Everything's in the record book. I'd like to save a few dollars for the department with someone on salary, rather than hire a temp."

Secora looked thoughtfully through the papers, as well as the armful of textbooks, and lesson planners she was handed.

Destiny hardly looked up from her work until her telephone rang. She ended the conversation with, "That's good news. When do we meet with Ms. Lambert and her attorney? Okay, I'll make sure we're there. Thanks."

"Something else to add to your calendar, Secora. The owner of the cave in Wyoming would like to meet out of court. Apparently, the land ownership title and documents with which we were presented were falsified. As part of the divorce decree, they had to sell the property and split the money. Her ex-husband wanted to claim ownership and jack up the price of the property with the footprints, so he could sell it at a profit for himself, but the wife actually holds the title – something like that."

"Then maybe it was the husband wanting to chase me away and preserve the first dates?"

"Either way, we'll get it sorted."

"Perhaps."

"Now, I believe you have all you can do to manage these extra classes for the next two weeks."

"True. I see one class conflict I'm worried about. Perhaps either Iris, or Jane could take it."

"Oh, I hadn't thought about that but... sure, I'll look into it." Destiny made a note on a long list.

Ten minutes later, Secora headed over to one of the new classes, leaving plenty of time to arrive before any of the Montana Archaeology students. Once there, she again reviewed the lesson book and opened the text to a bookmark, eager to meet the class.

THE DAY after Secora's office move, Bill and Tarkio returned to the university. Bill moved into her old office with Tarkio, which was as it should be. This way, they could work the information in their Bigfoot report into articles for the two publications which had served their needs before. Both Secora and Destiny were amazed at the results of their interviews in Colorado and had looked at some of the suggested videos.

The only downside to the trip was that Tarkio managed to twist his ankle while hiking the crags, west of Colorado Springs, and was now hobbling on crutches. Apparently, the climb was worth it, since they were rewarded with a brief view of a tree peeking Sasquatch.

Getting out to a road and back to their vehicle with Tarkio's bad ankle, was something neither of them hoped to experience again.

As a seasoned teaching assistant, Tarkio was able to help with Secora's lab class, since it conflicted with the Development of Culture Class she had temporarily taken on, until Iris could decide whether or not she could manage the extra lecture. She also asked the guys to present their report on Bigfoot Culture, to the class on Cultural Development. This was a great help because the injured instructor's broken leg wasn't healing and he would remain hospitalized until there was significant improvement.

# 14
# HOSTILITY

Because Secora was still dealing with morning sickness, Iris had been asked to assist with both of the new classes, and Jane was thrilled to take the bone lab. A month later, they learned that things for the poor instructor had gone from bad to worse. A fat globule from the broken leg traveled to his lungs, resulting in a pulmonary embolism.

Iris and Jane had to notify his students that their teacher may not return to his class that quarter, and that they would be finishing out the term for his classes.

The worst was yet to come. Two days later, Iris had to disclose the tragic news that the instructor had died from his complications. She told his former students where to find the obituary, and when the memorial would take place. Of course, the students were shocked and thoughtful when they learned he had "moved on," but Iris knew there was no use denying the truth, at least this way they could wish him well, and she offered to pray for his smooth transition with anyone who wished – outside of class.

THE STUDENTS in Secora's intro to megafauna class came up with some interesting views on the Ennedi Tiger. Many went as expected, but she shared a few emails with the class. One person suggested they might have seen one of these tigers with two cubs in the Mexican Sonoran Desert. Another shared that 'sand lions' once lived in what is now Israel. They looked very much like the strain of Ennedi Tiger which had the solid brown coat and a short tail – the one that actually looked more like a Smilodon.

Secora smiled. "I didn't know that. Thank you."

Another student said, "The Tibetan snow lion also had a short tail, at least as depicted on the Tibetan flag."

"Hmm... Perhaps you could check into information from the last sightings and let us all know?"

"Sure."

Another person offered an alternative opinion, "Tibetan Buddhists say it is a mythical creature, a protector for the Dalai Lama. It's a fanciful guardian, depicted on the flag and old coins. Not an animal you can look up."

Secora responded, "I believe is said to have lived in the eastern Himalayas, am I right?"

"It's a myth, but yes."

"Lions were found all over Asia, in India, in Persia, all through the mountain region. What do *you* think the chances are that they were also found in Tibet?"


THE NEXT MORNING, Secora and Destiny went to meet with the *actual* owner of the Wyoming rock shelter, Tanya Lambert, to resolve the legal issue. It followed that Secora and the department were cleared of charges, and Tanya made apologies to them for her husband's crude actions. Then, she asked if there was any information resulting from Secora's "scientific" efforts yet.

Something about her eagerness, and a certain glint in her eye made Secora suspicious about Tanya's sincerity. She risked a glance at Destiny who twisted her mouth in a way that seemed to convey agreement.

Secora said, "That sort of thing usually takes a while, often months."

They all signed the necessary legal documents in front of their lawyers, then Secora and Destiny shook hands with all there, and prepared to leave.

"Just a sec," Tanya called, "You will let me know what you find - right?"

"Absolutely," Destiny responded, before letting the door close after her.

Secora shook her head on the way to the car. "There was something left unsaid. I don't think that whatever this was, our troubles are over."

"Right, I wrote down the name of the estranged husband. I'll show it to you in the car."

Secora glanced at the name. "Hmmm... Bill Brown. If he exists, and that is his real name, I wonder if he had any other motivation besides money?"

"What if the source of the intimidation might be coming from somewhere else?" Destiny added, "I don't think the disruptive female student in your class was this guy in drag, do you?"

"No that was definitely personal. She was trying to discredit me in front of my class, and my boss. I doubt the two events are related. Maybe we aren't looking at it from the right angle. Maybe there's a bigger picture."

Destiny sighed, "Hopefully it will become apparent soon."

After a pause, Secora mumbled, "I can't help but wonder if it might have anything to do with either of the two of the criminals who went to prison. Both Chastain and a guy we called Blue Raincoat. We later found out his name was Tony Tobias Scott. He had extensive connections. I wonder if maybe Scott escaped again from Bolivia.

"So, what did he do?"

"He was the powerful leader of an international human trafficking and emerald mining operation, not to mention, he was responsible for a slew of murders. I'm sure he still has connections."

"Great, Secora. Not sure I needed to know all that - and I don't want to think about what Donald Chastain could be capable of."

They continued in silence as they waited at a red light. When it turned green, Secora said, "What if it was Tanya all along? This lawsuit thing could have been an attempt to draw attention away from some other issue."

Destiny turned on the blinker and turned into the parking lot to drop Secora off. "I suppose today's apology *could* have been an effort to deescalate and deflect. I could see Tanya being the power behind the problems."

"Who knows, Chastain may have known Tanya or her husband. Now that he's in prison... he might contact nefarious people... Oh, I've got it! With a black wig, *she* could have been the class heckler."

"Even scarier, was she inside the cave?"

Secora admitted, "I've got goosebumps."

"Me too." Destiny walked Secora upstairs. "I'm curious; did you hear anything on the materials you sent out?"

"As a matter of fact, I received a letter today which although, interesting, doesn't rule out the possibility of the 40,000-year-old dates. The same seeds were found in a 25,000-year-old level, plus or minus 600 years. Either way, the dates are early for humans and latish for the megafauna."

"Interesting."

# 15

# GROWING UP

J ane welcomed Kyah and Aparu to Missoula with open arms, and the three younger children just couldn't stop bouncing and squealing. After they collected their luggage and the dog, Aparu and Jane dropped Kyah off at Gideon and Secora's home, because they had a nice fenced yard for the dog to go to the bathroom and run around. It took the rest of the day before she was comfortable enough to come out of the crate and move around in the strange place. Kyah tried to rest, but his body could still feel the vibrations from the airplane hours afterward.

Later that evening L. W. and Sage hailed their return with a celebratory dinner and lots of hugs. Gideon mentioned that since their place was outside of town, Kyah might need a more permanent place to stay with Penny, closer to town since he had no transportation. As it was now, he had to drive Secora to work because their other car was totaled and they hadn't found time to replace it.

L. W. and Sage were overjoyed. They welcomed Kyah and Penny to stay in the rental house in their backyard. Their home in Missoula had some acreage which might be a good fit for the young man. They would need to fence in part of the yard so Penny wouldn't be tempted to wander off.

By the end of the week the fence was up and everything was set for their arrival. Kyah still felt tired and stiff from the long journey and it took a few days to settle in. His appointment with the local orthopedic specialist was still six days away. He'd brought a copy of his medical records from Bolivia for the doctor to review, and hoped to get a referral for ongoing physical therapy, with the goal of walking on his own - without crutches. In the meantime, it was a waiting game.

Seizing an opportunity, Aparu made arrangements for him to study under Jimmy Lizardeye to further his education. Jimmy was currently at the trailer in South Dakota, so Destiny took Friday off work, to take Kyah and Penny out for the week so he could learn the prayers for the living and the dead, and prepare himself to heal spiritual and psychological wounds. They would close up the trailer and leave it in the care of Clive Bull Bear, who had a married daughter who would be grateful to have a place for her family. Then Jimmy would pack up, and return Kyah to Missoula, where he would spend the rest of the pregnancy with Destiny while they figured out a more permanent solution to their housing needs.

It was also time for Jane, Aparu, and the kids to make arrangements to move out of Iris's house and into an apartment of their own nearby. As it was, they had also been moving back and forth between the trailer on Pine Ridge, and Iris's place. They decided to stay right in the thick of the family in Missoula, rather than taking that scenic place Gideon had found up in the Swan. It was much more practical for getting all of the children together to play. They also wanted to be closer to their oldest son.

When Kyah returned from South Dakota with Jimmy, he was most grateful to have a place to call home. The rental had privacy, where he could take care of himself and his canine companion. He never felt alone or far from help, and was near to family. L. W. frequently invited him to dinner, and made sure he had the groceries he needed.

Secora took Kyah shopping at least once a week. For these trips, they borrowed a wheelchair from L. W. so he could get out and about. Jane and Iris also took him out for ice cream, walks in the riverfront park, and to watch the carousel. He was grateful for these opportunities.

Still, being near his family wasn't like being in the thick of things when all of the kids had been around. Now that Kyah was a grown up – and pretty much on his own, it wasn't long before he felt a bit lost and lonely. Sometimes his heart ached almost to the point of tears. He also missed the regular rhythm of going to classes and seeing his friends at the university. This made him all the more determined to push himself with the physical therapy, until he could take walks on his own with the dog. They might eventually make it as far as the university and back. As it was now, Penny had to be let out alone into the yard, where exploration was limited because she had never been trained on the leash. Kyah hadn't been able to get around enough to take her anywhere, but that would soon change.

One evening Tarkio and his wife, Anida came over to visit. That helped a lot. Kyah especially missed hanging out with Tarkio and Bill. He wondered if they might know of someone who could build him a three wheeled conveyance, like a wheel chair but with an extended front tire, and with more ATV clearance, so he could get around outside, and move over obstacles like curbs, for more than the few minutes he could hobble on crutches.

Tarkio said, "It would need to be built to minimize the front end rising so high the contraption would flip over the way dragsters occasionally do." Anida thought she might know somebody. She would ask and let him know.

After that, Kyah's mood started to pick up. He had something to look forward to, along with the PT – whenever that actually got started.

He took more trips outside with L. W's wheelchair after she assured him, she hardly ever used it anymore. After the first attempt at a walk failed, Kyah was left helplessly holding a leash and empty collar, and the dog was on the loose for several hours. After that, Sage took pity on them, employing a two-collar system and lots of practice walks in the backyard. Three weeks later, the daily walks were almost foolproof. Even so, Sage joined the pair for walks off the property for another week, holding the ubiquitous doggie bag.

"Don't think a thing about it kid," Sage had said. "I need the exercise or, at least that's what L. W. tells me. Frankly, I think she enjoys the quiet time.

Though he was nervous at first to be on his own, he managed a few excursions with Penny, who still wasn't at all sure the collar and leash were good things. She'd been a stray – or at least, had roamed unconfined. It was taking her a while to adjust to city life and learn to trust Kyah as a partner. He was grateful he had finally taught her the basic commands, like come, stay and sit.

ONE DAY, a stranger pulled into the driveway with a flatbed truck. Shortly afterward, Tarkio and Anida pulled in too. The reason for the visit became clear when Kyah noticed through the window that Tarkio helped the man lift off a custom wheelchair from the back of the truck, and carefully set it down. They used a remote control to drive it up to the door. Anida stepped out of the car with fast-food bags and a drink carrier. After she closed the car door with her elbow, she and Frederick followed the men inside.

They shared a meal, and then paid the mechanic for his creation. After that, everyone spent the next couple of hours joyfully taking turns driving the chair over obstacles, including the large broken branch from the elm in the yard that no one had been able to clean up from a hailstorm earlier that month. Frederick couldn't stop giggling during his turns. L.W. even challenged him to a race in the regular wheelchair – and won!

When it became dark and the mosquitos became obnoxious, L. W. called them inside and fed everyone tacos and salad, then they visited more quietly as Frederick drifted into sleep.

Even with the assistance of the new vehicle, Kyah could not overlook the fact he would need to somehow acquire a used car, though he had no idea where he would earn money for it. It had been months since he had a job, and what little savings he had was used up by the time he left Bolivia.

The next weekend, Sage and L. W. took him up to Jamal Hasan's Resort for what would likely be Sage's last major public presentation. They hoped it would distract the boy from his worries.

# 16

# THE COMPLEXITY OF EARLY
# RELIGION

Gideon and Secora arrived at the Hasan Resort at West Glacier, and picked up information packets by the door. They quickly found seats, and Secora's stomach was happy when she read there would be a dinner break halfway through, and dessert at the end.

Today, the audience was charged with excitement. Sage's talks were always interesting. He was enthusiastic about the concept that God regularly sent Messengers to earth, one following another, throughout the ages bringing the Creator's message of love. At times, of great duress - or greed for personal power reared its ugly face, but each time, God sent a Prophet or Messenger to restore the beauty of the world. Baha'is called it progressive revelation.

Sage was an archeologist who became interested in the prehistory of religion, and he had come to some amazing conclusions over the years. One of his favorites was that if God never left us alone, without the guidance of His Educators, the vast majority of them would not have been modern humans. He'd say, "Off the top of my head, I can think of 16 different expressions of humanity over nearly *seven million* years. How many of them can you name? Let's remember that only the very last on the list, is modern Homo sapiens, sapiens."

He was also fond of the realization that, "Eurasians, Pacific

Islanders, East Asians, Central Asians, Americans, and Africans - share tribal descent. We must proudly acknowledge our roots."

Decisively, Sage figured these ancestors passed through three cultural stages dictated by the abundance, or scarcity of food. Also, for the last 20,000 years, at the very least, most Proto-Indo-Europeans have believed in the oneness of God.

During one of his previous talks, Sage had mentioned the enigma of Yima or Yama, Lord of both the Zoroastrian and Hindu scriptures, who was remembered for *several* revelatory ages. The innovations assigned to Him took place over a period of perhaps three or four thousand years. Since His expansive story was so full of cultural and communal development, it would need an entire day in itself. Some members of the audience were eager to make that happen.

So, Sage worked with Jamal Hasan to schedule what would likely be the last of his major talks on prehistory.

It took an extreme dimming of the lights to get people to simmer their conversations. Then a beam highlighted the banner above the stage, which read:

*For He dwelleth in the ark of fire, speedeth, in the sphere of fire, through the ocean of fire, and moveth within the atmosphere of fire. How can he who hath been fashioned of contrary elements ever enter or even approach this fire? Were he to do so, he would be instantly consumed."*

— BAHA'U'LLAH, GEMS OF DIVINE MYSTERIES, #110

Foot lights came up as Sage walked to his favorite chair, fashioned from a tree stump, and said, "Certainly, God is far beyond human conception as this banner expresses. The unfathomable creative force we tend to label as God could not safely interact with us, His fragile Creation. Throughout the glimmerings of our human evolution, He sent intermediaries to earth, to manifest His love, desires, and expectations. These Prophets not only spoke in different languages and dialects, but they also spoke with the tongues of different evolved states of humanity. A great Zoroastrian scholar, K. E. Eduljee disclosed that ancient human varieties have occupied sites in the Central Asian area now known as Tajikistan, for as long as 900,000 years. And, in 1991, a Homo erectus skull was found in a Georgian cave at Dmanisi, ninety miles southwest of Tbilisi, in the Mashavera River valley. It dated back to 1.85 million years - not far removed from *Australopithecines* – and nothing short of stunning! It means that some Homo erectus stepped out of Africa and into Eurasia almost two million years ago, maybe even sooner. But this is the clearest date so far. That's the early Pleistocene, my friends! Who knows what we'll find next?" Sage came to center stage. His words became deliberate. "Humankind has been on our planet for almost seven million years, and so-called modern man for only a quarter of a million years in Africa, nearly that long in Eurasia. Since God promised to never leave us without guidance, it should be no surprise that the *vast majority* of *Prophets* were not Homo sapiens, sapiens. Right? God's Messengers did not just pop up a few thousand years ago, and most didn't look like us." Sage returned to sit on the stump, and looked to his friend, Jimmy Lizardeye. "I would like to ask my friend, Jimmy, to offer a prayer before we get started."

Jimmy stepped to a microphone in front of the audience, with his beaded pipe raised.

He said, "Grandfather, Source of all things, please assist our understanding of the ancient peoples' ways, and bring about harmony between our past, our present, and our future. From the Earth, our mother, and the four directions – we ask a blessing for the people here today, in their endeavor to understand one another as they attempt to live in grace with other human beings, the plants, the animals, and the minerals of the earth - as one family and one community."

Jimmy finished, "May the six grandfathers honor our prayer. Hetchetu 'alo. Thank you." He then quietly took his seat next to Destiny.

Sage rose again, this time with a notebook from beside his chair. "Thank you, Jimmy, for the reminder." He scanned the crowd and smiled. "I will read you a few excerpts from various scriptures today, to give you a taste of their beauty. The *Svetasvatara Upanishad* is hauntingly beautiful. It rings as true as if it was written *yesterday* rather than in the Stone Age! I suspect it came from around 14,000 years ago, when the earliest monuments were built. This verse might have been brought by Lord Rama, but the actual time or name of the Prophet doesn't matter. It is a spiritual treasury, part of an oral tradition protected by pure hearted Rishis - the seers and ancient sages who bore these Eternal Truths in mind until they could later be placed on paper. It is a candidate for the oldest remembered, and eventually recorded prayer; a deep rendering of God's relation to the cosmos and its creatures in the heroic Aryan tradition. The original is long; here is a thinly scraped excerpt:

*O Brahman Supreme! Formless art Thou, and yet Thou bringest forth many forms; Thou bringest them forth, and then withdrawest them to Thyself. Fill us with thoughts of Thee! Thou art the fire, Thou art the sun, Thou art the air, Thou art the moon, Thou art the starry firmament, Thou art Brahman Supreme; Thou art the waters—Thou the Creator of all! Thou art woman, Thou art man, Thou art the youth, Thou art the maiden, Thou art the old man tottering with his staff; Thou facest everywhere... Thou art the dark butterfly; Thou art the green parrot with red eyes. Thou art the thunder cloud, the seasons and the seas. Without beginning, beyond time, beyond space... Thou, sole guardian of the universe. In the hearts of Thy creatures, Thou hidest thyself.*

*The Source of all scriptures Thou art; and the Source of all creeds. Of all religions thou art the Source... Yet what shall scriptures avail if they be smooth on the lip but absent from the heart? One Thou art... born from many wombs Thou hast become many: Unto Thee all return. Thou art ruler of the beasts, two-footed, four-footed: Our heart's worship be Thine! There is no day nor night, nor being nor non-being—Thou art alone. Great Glory is thy name... Invisible is Thy form, the seers, in their hearts purified— They alone see Thee... Thou dost pervade the universe, Thou art consciousness itself, Thou art creator of time... Thou art the Primal Being. Thou appearest as this universe of illusion and dream. Indivisible, infinite, the Adorable One—let a man meditate on Thee within his heart, let him consecrate himself to Thee, and Thou, infinite Lord, wilt make Thyself known to him.*

*O Thou womb and tomb of the universe, and its abode; Thou Source of all virtue, destroyer of all sins—Thou art seated in the heart. When Thou art seen, Time and form disappear. Let a man feel Thy presence, let him behold thee within, and to him shall come peace, Eternal Peace: All his fetters shall be loosed.*

"The Revealer of this piece uses concepts with which we are familiar today: *O Thou womb and tomb of the universe – and its abode. The Source of all scriptures Thou art; and the Source of all creeds.* Did you expect that sort of complexity from a Stone Age Prophet? Doesn't it make you wonder what *other creeds* could *possibly* be present that far back?

"The first portion is precious, because the Speaker mentions that God is the spirit in every part of nature, rather than some random sprite, or a god. In college, I was taught religion began with fear - fear of natural events like death, thunderstorms, or eclipses. But as this ancient piece clearly explains - spirituality is conscious awareness of a Creator - earthly life is illusion. This prayer demonstrates that early mankind was capable of knowing God as the source of *all*.

"If you choose to embrace a revealed religion, you likely recognize words in this verse from each and every Prophet – Rama, Krishna, Abraham, Moses, Zoroaster, Buddha, Christ, Mohammad, the Bab, or Baha'u'llah - as if they belonged to your own personal savior. Because they are Emanations of a united Holy Spirit, an umbilical thread that connects us to our Creator.

"In the Bible, as with other scriptures, we begin with a Creation piece. We learned from the Old Testament that, 'In the Beginning was God, and the Word was with God'. Then followed the story of the design and construction of the earth and its features. But what is this 'Word?' How have humans been able to recognize it? I refer again to the banner today. How can that Central Creative Force of the universe commune with human specks? Through His Emissaries, of course, the Great Prophets of the ages."

"Today, we'll feature the Central Asian or Aryan scriptures. Please note that these people lived in the ice-free lands of the Arctic Circle perhaps earlier than 20,000 years ago. Yes, we're going to be talking about the **Aryan tribal people** – IN NO WAY to be confused with Hitler's specifically twisted concept of Aryans."

Sage turned on a PowerPoint image that spotlighted an immense map. "I love this map! The best of its kind. In this part of the world, humanity survived three remembered global stages. *First*, the hunter-gatherers basically lived in times of plenty. *Next*, a drying climate caused starvation and cannibalism. *Finally*, came domestication and the glimmerings of civilization.

"At first, wild food sources could usually maintain human life, but over thousands of years, the land became drier in southern latitudes." Sage pointed at the map. "As the southern ice pack began to melt and recede, waves of Proto-Indo-Europeans were freed to travel southward, in several directions, as we can see from this map. Broad valleys and passages lead them east of the Urals, following great rivers and even further, to the coasts and the islands. It's estimated that tribal people crossed into the Americas anywhere from 20,000 to 14,000 years ago. Of course, those estimates change from time to time.

"Many other travelers passed west of the Ural Mountains, into the vast lands of Central Asia, then later into Europe and its surrounding islands.

"In the second age, global warming caused the rivers, game and fish to dwindle. The ravage of severe drought and hunger demanded the need for domestication if people were going to survive. Later, slowly increasing populations prompted tribes and clans to find fresh pastures for horses, camels, sheep, goats, and cattle.

"Eventually, barely enough - gave way to a production of excess. People gathered in agrarian communities for protection, and in time, generated a surplus of products like meat, milk, cheese, or leather which could be traded or sold – leading to the organization of trade routes and cities.

"As we look at these three stages in more depth, we find Stone Age Prophets who might have lived a long, *long* time before the coming and going of glaciers, or after ice melt. The land was still relatively lush, and generally, humans could hunt or fish to fill their needs. Scraps of text and lore give us a sequential record of their physical, spiritual, and cultural development.

"Almost every tribe or culture has its own name or names for the first man or woman.

The concept is not limited to societies represented by written scriptural accounts. Such Beings have left their marks on all of us. Acknowledging that our most ancient roots lie in Africa, it makes sense that we remember a most primordial, *female* African Educator - **Nu Wa,** the **Remote One**. She is referenced by a number of other names among tribes now encircling the planet, and would most likely have nurtured mankind from primordial human memory, even as far back as the Australopithecines two to four million years ago, before varieties of humans fanned out from Africa into Asia. So far, the oldest archaeological sites in the world are found in Turkana, Kenya.

"Nu Wa is said to have brought a degree of integrity to our earliest human ancestors as they explored life beyond the safety of trees. Until then, there was a social structure not much different than that of other primates. She brought a sense of community to an early humanity without moral guidelines, starting us on a path which one day would lead us toward civilization. A path we are still learning to walk.

"Jumping a couple of million years ahead, early Eurasian believers in God called themselves *Mazda Yasnis,* or worshippers of *Ahura Mazda,* God, in the ancient tongue. They considered themselves **Aryans,** meaning the '**Noble Ones,**' because of their submission to the Creative Force. As one traces the scriptures from this age, Prophet's names may vary due to region. Some people were more distant from the source of a revelation, or spoke different languages, and even the dialects have changed over tens of thousands of years.

"Just as paleontologists and geologists carefully peel through layers of the earth's history, we can begin to lay out a developmental framework for the northern continents over the last two million years. As we introduce and compare major Prophets from multiple scriptures, the older records we have currently might center near 20,000 years ago. The individual reign of a "Prophet-King" might seem to last thousands – even *millions* of years, but there's usually a focal point which coincides with one of humanity's historic ages, for instance, the Stone Age, or the Iron Age. As I introduce these Messengers, there will be a number of referential names for each. Mr. Hasan will kindly feature them on our PowerPoint, in case you come from a part of the world where a different name makes sense. Thank you, Jamal.

"Zoroaster's *Avesta* unequivocally states **Gayomart**, was the first man – *before all others*. As with most of the earliest Prophets there is a Creation piece that precedes the coming of mankind to earth – perhaps, even preceding Creation itself. Gayomart was the first mortal. His other names include Gaya-Maretan, 'Gaia' meaning *life* and 'Maretan' meaning *mortal*, **Gar Shah**, the 'King of the Mountains,' and later **Keyumers** - shortened to **Q-mers** in Farsi.

"The Avesta calls Gayomart the Pure and Righteous. The 'First' Prophet, as well as the first human Ahura Mazda created. His story is a collection of extremely old human memories about the First King, from the Yasnas and elsewhere. At first, He had no flock to preach His Revelation to, but from Him the family of Aryan lands, and all Eurasian Teachers of Faith developed."

Sage turned the page in his notebook and read. "From the Zend Avesta.

*First the sky was created from rock crystal in the shape of a hollow sphere so that it was both above and below where the earth would be. First water was created and then earth. The first tree grew, the Saena-mother of all trees. Its crown provided a place for the first nest for the first bird, a falcon. When he beat his wings the dropping tree leaves became the first plants.*

*After some plants were created, then animals began to appear, then the first Mountain, Alburz (also known as Mount Hara or Harbatz), grew. The first animal that came into existence was a white bull, a primeval ox (aurochs) as bright as the moon. It lived on the banks of the Vah* (River) *Daiti in Airyanem Vaejah, the ancient homeland of the Aryans.* (This is thought to be the Polar or Siberian homeland prior to the advance of ice.)

*The Primal Man was created immediately after the Primal Bull that was to supply him with food and help him fight evil. These two beings stood on opposing banks of the river, the good Daiti, which flowed from the center of the world. When Gayomart and the bull appeared, Ahriman, (AKA, Angra Manu,) 'the source of evil and darkness was laid low in awe.*

*Gayomart in His radiant beauty was created spontaneously by the Force of Creation to assist Ahura Mazda in the fight against the Evil Spirit. His body was created from earth, its divinity and sperm were fashioned from the light and brightness of the sky. He measured four medium reeds in height and in breadth. He was round, white and brilliant, and shone as the sun.*

Sage continued, "He was eventually sent to earth in noble beauty, *'as a fifteen-year-old Boy',* His purpose was to oppose evil. He was granted the supernal farr, a radiant, shimmering halo, or aura, shining brilliant as the sun - reserved for spiritual Kings and Luminous Beings.

"Muhammad ibn Jarir al – Tabari, a pure hearted 10th century Persian scholar, linked a collection of wise sayings, or *Apothegms,* to Gayomart. Verbal tradition allowed people to easily recite bits of sacred wisdom before of the advent of writing. 'Know thyself' may be such a gift.

"Jamal could you help with the Power Point for the Prophets?"

Their host strode to the computer and nodded.

"Gayomart became the first Shah, or King of the world. Like the other *'Firsts',* He lived thousands of years, in stages. First, He was alone, then He was the first Great King to arise among humans. Next, He ruled over men and beasts with unparalleled wisdom, and a gentle, but potent nature. Later, He was the first man to practice Justice, and is called the first *Lawgiver.*

"The Quran says **Adam and Eve** were created in heaven, then sent to earth. In the Torah and the Bible, Adam is made from mud, and Eve, from one of His ribs. As mortals, they became His representatives, and lived a life of plenty in Eden. Adam's Revelation was followed in sequence by those of <u>Seth</u>, then <u>Enoch</u>. In *Genesis,* Adam is considered the first man, but He was also part of the time of a great starvation, as we will see later. Finally, He and Eve were noted as parents (or more likely ancestors) of farmers in times of domestic herds and crops in the area of 13,000 years ago. Portions of their story continue until around 5,000 years ago.

Sage detoured to the stump to grab a bottle of water stashed there. He took a long drink, then nodded to Hasan to change the image to reflect the various names of each Prophet.

"In China, the *First* remembered would be **Fu-Xi**, followed by *Shennong* and *Huangdi*. Together the three were known as the San Huang Trio. According to Ban Gu, a Chinese historian, politician, and poet who lived during 32–92 AD, **Fu-Xi** is known as the first <u>Supreme Ruler</u> and <u>God-Emperor</u> of China: *Then came Fu-Xi and He looked upward and contemplated the images in the heavens, and looked downward and contemplated the occurrences on earth.* As with the others, His contributions over the ages contain an extensive list of accomplishments, suggesting layers of prophetic stages.

Mr. Hasan changed the PowerPoint display. "Then there is **Yima**, whose extended reign could be an entirely separate Creation thread, the remnants of which are mashed in with the rest of the Persian Avestan story. He is the connection between two ancient religions; Persian and Hindu. For the people of the *Rig Veda,* **Yam**, or **Yama** was the first mortal. In an Old Persian tablet found at Persepolis He is **Yima**, other texts refer to <u>Yama-kshedda</u> or <u>Yima Khshaeta</u>, meaning <u>Bright Shining as the Sun</u>. The renowned Zoroastrian historian, K. E. Eduljee, says, He is also called <u>Yima-Srira</u> or <u>Yima the Radiant, son of Vivanghat</u>. He is closely entwined – at least in part, with the names of *Ram* or *Rama*, in India; and *Atrahasis* and *Gilgamesh* in Babylonia and Mesopotamia.

His reign covered enough time for at least the first three remembered prophets in that line, and He has many names which have changed with the languages over the years.

"Yima's later form, **Yam** or **Jamshid,** was, perhaps, the fourth king of the world *after* Gayomart. In Middle Persian Pahlavi, his name transformed to **Jamshid,** as you see on the Power Point it's pronounced as Yom-shed. Edouard Schure tells us Jamshid was his anointed name, taken from the root words 'Jam' or 'Yam,' which means 'Bright Shining' and 'Shed', meaning 'Radiant Sun.' He was surrounded by a burning light; a radiant splendor which burned about Him by divine favor. The brilliance known as the **'farr'** is a shimmering aura which can overwhelm onlookers at the time a Divine Being reveals the Word of God. Sometimes it is portrayed as a halo, as with Christ. Though Jamshid remained humble, this radiance allowed Him to command mortals, angels, and demons; banishing evil and rewarding good people. He was distinguished as an ancient Indo-European Prophet who raised the call for humankind to return to Faith in one God rather than worshipping many."

Jamal brought up a fragment of a Baha'i tablet.

"This shrunken selection from the *Tablet of the Immortal Youth,* describes how difficult it must be for God's Revealers - to descend from Paradise where they are cherished and honored, to a strange earth where they are beset by the contrary winds of human emotions and greed. They and their followers suffer terribly, and the Prophet often dies in the quest." Sage read:

*Lo, the gates of Paradise were unlocked, and the hallowed Youth came forth... Rejoice! This is the immortal Youth, come with crystal waters...This is the immortal Youth, come with a mighty name. Upon His brow there shone a beauteous crown, which cast its splendour upon all who are in heaven and all who are on earth... By God! A most noble Angel is this. And the hearts of the inmates of the eternal realm cried out: Rejoice! This is the immortal Youth, come with an ancient light...This, verily, is the Horseman of the Spirit Who circleth round the fount of everlasting life. ... He stood, even as the sun in the*

*midmost heaven, arrayed with a beauty at once peerless and tran-*
*scendent...*

*... Wherefore, O ye lovers of the beauty of the All-Glorious! ...It*
*behooveth you to be free from all attachment, whether to yourselves*
*or to others; nay, ye should renounce existence and non-existence,*
*light and darkness, glory and abasement alike...that ye may, pure and*
*unsullied, enter the realm of the spirit and partake with radiant hearts*
*of the splendours of everlasting holiness ... Cast off the burden of love*
*for this world and every attachment thereto, and, even as luminous,*
*heavenly birds, soar in the atmosphere of the celestial Paradise and*
*wing your flight to the everlasting nest.*

*— BAHA'U'LLAH*

"Those of you who follow the Norse Eddas will probably recognize the phrase, 'This, verily, is the Horseman of the Spirit Who circleth round the fount of everlasting life.' as being very similar to the 13th century Edda, which describes Odin riding Sleipnir up and down Yggdrasil, the Tree of Life in every age. In the longer version you might recognize the horseman and the Trumpet Blast from Revelations. In retrospect, it is key to know, that our Creator has sent the Holy Spirit to earth time and time again – clothed with a different body and a new name.

"Once these first remembered Prophets arrived – what happened? **Gayomart's** followers were cave dwellers, possibly in the Carpathian or Alburz Mountains. He wore the skins of leopards; His followers also wore animal hides or girdles of leaves. Timewise, this could have been anything from Homo erectus times to Neanderthal, or even later. Who knows? He is celebrated as the first Righteous man to embrace the Will and Commandment of God, known as *Ahura Mazda* or simplified to *Ormuzd*. Gayomart or His lineage - lived for 3000 peaceful years before the evil *Ahriman* or *Angra Manu* awakened, and took the form of a fiery dragon. This could mean the people did not yet pray to personal idols for that length of time; as also noted in the Atrahasis and

Gilgamesh Epics. In the second cosmic stage, Gayomart and the bull were attacked by Ahriman because they withstood his attempts to spread world-wide destruction by Want, Sloth, Lust, and 1000 diseases. On the first day of the spring the Evil One himself leaped onto the earth as a dragon (a snake with legs), to defeat the forces of good. The ensuing combat between the forces of Light and Darkness came to an end by the arbitration of angels, but the bull had been mortally wounded. Foreseeing the Bull's death, God administered a soporific to ease its pain. From the dying Bull's blood all vegetation sprang forth. From its seed, came all the animals we see today.

"Ahriman then sent the demon of death, but he could not kill the Prophet because His fate had not yet come. Gayomart was destined to live for thirty more years. The prophetic counsels were subsequently carried on by His wife, Masia, and others, until the time of the next Revelation.

**Adam and Eve** present a mixed bag of events: arriving on earth, making the material choice between good and evil, also by a snaky tempter, then being evicted from the Edenic state, perhaps a physical place. Realizing their grievous error, they felt a great remorse, and were unable to find food. Along the line they became parents, or ancestors to farmers.

"**Fu- Xi**, a name likely remembered throughout multiple early revelations, guided humanity from 1.8 million years ago to 6,000 years ago. His many gifts include: cooking with fire, showing us how to offer our first sacrifices to heaven, and the use of fasting for physical and spiritual cleansing. He discovered divination by the use of yarrow stalks, and is known for medicinal plants, which were also utilized by his contemporaries, Yima, Rama, Abaris, and Aesculapius. Fu-Xi also encouraged fishing by adding nets of willow wands, and helped us tame wild animals. He united man and wife, personally choosing the one hundred Chinese family names, and decreed marriages should only take place between persons bearing different surnames. He regulated the five stages of change, and laid down the laws of humanity. He also endowed us with social laws, art, and technological inventions to help civilization advance.

135

"His seemingly endless event line crescendoed around 7,000 to 5,000 years ago, the same time associated with the deeds of Lord Krishna. It seems possible that Krishna's East Asian disciples graced their homelands with tales of this Prophet as the mighty **Fu-Xi**. His gifts during this time included; the farming of silkworms, and the eight trigrams of the I Ching or Pakua, said to be the basis for Chinese writing. According to the author Ban Gu, Fu-Xi had the arrangement of the trigrams revealed to him supernaturally on the shell of a turtle's back, in order for Him to gain mastery over the worlds. During the Iron and Bronze Ages, Fu-Xi instructed mankind to hunt and fight with weapons of metal. His people lived in thatched huts, made pottery, and fashioned iron jewelry." Sage nodded to Hasan to shift the image.

"Although musical tools, like vocal calls, Neanderthal's flutes, the long-horn, (didgeridoo or alphorn), and wood-knocking (drumming) were used tens of thousands of years earlier in cultures across Africa, Asia, and Europe. Fu-Xi showed us how to create music on a 7 stringed guqin zither, a short clarinet with strings, and with the arched harp that may have originally developed from the bow. It eventually became the lute used by the minstrels of Europe, and featured a broad wooden or hide-covered sound box, joined with a curved branch. The number of gut strings varied between three to ten. Players kneeled, and used both hands to pluck the strings, as noted in Egyptian funerary art. It is still used to accompany performances of oral history and myth in Africa, and elsewhere. Clearly, His story was an accumulation of divine gifts.

"From early Aryan beginnings, **Yima's** lore covers two spiritual paths. *Ahura Mazda* was the Avestan name for God. But in the Rig Veda of Hindu scriptures, God was referred to as *Asura Varuna*. The most ancient parts of the **Vedic** record refer to **Yama** or **Rama** as the "first" primordial man. Yima was the <u>Son of the Sun</u> - Apollo-like. He is listed under "Firsts" because of this interesting answer to Zoroaster's query, an interchange between the Prophet, and God:

*"Zoroaster asked Ormuzd 'O Ahura Mazda, righteous Creator of the corporeal world, who was the first person to whom You taught these teachings? Who is the first man with whom you conversed?"*

*Then spoke God (Ahura Mazda): "Yima the splendid who watched over His subjects, O righteous Zarathushtra, I first did teach the Aryan religion to Him prior to you.*

— THE VENDIDAD

"He may have been the 'First' – but he was not always the Revealer of God's guidance.

We are told in the following passage, 'He became the mightiest king the Aryans had ever known'. Later, he received a portent of domestication in the form of a Golden plough, a long dagger with golden forks - the ard mentioned also, in the Fu Xi and Shennong stories. Sage continued reading.

*"Yima spoke to me, and said he would like to spread the religion among mankind by teaching others. It was then that I replied O Yima you are not created for this task by Me. You are not learned enough to increase the religion among mankind. – you are not the Messenger of the religion. I made [My pleasure] known to Yima. And he proceeded south, towards the path of the high sun, increasing the land with his golden plough, conquering and cultivating the lands. The boundaries of the Aryan kingdom were thus extended in breadth, one third greater than before.*
*Ahura Mazda visited him once more, warning him again of overpopulation. Yima, shining with light, faced southwards, once again* (towards lands freshly freed of ice).
*"When Yima's rule extended to 600 years, the state of abundance* (overcrowding) *recurred. This led to Yima proceeding again towards the south and the west, extending the boundaries of the Aryan kingdom two thirds greater than before. Thus happened the second great migration of the Aryans.*

*"When Yima's rule extended to 900 years, abundance again led to Yima increasing the land with his golden plough, towards the south and west. This third great migration made the [lands] three times larger than before... In the first 1000 years of his rule, Yima the splendid enjoined righteous order on his subjects. He controlled invisible time itself, making it so much larger in size so as to praise and spread His righteous law."*

"During the first 1,200 years of the Yima/Jamshidi Era, Airyana Vaeja expanded by four and a half times towards the south into Afghanistan and even the upper Indus valley. These vast migrations displaced other local groups or bands, who were also struggling to make a living - especially in the light of climate change. Floods, dust storms, and fires devastated natural resources, triggering drought and famine. Moreover, a sudden climate chill, a mini-ice age struck 12,800 years ago, coinciding with the Younger Dryas, lasted approximately 1,200 years. There were several cold spells, each lasting approximately a hundred years. Accounts in the Avesta and other Zoroastrian scriptures, mention that seven warm months in a normal year was shortened to only two in the frigid times. The next part of the story tells of a meeting between Yima, Ahura Mazda, and the Venerable Beings in Airyanem Vaejah. Here Ahura Mazda warned of an upcoming catastrophe: an ice age!"

*That glorious age of the Aryans did not last forever, O Zarathushtra! It was time for the evil one's attack. I Who am Ahura Mazda spoke then to Yima Kshaeta: 'O splendid Yima, towards the sacred Aryan land will rush evil as a severe fatal winter... thick snowflakes falling in increased depth. From the three directions, will wild and ferocious animals will attack, arriving from the most dreadful sites...O fair Yima, son of Vivanghat! Upon the material world the evil winters are about to fall, that shall bring the fierce, deadly frost; that shall make snow-flakes fall thick, even an aredvi (glacier) deep on the highest tops of mountains... Before this winter, any snow that fell would melt and convey the water away. Now the snow will not melt but will form an ice cap. In this place, O Yima the corporeal world will be DAMAGED. Before in this seed land the grass was so soft the foot-print of even a small animal could be observed. Now, there will be no footprints discernable at all on the packed sheets of hard ice that will form.*

*Ahura Mazda advised Yima to construct a Vara (ark-like enclosure) in the form of a multi-level artificially lit cavern; two miles long and two miles wide. He must stock it with two of every animal, bird and plant, and nearly 2000 of the fittest people, and build a supply with food and water gathered the previous summer... Yima; make a mighty VARA, an enclosure as long as a riding ground, with four equal sides. Here bring the families of men and women, cattle, dogs, birds and the red flaming fire... the symbol of the undying Word of God. Inside the Vara, make water flow in a canal, one Hathra long. Keep earth inside the Vara, to grow green vegetables as food. Make cattle pens, to house the cattle of the Aryan people. Let love blossom unfailing in the enclosure.*

— TILAK (SAGA OF THE ARYANS) 1925

"To survive the small ice-age, the herders and their settlements had to adapt by creating a self-contained unit capable of sustaining communal life, using a strictly laid out urban plan which even allowed room for worship, storage, newlyweds and newborns. Yima oversaw the construction of shafts for light and air flow, streets, and living quarters built from clay and wooden pillars. The undertaking was an impressive challenge for a community thousands of years ago; it would be terrible even now. Yima's design enabled people to live within their lands, rather than battle their way further southward with herds and families toward milder climates. He brought in nearly two thousand people, then sealed the Vara with a golden ring.

"The Vendidad tell us the enclosure provided sustainable housing in unbearable winters. People in northern mountainous regions continued to use the varas - snowed in and cut off from the rest of the world. Even today, the Yagnobi people living near the Pamirs in Tajikistan, survive frigid winters in that same way. K. E. Eduljee says settlements were built according to three distinct plans. One settlement contained a thousand dwellers and had nine streets. Another had six hundred dwellings and six streets. And those which held three hundred people had three streets.

"Here's the thing, maybe we should have been looking *underground* for the Ark – like the huge construction in Cappadocia, an area in Central Turkey outside a city called Derinkuyu. The place is thought to have been built in deep antiquity. Its engineering is superb, with extensive ventilation shafts that bring air to every square foot of the **thirteen-story underground dwelling**. The supports are excellent, no sign of collapse. There is room for 20,000 men, women, and children, religious centers, store rooms, stables, and even wine presses. If you're interested, I recommend watching the History Channel /Ancient Aliens episode "Underground Aliens". They filmed the site, and showed blueprints.

"These early Prophets took on the forces of evil idolatry, and drew a path for the civil, just, and compassionate organization of society. In cross-referencing, we find commonalities in these tales that overlap. Sage signaled Jamal to tap each topic as needed.

VIRGIN BIRTHS AND RADIANCE: **Krishna** was referred to as the Radiant One by his people of the mountains. His mother, Devaki, fled from her greedy brother's palace to the forest when she learned from an elderly sage that he intended to kill her. The king's wife had been surprised to find that it would be Devaki's child who would rule the realm, and the world, instead of hers. In the quiet forest, Devaki found an ancient sage who told her she would become pregnant, as a grace from God, and would bear a precious child, a Radiant One.

"**Fu-Xi** was also born of a virgin. His mother was made pregnant by the vision of a rainbow and a white elephant. As a boy, He was described as 'radiant as a rainbow.'

**Yima** was also known as the Radiant One - until the farr departed him when he stopped being a Prophet, and instead became a mighty king. Prophets are enshrouded with a bright light that makes it tough for onlookers to make out details.

The virgin birth most of us know is that of **Christ**, but even more recently, in early American lore, **Deganaweda** the Peacemaker, an American Messenger, was also said to be born of a virgin.


PLAGUE HEALERS: "In the Great Initiates, Edouard Schure tells us **Rama** – as well as **Yima,** were bestowed a cure for an otherwise incurable plague. Until then, everyone infected had died. *He put an end to an epidemic with a plant called homa or haoma (*Greek *amomum,* and Egyptian *persea) from which He extracted a healing essence. This plant became sacred among His followers, replacing the mistletoe of the oak tree, preserved by the Celts of Europe."* To this day, it remains a healing medicine, and also a sacrificial offering. A staff bearing two intertwined snakes was given to the Prophet as a sign of this healing. Parallel stories of plague, healing, and the staff are recorded in the narratives of **Atrahasis, Abaris,** and **Aesculapius.**


LENGTH OF REIGN: **"Gayomart** is clearly depicted as the only human on the earth in the beginning. The cave dweller later ruled over men and beasts by His gentle but potent nature and unparalleled wisdom. Next, He was known as Pure, and Righteous, the peaceful and pious King who rendered the primitive world prosperous and habitable, likely an early reference to domestication. Following that, He was also the first man to practice Justice and was called the Lawgiver. After He died, the Word of God and prophetic counsels, were kept by His wife, Masia, then somehow, Mashya and Mashyana, and the giant twins figured in the line of descent – maybe like the 'Begats' of the Bible – until the Revelation of Siamak.

"Most Christians see **Adam** as the first man that was created – but was that 7 million, 13,000, or 3,000 years ago? Adam and Eve are said to have covered themselves with fig leaves in Eden, but their family is said to be fully clothed farmers living among other people. This pair was evicted, and likely died outside of Eden unable to hold onto the Revelation or even sufficient food for survival during the starvation, yet, on the flickering cusp of domestication.

"China remembers **Fu-Xi,** as the first God-King who taught us to fish, and also inspired agriculture. A shift to farming led to societal development, courtesy and compassion, and even royal fashion and throne rooms. Fu-Xi died after 197 years at a place called Chen, where one may still visit his monument.

"Certainly, nobody can remember all the layers of God's educators, so **Yima's** was handed down for countless centuries of cultural prehistory. As Jamshed he lived until the Bronze Age. He was also the first man to practice Justice and was called the Lawgiver. He did not 'end' in this age. But as the Revelation became old and degraded by human preferences and additions, it became sullied.

"In Summary, early Prophets like Gayomart, Fu-Xi, and to some extent, Adam and Yima, had one goal - for humans to worship the Supreme Creator: to purify their hearts, and to turn away from the materialistic devas or gods, to refrain from making offerings to various elements, talismans, idols or icons in order to get something in return. These first remembered Prophets added with Nu Wa, paint for us a tremendously long prehistory. They bring a richness and noble beauty to the development of human religion, society, and culture. Thank you, friends."

Sage and Jamal stood together, and Jamal invited everyone to a marvelous roast beef or vegetarian lasagna dinner. "Lovely desserts will be offered at the end of the evening."

# STAGE TWO: STARVATION

After the audience had once again taken their seats, Sage came out to center stage. "I'd like to thank Jamal, William, and the staff for another elegant meal this evening. Weren't those salads fantastic?" The audience heartily agreed – and about half of them gave a standing ovation. Sage thought he could see Jamal's cheeks redden. "In a few minutes, we'll be able to sample some lovely desserts." Again, the audience shared their delight.

"Now, if you are ready, we can take a look at the next stage noted in the scriptures, the starvation." The group settled and quieted. "Between the ages of the 'firsts' and the 'seconds' life became insecure. Little is remembered from this desperate time of overpopulation and tragedy. What we do have are the names of Siamak, Seth or Shiith, Shennong and, of course, Yima. Until then, people sustained themselves as hunters, fishermen, and gatherers of fruits and vegetation for their diets. But the climate changed. Global warming became the focal issue. Communities of different types of humans had increased in size, but water and food resources were dwindling. As the weather became more irregular, droughts increased, caused by post glacial drying of the rivers and land. People crowded around dwindling resources, resulting in conflicts, starvation, and die offs.

"**Siamak**, the second great Prophet to lead the tribes of Eurasia after Gayomart, was beloved of all except the devil, called Ahriman, or Angra Manu. An angel named Soroush had warned Gayomart of the danger of rising idolatry - represented by Ahriman; but in this age, the noble Siamak led an army of His own, accepting the challenge of hand-to-hand combat with the evil son of Ahriman. So it was that the beloved king died at the hands of that demon. This may seem reminiscent of the story of Cain and Abel? Or the battle of the spiritual sons of the Sun, against the materialist kings on the Kurukshetra Plain, where Arjuna and Krishna fought the sons of the moon, who were acclaimed idol worshippers. In each case, descendants from the line of the 'firsts', continued the fight between good and evil. In the next era, Hooshang led the army that ultimately defeated Ahriman's son. So, from the legend one might imagine that idol worship was quelled for a time, and humanity again turned to peaceful worship of a single God.

"**Seth**, Adam's son, or more likely a linear descendant, took over the responsibilities of prophet hood from Adam. The Qur'an, 87:18, asserts that Seth was *'the Receiver of Scriptures,'* perhaps fifty psalms. Medieval historian al-Tabari and other scholars say Seth buried Adam, *and* these *'secret texts'* in the 'Tomb of Adam,' referring to it as the 'Cave of Treasures.'"

Sage selected a page from his notebook. "In *Antiquities of the Jews,* Josephus refers to Seth as virtuous, and of excellent character.

*His descendants invented the wisdom of the heavenly bodies, and built the 'pillars of the sons of Seth', two pillars inscribed with many scientific discoveries and inventions, notably in astronomy, in order to protect the discoveries so they might be remembered after the destruction. One was composed of brick, and the other of stone, so that if the pillar of brick should be destroyed, the pillar of stone would remain, both reporting the ancient discoveries, and informing men after the coming flood, that a pillar of brick was also erected.*
*Josephus reports that the pillar of stone remained in the land of Siriad in his day.'*

"The land of Siriad refers to modern day Egypt.

"**Shennong**, second of the three Noble Emperors and an *ancient forebearer of modern humans,* succeeded Fu-Xi, in mission. He overlapped the time of hunger and early agriculture. Food production and storage techniques slowly began to allow humans some control over the periodic, horrifying famines. Eventually, during the time of Huangdi, farming would provide an excess of products, anticipating the glimmers of commerce.

"He disseminated a mass of medicinal lore, but his greatest contributions lay in farming innovations. According to Ban Gu of the Han Dynasty, '*in ancient times people only ate animal meat. By Shennong's time, there were too many people and animals were too few. He taught farm techniques and the people called him the 'god of farming.'*

"Shennong graciously shared basic Mesopotamian types of agriculture, and is associated with growing barley, beans, hemp, millet, oats, peas, rice, sesame, and soybeans. He brought about the use of the plow called the ard. Oxen were hooked to a simple shaft, an angled stick, which was dragged through the soil to loosen it. The farmer grasped another stick, projecting from the top of the shaft for guidance control.

"**Yima or Yama**, along with his sub stories like the Akkadian Epic, Atrahasis, and Gilgamesh of Sumeria - described vivid images of a disturbing test of the various human species – some of which did not survive past this stage. Before the flood, the crises of global warming and ensuing deprivation pop up quite graphically in these narratives. The disappearance of rivers and fishes is specifically mentioned. Households, tribes, and clans suffered horrendous famines. Starvation or cannibalism seemed to be the only choices until the first flickers of domestication. Family members were killed and eaten, starting with the young and the old.

Yima's long lineage of thousands of years, likely included one called **Atrahasis**, whose story is a parallel. Like Yima, he lived in three shifts, each lasting 1200 years, totaling over 3600 years. The tale of Atrahasis is thought by some to be the oldest account of the Great Flood story, yet it begins with a layer that precedes the Creation of mankind. Atrahasis 'The Wise' was sent to earth well before the flood. Some people think He may have been the Stone Age king of Shuruppak, a bustling city-state along the Euphrates River. As Stephanie Dally explains:

> *Tragedy loomed as the people of Atrahasis' time grew to the point of overpopulation and noisiness. When they became as noisy as a bellowing bull, they were struck by a plague. After Atrahasis prayed for relief, Enki told Him to have the people stop praying to their personal gods, and pray to the Almighty God, specifically, to have the plague healed.*

> *"Now there was one, Atrahasis, whose ear was open to his god Enki and he spoke to his lord. How long will the gods make us suffer? Will they make us suffer illness forever?"*
> *Enki responded with a Me, an edict, a universal decree of divine authority.*
> *Enki (God) made his voice heard and spoke to his servant:*
> *Call the elders, the senior men! Start an uprising in your own house,*
> *Let the elders proclaim... Let them make a loud noise in the land:*
> *Do not revere your gods, do not pray to your goddesses.*

"Also, **Gilgamesh**, who sat on the throne of Erech (Uruk) on the Euphrates above Eridu and Ur in Iraq, was central to a tale told by **Utnapishtim**, a survivor of the flood. He was most likely the son of Ubara-Tutu, **Enoch**, who was the last antediluvian king of Shuruppak of Sumer. *"He saw what was secret and revealed what was hidden... He brought back tidings from before the flood... Though a bleak, prolonged famine ravaged the people, it finally ended when Enki increased the waterways and sent large quantities of fish into the rivers. Total annihilation was averted.*

"Climate change and unyielding drought are remembered by tribes throughout the planet. In Egypt, the great Sahara Desert began to eat up greenery around drying lakes, and rivers about 11, 000 years ago. In the America's, people followed fish and game along the coasts and through the ice corridors, seeking fresh waters and enough game to survive. By the time of the European invasion, many indigenous people were fighting over game and resources - at a cultural crossroad between hunting and farming.

"The names of the 'Seconds' are remembered from dangerous and dramatic times. There may not be many enduring references, but we retain pervasive global memories of tremendous famines, where game, fish, and perhaps even the rivers disappeared. Outcomes included the cannibalism of the weak, young or debilitated; as mentioned in Aryan, Chinese, Egyptian, and Biblical scriptures. Massive die-offs may have encouraged newer types of humans to step to the forefront. And it was also a time when some Prophets may have had a change of heart.

## FALLS FROM GRACE

"Service to God is about purity of heart, becoming a clear channel. It's not the same as giving in to the temptation of the easy, or materialistic way – sacrificing to 'idols' for personal purposes, as for rain, food, wealth, or protection; in other words, adding any gods to God. When that happens, religion often slides into rituals and ceremonies, honoring tyrants, gods, saints, or embodiments of some perceived desire. Under dire circumstances the order of things crumbles.

"During times of increased idol worship, the vast Aryan Nation split into two or more camps as it has today, freedom or oppression. Not only religion, but politics pit one nation against brother nations, with disastrous results. Think of Russia, Turkey, Armenia, Afghanistan, and the Ukraine. People subjected to torment and suffering at the hands of materialistic tyrants. Dictator worship, *temporarily* triumphs over belief in One Creator.

"The sacrifice and endurance of Each Prophet - a pure angel - is

147

tested by this harsh Earth. Not all of them choose to continue the engagement. Rama was offered a mortal crown to rule over humankind. Lucky for us, Rama did not accept earthly glory, choosing instead, to continue His difficult path. Consider the choices of Moses; or Christ in Gethsemane, as He laments about the upcoming betrayal, capture and death; wondering if His followers would be able to establish the renewed Faith. Similarly, Mohammad's forbearance was grievously tested when his daughter was run through with a spear in front of Him, then the killer immediately begged for, and received His mercy. During Baha'u'llah's plea to God in the *Fire Tablet*, God encourages Him to remain patient, to continue to bear pain, and sacrifice everything in the path of Faith. Which, of course, He does with magnanimity.

"The name of the American Prophet, Quetzalcoatl, represents that choice for humans very well. At any moment we may choose the bird of the spirit, 'quetzal' flying toward heaven, or the snake 'coatl,' ignoring issues, and binding oneself to the day-to-day grind of earthly life. Just getting by - not making a difference."


"Now, let's talk about Mashya and Mashyana There is an incongruous time break between Gayomart and other types of humans. He foretold as He died, that despite His death the modern human race would be born. Long after His death, a rhubarb plant shot up. The top split into two branches, creating a male, *Mashya*, and a female *Mashyana*, known as 'Ask' and 'Embla' in Norse Mythology. Some call them 'Adam' and 'Eve'. They became the first mortal couple. Okay! Rhubarbs! Yes! But is that any weirder than coming from a rib, or earth, or mud? After fifty years, these first humans of a different stage bore twins. Unfortunately, *Angra Manu*, the Evil One, took the form of a snaky, fiery dragon, who tricked Mashya and Mashyana into worshipping him as their creator instead of God, Ahura Mazda. You could say it was the tasting of the fruit of the Tree of the Knowledge of Good and Evil. Was *this* the first sin? Given a choice, they put something or someone before God and it filled the world with corruption and evil. Things changed. Humanity suffered horrible famines and they were forced by starvation to eat their own precious children. After a long, long time, Mashya and Mashyana bore another set of twins, from which a more modern humanity arose."

Sage smiled and snapped his fingers. "Now let's skip to the version most of you know. In a place referred to as Eden, a place where all their needs were met, Eve gave Adam the fruit from the tree of the knowledge of good and evil. In the Qur'an, it is claimed that *Adam* gave *Eve* that forbidden fruit. Either way, they became enmeshed in the conflict between Good and Evil on earth. Perhaps they were unable to cling to the Revelation that was the purpose of their existence. There were reasons – sanity was falling apart. People everywhere were starving to death, fighting over scraps, and resorting to cannibalism. Quite possibly, Adam and Eve starved to death along with them.

"We are told that after leaving Eden, Adam and Eve also suffered from a horrible famine similar to that experienced elsewhere in the world." Sage flipped open a Bible which William left for his use by the stump chair, and read,

*"When they were driven out from paradise, they made themselves a booth, and spent seven days mourning and lamenting in great grief. But after seven days, they began to be hungry and started to look for victual to eat, and they found it not. Then Eve said to Adam: 'My lord, I am hungry. Go, look for (something) for us to eat. Perchance the Lord God will look back and pity us and recall us to the place in which we were before.' And Adam arose and walked seven days over all that land, and found no victual such as they used to have in paradise."*

— FROM THE KING JAMES BIBLE, GENESIS

"In Adam's case, the 'snake' may represent human frailty, a need for attachment to the earth and a material existence. It led to corruption when people sacrificed to the rain god, or the fertility goddess in desperate times. Many chose idol worship; praying to elements as gods, or calling on personifications for specific help, or personal favors."

"Did God punish Adam and Eve, and *make* them leave Eden? In the Quran, it was *they who* turned away from *their Creator*; turning towards something more worldly for a time. They later grieved the loss of connection with God, when they realized their mistake, and they knew His disappointment and displeasure. Was *this* the first sin? Probably not. Leaving Eden means so little as a sentence, but understanding the real-life drama gives significance to the words. Our ancestors could no longer satisfy their needs from the forests and the waters. Starvation was the engine which impelled humanity to eventually tame plants and animals in increasingly desperate hopes for survival. In time, they learned to raise herbs, vegetables, grains, and fruit. They confined animals in small flocks to meet basic needs. Some humans endured. Perhaps Adam and Eve did not.

This is *our* human history – and may God forgive us – maybe our future too. We could take a lesson here. Zoroaster tells us that at the time of the end, evil will be purged when the world will be bathed with the purification of fire. Makes me think of global warming."

"**Yima** also changed his mind about how he wished to serve the Source, and humanity. He decided not to be a Prophet, but a king who would bring prosperity back to humanity. Even so, God cherished him at every turn. He gives us free will. There's no reason to think this doesn't include the Prophets.

Toward the end of his reign Yima, or more likely, a Jamshidi king of that line, fell out of favor because his pride made him see himself as a god – and therefore a polytheist. Perhaps his pride grew with his power, and he forgot that all the blessings were due to God. Jamshed's misguided or idolatrous followers boasted that all good things came from the king, not from God. They demanded that He should be accorded divine honors as if He were the Creator. Jamshid became vulnerable as His faith waned. The brilliant **farr** deserted him and he was disgraced in the eyes of the Aryans. The encroachment of idolatry led to the end of a Golden Age. In the Gathas, Zoroaster laments that King Jamshed lost his path and became a sinner. His arrogance weakened the entire Aryan nation, allowing them to be conquered for a thousand years until they were again liberated. Eduljee sums it up. 'Jamshid is considered one of the wisest and greatest kings ever, but one who would nevertheless fall from grace, thus heralding the start of tragic epic cycles in Aryan history, cycles that rotated between good and evil times. As Yama, he was still revered by Hindus, many of whom had been polytheistic for a very long time.

"The earth and life forms suffered in that devastating era. In that particular phase of evolution, perhaps humankind was meant to become more consciously aware of themselves, and the consequences of their thoughts, choices, and actions. Even the Prophets were held accountable. Without law and accountability, how could social aggregations and nascent cities become civilized? The good news is that some of the humans and animals did survive.

"To me, it seems apparent that the Prophets and Messengers listed in scriptures and historical traditions, for these times and earlier, were physically different types of humans.

**Gayomart,** as noted by Zoroaster in the Vendidad, is *different from men later born of his seed.* In the Book of Giants, Enoch tells us that **Masha** and **Mashyana's** twins were giants – so we might assume the parents were also. Other notable giants were Nimrod, Goliath, and the Armenian hero, Hayk.

**Siamak** was different from Gayomart, the Giants, Masha and Mashyana and probably Hooshang.

**Shennong,** second of the three Noble Emperors, was an *ancient forebearer of modern humans,* and He succeeded Fu-Xi, who was therefore an ancient form.

**Gilgamesh,** according to Enoch, was a giant. The Epic of Gilgamesh, (a Mesopotamian parallel story of **Yima),** is known from a series of eleven clay tablets in cuneiform. In the first tablets, God sent a wild man named Enkidu to stop Gilgamesh from oppressing the people of Uruk. Let's see; a giant, a wild man, and the people of Uruk

– hmm, sounds like three types of humans in the same place? Probably not unusual.

God said He would never leave us alone without guidance, and we have unearthed so many human types in the last few years, that it becomes easier to believe they didn't all look the same as you and me. I hope you find the possibilities as intriguing as I do.

# 18

# STAGE THREE - ABUNDANCE

"The *Third* remembered Prophets are associated with the beginnings of domestication, and during an unnaturally extended time frame - early glimmers of a time of plenty. Ultimately, domestication was the remedy for the famines, and initiated the onset of trade, communal society, and cities.

"Husbandry was feebly set in motion during the starvation times of Siamak, Seth and Shennong and kings of the Yima dynasty. Managing animals and other crops became imperative. This eventually led social groups into more plentiful times of agricultural surplus, metal work, and trade routes. Society became more organized. Communities developed into great cities and fortifications. Laws were established, and civilization progressed.

"As communal living expanded, personal power over others seemed beneficial to greedy individuals. Rumblings of strife and separation became more common. Those who believed in one Creator, tried to hold fast in opposition to others who worshiped individual *personalities* and inanimate *objects*. Sometimes groups acknowledged God - but also a number of gods or natural forces. In places, religion devolved into rituals and ceremonies. Blood sacrifices arose as a portent of idolatry and personal power. From the most ancient times great Prophets tried to bring people back to the path of love, respect, kindliness, and oneness. This has been a recurring cycle – darkness and light, **yin** and **yang.** No evil counterpart to God is needed – we bring it into being ourselves."

Sage signaled Jamal who highlighted the Prophet's names on the PowerPoint. "Farming innovations may have begun with **Gayomart,** who at some point in a long lineage, was peaceful and pious and rendered the primitive world prosperous and habitable. He befriended an auroch, a 'moon white bull', perhaps, a reference to domestication.

"**Hooshang** was a powerful Prophet who became the third Aryan leader or king of men. He beat back the oppression of cruel deva worshippers and greedy idolaters. For a time, the world was renewed, purified by love and virtue. People were kinder, especially to the poor. Men of good will could, once again, live in peace. The Mehr religion, attributed to Hooshang's time, was the popular religion for all Iranians before Zoroaster. Such is the rhythm of religion: Degradation and dissolution caused by the wills of men – then purification once more!

"Herds of cattle and goats grazed pastures that were ringed with the awe-inspiring pinnacles of Inner Asia. Sometimes these were not enough to protect the tribes from cruel raiders who attacked them and their herds. Communities needed to defend themselves with the aid of warriors. During Hooshang's time, horses, donkeys, and oxen plowed fields and carried loads. They transported people during daily chores, marketing, and warfare. Sheep and cattle herds flourished, so meat, dairy products, and hides became plentiful. In addition to surplus bounties provided by animals, grains, fruit, bread, and woven goods could be traded or marketed. This provided a way to pay taxes for maintaining an infrastructure like roads, irrigation canals, and aqueducts to enhance the crops and their transportation. Abundance led to the establishment of trade networks like the Silk Road.

"**Enoch** also known as **Hermes, Thoth, Khonoukh,** and **Idris -** renewed Adam's and Seth's religion for the Babylonians. As often happens, most people turned away, only a handful listened. Most citizens failed to grasp His revelation, and wanted to kill Him - *several* times. He was forced to abandon the land of His birth, but His teachings did succeed famously in other parts of the world like Egypt and Greece. Like the other Messengers, He was often shown as a shepherd of men - in the company of a lamb, or ram."

Sage again referred to the notebook. Eduard Schure told us

*He led his brave followers out of Babylon, headed for Egypt. There as Thoth to the Egyptian, and Hermes to the Greek, He carried on His mission, (having) His greatest effect on mankind from Egypt where the effect of His Illumination was gargantuan and mysterious.*

*Beneath the seeming idolatry of its external polytheism, Egypt preserved the ancient foundations of esoteric theology and its priestly organization... for a period of over 5,000 years, Egypt was the stronghold of pure and exalted teaching. In Egypt, Thoth is considered to be Ra's Will, translated into speech. He is associated with the arts of magic (dealing with Angels and Demons) and a system of writing, as well as, the development of science. He became associated with the judgement of the dead.*

In the *Vision of Hermes* Schure spoke about death and salvation - even the possible destruction of a soul as described by Osiris, the Lord of Light.

*From one Soul of the Universe are all Souls derived. Of these Souls there are many changes, some move into a more fortunate estate, and some quite contrary. . . Not all human souls, but only the pious ones, are divine. Once separated from the body, and after the struggle to acquire piety, which consists in knowing God and injuring none, such a soul becomes all intelligence.*

*None of our thoughts can conceive of God, nor can any language define Him. The incorporeal, invisible, and formless*

*cannot be comprehended by our senses…God is ineffable. …the*
*First Cause remains hidden*

*Therefore, strengthen your soul, O Hermes, and quiet your*
*clouded mind by watching these distant flights of souls' mount*
*to the seven spheres and scatter like hosts of sparks! For you*
*too can follow them; it is sufficient to will it, in order to lift*
*oneself.*

"Enochian knowledge and Hermetic ideas were basic to the turn of the last century's secret societies like the illuminati, and social sororities and fraternities. All of which began with the Greeks and Egyptians, and continues even today with charitable groups like the Masons."

"Similarities between them include:" Sage signaled Jamal to highlight several topics on Power Point.

"REDEMPTION: **Huangdi,** the Yellow Emperor, was named after the yellow Phase which represented the earth, dragons, the center point, and up and down. He was both a cosmic ruler, lord of the underworld, and a patron of the esoteric arts. His homeland was said to be the Sheep's Head Mountains just north of Goaoping.

"He continued the bloom of farming technology initiated by Shennong, and laid down social patterns to sustain it. His numerous inventions included carts, like the 'south pointing compass' which is key to this tale. 'The Yan emperor begged for the Yellow Emperor's help in battle. Huangdi employed his tamed animals, but the evil enemy gained the upper hand by darkening the sky, breathing out a thick fog which confounded his adversaries. To overcome this, Huangdi invented the South Pointing Chariot, a small two-wheeled vehicle which carried a movable figure with an outstretched arm as a pointer to indicate south. No matter how dark the skies, the chariot turned unerringly to lead his army out of the fog.'

"Huangdi inspired the use of boats, improved the practice of medicine, and sought immortality. His teachings are said to be the basis for the Five Phases, the Five Virtues, the Five Cardinal Points, and Five Elements: wood, fire, earth, metal and water that are used for describing interactions and relationships between phenomena. They are employed in several fields of Chinese thought, including geomancy, music, military strategy, and the Shao Lin martial arts. He set the Chinese calendar, created the Chinese diadem, throne rooms, and 'cuju'- an early version of football.

"The three legendary Emperors: Yao (Fu-Xi), Shun (Shennong), and Huangdi (Yu or Yenti), were each credited with improving the livelihood of the nomadic hunting tribes; teaching them to build shelters and tame wild animals. They ruled by virtue and wisdom, and dedicated themselves to creating a remarkable political culture based on responsibility, respect and trust.

"Over 8,000 years ago, a young shepherd, became King **Jamshid**, the shepherd of his people. He instilled law and justice, and initiated the castes to balance the necessary vocational skills. He was also responsible for a great many inventions that made life more secure for his people." Sage read.

*Yima the righteous told me then: O Ahura, if I am not created for the task of increasing the good religion, then I would like to advance the world, to increase it and be a righteous king and protector. I ask You this, that in my kingdom there be neither cold wind nor hot wind, neither extreme winter or summer, there be no sickness nor death, that my subjects be undying and unwanting and gloriously happy under my reign.*

*I Who am Ahura Mazda, was pleased with this. I brought Yima – a Golden plough which was dagger shaped with golden forks to signify that His authority was divine, sanctioned by Me... and gave him a different mission: to rule over and nourish the earth, to see that the living things prosper. This Yima accepted, and Ahura Mazda presented him with a golden seal and a dagger inlaid with gold... I told him to watch over the worlds which belong to me, and I gave him a saber of gold and a sword of victory. And Yima moved forward on*

*the way of the sun and assembled the courageous men in the famous
Airyana-Vaeja, created pure."*

— ZOROASTER IN THE ZEND AVESTA,
VENDIDAD-SADE, 2ND FARGARD

"For a long time, his people prospered in peace. Stone Age people
in loin cloths were able to construct great temples and cities. Technological improvements became standard, and Yima strove with great
dedication to keep people free of spiritual and physical disease.

"**Yima** became the greatest monarch the world had ever known,
endowed with a radiant splendor that burned about him by divine
favor. As Rama, He set the festival of *Naw-Ruz*, meaning the 'New
Day' a "Spiritual Springtime". It represented the renewal of God's
Faith, celebrated at the time of the earthly renewal – the spring
equinox. The holy day features signs of birth and renewal, such as
flowers, grass, eggs (sometimes highly decorated, as in pysanky),
bunnies, chicks, young fish, and other signs of springtime. This day is
celebrated by Zoroastrians, Muslims and Baha'is. It is also the heart of
Ostara, the backdrop for Christian Easter. He set the other quarterly
holy days, summer harvest, autumn, celebrating children, families, and
feasts, and the midwinter solstice, Yule - honoring souls – eventually
becoming the backdrop for Christmas.

"During the first 3000 years, the Aryans had prospered. Sacred
fires flamed in the house of every noble man, as a reminder of the
Word of God *flaming* in the hearts of His servants. Jamshidi kings
ushered in a Persian golden era - one that fostered significant societal
change.

CLOTHING: **Hooshang** and **Yima** instituted special sacred clothing,
such as the sudreh - a garment worn under the outer clothing. It
contains a small pocket in the front to collect one's good deeds –
similar to a Jewish prayer shawl. It is worn to protect the wearer from
perpetrating, or receiving evil acts. The Kushti is a sacred string or

158

cord belt, representing the umbilical connection to God. During this time, woven arts employed linen, silk, cotton, wool, and the hair of other animals, to produce fine fabrics like brocade.

"**Huangdi** also instituted elaborate clothing. His wife, Leizu, introduced the weaving and dyeing of cloth made of wool, linen, and silk.

COUPLES: **Atrahasis** explained that after Enki (God) sent large quantities of fish into the rivers, there was enough food for families. 'Children became a source of joy and a fulfillment of love during the ancient conditions of marriage and childbirth. A wife and her husband chose each other, in gardens and waysides, when the girl (had a) bosom and a beard was seen on a young man's cheek. – Dalley

'**Yima**; In the mighty Vara, *'Here bring the families of men and women, cattle, dogs, birds and the red flaming fire, the symbol of the undying Word of God...... make for them* (young couples) a residence; with rooms, pillars, long extended walls and an enclosing wall (for privacy). Tilak, in *Saga of the Aryans* 1925

MEDICINE: **Enoch,** the first to define psychology, was a healer with Stone Age roots and His head in space observing the spheres.

**Huangdi** furthered healing arts in Chinese medicine and sought immortality.

**Yima,** as **Rama**, eventually banished starvation and ended a formerly incurable epidemic, with a potent elixir made from a plant from which He extracted a healing essence. This plant became sacred, replacing the healing mistletoe of the oak tree, and is preserved by the Celts of Europe today as a major healing medicine, and sacrificial offering. Similar blessings were bestowed by **Aesculapius** and **Abaris**. In these cases, the staff encircled by two intertwined serpents was bestowed as the sign of the sacred healing of this incurable disease, and remains a sign of healing today as the caduceus.

<u>Castes, Justice, and the Law:</u> Imagine that during the dawn of agriculture, people here and there managed to grow a small crop of grain, or catch a couple of cows for themselves. Desperate or fierce people may want to take their crops or herds for themselves – perhaps even killing the original owners. Law and justice were necessary for peace and prosperity. In order to protect and balance the settlements, special professions – castes, were instituted and maintained.

Regulations prevented everyone from clumping into one or two groups, like *just* warriors, or *all* priests. Individuals worked their particular trade with freedom and dignity.

"**Hooshang** built the social patterns on which civilization was based, and started a hereditary kingship that ruled with justice and grace. He ushered in the Divine Right of Kings, since the first kings were actually Prophets. His titles included first King, and first Lawgiver. Law was the concept of common justice. In this system of governance, kings had a sacred responsibility to protect the people, to establish and uphold just laws that encouraged community development and the advancement of society. Those who maintained this sacred trust were said to rule an ethical path in **grace**. Greater Iran was a vast region which included most of Asia. The Mehr religion divided people into seven stages, or ranks of labor. Ferdowsi says in his Book of God: *We are not ashamed of an ancient faith, no world had a better faith than Hooshang's faith; All was righteousness and justice, the Mehr code.*

"**Enoch** was the first of the 'children' of Adam to be given prophet hood after Seth. Later on, He was called Hermes Trismegistus, or 'thrice great'; Excellent as a great king, a legislator, and a priest. He was a Prophet, a philosopher, and author of esoteric – even magical work, which became the source of occultic philosophies and rituals.

*He bade people to do what is just and fair, teaching them certain*
*prayers and instructing them to fast on certain days, and to give a*
*portion of their wealth to the poor. He shared a vast amount of divine*
*knowledge.*

— (1899) E. A. WALLIS BUDGE

"**Shennong** in Chinese texts, and **Jamshid - Rama** in Vedic texts, divided a community into four necessary occupational castes. Specialist occupations included: priests; who conducted the worship of God; warriors who protected the people by the might of their arms; farmers who grew the grain and animals for food, cultivation, and transportation; and the artisans who produced necessary farm implements, and goods for the ease and enjoyment of life.

"During the **Jamshidi** dynasties, the incipient rule of law was grounded in grace. Justice heralded a *golden age* in which the tribal Aryan homeland became *paradise on earth*. Eduljee, said, 'In an effort to extract historical developments from the myths and legends, we will say that the Jamshidi age followed the age of Hooshang.'

"In the **Vedic** thread, farmers had undisputed parcels to work to the best of their abilities. Professions were called varnas which meant enclosed. Arjuna's varna was warrior. That was his particular profession. Brahmins were the learned and the priests. Nobles and warriors were the Kshatriyas, merchants and farmers were Vaishyas, laborers and artisans, the Sudra. Each individual knew their designated path or dharma. All were treated with equality and dignity. It was a system of guidelines, rules, or laws for both Hindus and Zoroastrians. Once a child reached the age of about fifteen, they joined their particular fold, or group, and began wearing a sacred thread belt, or sash to mark initiation into a guild.

"Originally, these categories bore no *stigma*, but powerful 'leaders' seeking material wealth, managed to turn a useful system into an oppressive yoke, riddled with prejudice. Guilds morphed into a cruel system that flew in the face of the loving and just principles of the Aryan and Vedic Prophets. People traced belief in *Asura Varuna* and the Lawgivers, for gods and idols. Prophets of each age, must weep when they see how tainted the faith of some who profess to be their followers becomes.

"**Huangdi** was known as the originator of the degree of unity known as the centralized state and He is regarded as the initiator of modern Chinese civilization, which was governed by a sound code of laws, and respectful behavior.

WRITING: "**Enoch** fled to Egypt, His mind filled with wisdom and his heart with justice. There, He was known as **Thoth** and had a powerful influence on both clergy and royalty. The Greeks who visited Egypt in search of wisdom called Him **Hermes**. He was the first to invent a basic form of written language. Although there have been subsequent variations and improvements in writing, He is credited with filling several Egyptian halls with collected spiritual wisdom, science, and magic. The Egyptians attributed forty-two books on esoteric science to Hermes. The *Doctrine of the Fire-Principle* and *Words of Light* contained in the *Vision of Hermes* became the climax of initiation into the Egyptian priesthood.

"**Huangdi** is regarded as the father of Chinese characters, said by some to be the oldest continuously used system of writing in the world; an oracle bone script found on animal bones or turtle shells, which was used in divination during the Bronze Age.

METALLURGY: "During **Hooshang's** time, smiths melted metals from ore to create household and farming tools: saws, axes, hoe-like mattocks, and knives, as well as other weapons. The Shahnameh mentions that gold was used in ancient times to make surgical knives for performing 'Caesarean' operations, well before Caesar's time.

"**Huangdi** shared with humanity alchemical secrets, the making of gold objects, and improved metal farming implements.

"**Yima's** times saw improvements in the mining of jewels and precious metals, allowing the manufacture of armor and weaponry to protect the new cities. Golden implements aided surgery. Iron was used to make helmets, chain-mail tunics, breastplates, and coats of armor for man and horse.

SCIENCES: **"Hooshang** is associated with the expansion of world navigation in sailing ships, mining, fine brick masonry and the use of architectural plans.

**"Enoch** not only filled libraries in Egypt with scientific volumes, but laid the foundation of philosophy. According to Baha'u'llah,

> *'The first person who devoted himself to philosophy was Idris. Some called him also Hermes. In every tongue he hath a special name. He it is who hath set forth in every branch of philosophy thorough and convincing statements. After him Balinús derived his knowledge and sciences from the Hermetic Tablets and most of the philosophers who followed him made their philosophical and scientific discoveries from his words and statements.'*

— TABLETS OF BAHA'U'LLAH

**"Huangdi** oversaw the chemistry of perfumes, fermented beverages, and clothing dyes. He expanded the use of boats and navigation, improved astronomy, and math calculations.

**"Yima** instigated the use of chemistry to make perfumes and wine. According to Persian legend, the king banished one of his wives from his kingdom causing her to become despondent enough to wish to take her life. She went to his warehouse, where she found a jar of spoiled grapes that were deemed undrinkable. The fermentation that she thought was poison, was pleasant and lifted her spirits. She took her discovery to the King, who was pleased.

"These Prophets led us into an age of bounty and civil organization. In the end, **Hooshang** left the throne to his son, Tahmuras, after forty years. The Bible says **Enoch** was taken by God at the age of 365 years. **Huangdi,** the Yellow Emperor, lived for over a hundred years before meeting a *phoenix*, a symbol of high virtue and grace; and a Qulin, a hooved, lion-headed, horned horse creature - sometimes depicted as a giraffe. These animals are known throughout various Asian cultures to signal the imminent arrival or passing of a wise sage or illustrious ruler.

**Jamshid** was given a seven-ringed cup filled with the elixir of immortality which allowed him to observe the universe. He commanded the angels and demons of the world and in Heaven. He was both a King and the divine Representative of Ahura Mazda until He became self-important and stopped serving Him.

One day the Shining Beings raised His throne into the air and flew it all around causing his subjects to think *He* was a god. The farr departed when his ego caused him to become arrogant. He was disgraced, his kingdom fell to ruin, and the religion degenerated into darkness. People began to murmur and rebel. He repented in his heart, but glory never returned to him. He was overthrown by Zahhak the Arabian, and fled, but he was finally trapped and brutally murdered. After a long Golden Age, humanity descended from the heights of civilization back into gloom, making it vulnerable to foreign aggression and destruction.

"IN SUMMARY, rather than blond Valkyries, the Aryans were known as 'the Noble Ones' because of their submission to the will of God, plain and simple. The purity and unity of the Old Aryan Homeland was its belief in One God! Not in a purity of skin tone or hair color.

"Scriptures and historical traditions were instituted by physically different types of humans. Throughout millions of years of history, most of Them did not look the same as us.

But three cultural developmental stages coincided with the earliest recorded Prophets. It would be fair to say ancient Revealers of God's Word have shepherded humanity from its meager beginnings. It carried us through times of sufficient food; through worldwide catastrophes, crises like climate change – ice ages, floods, fires, and the drying of rivers due to severe drought, where increasing populations were decimated by starvation. At least a portion of humanity survived, and scrabbled into times of domestication and civilization.

"Some Prophets apparently failed in their revelatory gifts due to extreme circumstances. Yet all are treasured Emissaries of the One Source, related in a special choir of souls: Nu Wa, Gayomart, Yima, Rama, Jamshid, Fu-Xi, Krishna, Abraham, Moses, Zoroaster, Buddha, Jesus the Christ, Mohammad, the Bab, and Baha'u'llah - never competitors. They are literally soul brothers as bearers of the same Holy Spirit, and always have each other's backs... praising the Blessed Person who came before, and mentioning at least One who will come after them. For example, 'the Glory,' or the 'Spirit of Truth,' or, 'He will come again from Sinai...thence from Seir.' Given all of that love and respect there shouldn't be rivalries or arguments between faiths. But putting the Great Being first has been a difficult lesson for humankind to retain. It bears repeating in every age. That is in essence, *why* the Ancient Religion of God must be renewed and cleansed, from age to age.

"Thank you for your time. If you have any questions, maybe we could chat over dessert! For those of you, who have questions but can't stay, can reach me through Jamal. You have been a great audience."

19

# ON THE JOB TRAINING

Kyah was feeling extreme angst. Family visits were decreasing and he couldn't get out and about to see friends or take classes – or even get to a store on his own. His electric wheelchair could only take him so far. Outside of Sage and L. W., he was cut off from the world he had known, a world where he had been a center of attention and action. He missed daily contact with his mother and Aparu, though they stopped by several times a week to take him into the country, to appointments, or to do shopping. That helped a lot. Still, he couldn't reach out and hug his brothers and sisters whenever he wanted.

It had taken a couple of months of focusing on physical therapy, before he could leave the wheelchair and walk on crutches. The bones were mostly healed, but he and Penny had a long way to go before they could prove their capabilities in the field. While he worked on strength training, he continued to practice basic commands with Penny. He was now ready to teach her how to "search". Kyah took one of Gideon's socks for her first experience. He asked her repeatedly to "sniff" the sock while Gideon hid. She had no idea what he was asking. It took several times with him hobbling on the crutches with her to find Gideon. Eventually, it clicked and Penny began to enjoy her daily training exercises and excelled at her new favorite game - "search". The whole family got involved, including his brothers and sisters, who hid, while he gave Penny an article of clothing to "sniff" then told her to "search" for the "missing" family member.

Kyah bragged about his success with training Penny to Tom, his physical therapist, when they talked about him starting to walk on his own. He would soon be able to donate his extraordinary wheelchair to someone else in need. Tom was overjoyed. Then he told him he knew another man who had a search and rescue dog. If Kyah wanted him to, he would give his number to that friend. Kyah eagerly agreed, and was definitely feeling better after that visit.

THIS DAY WAS overcast when Kyah stepped outside to the porch. He had been trying to increase his stamina, but found it was no easy task. He rarely used his crutches now, but he still had a long way to go to rebuild his strength.

Penny looked up and wagged as he yawned, and then shivering, he returned to the house without taking a walk. Penny looked disappointed, or was he just imagining it? He got a cup of coffee and sat in his comfortable chair. It felt good to be off his feet.

Penny looked into his eyes and he rubbed her face, but he jumped when his phone rang. Hardly anyone called him. The caller said his name was Garrett Mackay, Tom's friend. Kyah wasn't sure where this was leading, until the man said he shared Kyah's interest in search and rescue. He and his dog, Sally, were actually a team in the Granite County SAR.

"So, this is why I called, we have a situation up in Schwartz Creek – in your neck of the woods. A young woman disappeared yesterday. She was last seen on one of the logging roads, with a group of young people who were drinking beer and target practicing. Apparently, she went off to take a leak and never returned. The kids told Deputy Khiergan Sparks in Missoula that they had looked for almost two hours before giving up and reporting her missing.

"I'm in Philipsburg now, but I'll be taking Sally over there in a few minutes. We could meet in Clinton, and I could take you and Penny along for a trial run, what do you say? Oh, bring a jacket, it might rain."

Kyah had to close his mouth before he could answer. "Uh, I guess that would be great. I'm a little nervous, but I think we are ready. When do you think you'll be in Clinton?"

KYAH PACKED A DAYPACK, and Sage drove him over and they met up near the bridge on the Clark Fork almost an hour later. After letting the dogs greet each other, Kyah and Penny hopped into Garrett's pickup and they crossed the river and headed up the canyon. After hesitating at a fork in the road where Garrett checked his directions, they continued to climb the side of a steep hill until they found a pull out near a practically dried up stream. Unfortunately, the kids, or someone else, had left a pile of trash next to the trickle of a creek.

"Maybe we can pick this stuff up later?" Kyah suggested.

Garrett didn't answer right away; he was looking at his notes. "She supposedly went upstream, then turned to the left, according to the witnesses."

Kyah winced. "I imagine the others went after her and mixed tracks and the scents. How can we work with that?"

"Luckily, the kids gave the deputy the sweater she'd been wearing, but left it behind when she went to relieve herself. He should be meeting us here with the evidence any minute. In the meantime, we wait." He fished two candy bars from his pocket and offered one to Kyah, who accepted it with a grin. Not five minutes later, a vehicle pulled up behind Garrett's pickup. A man dressed in a Missoula County sheriff's uniform stepped out to stretch. "Hi, I'm Deputy Khiergan Sparks. I take it you two are Garrett and Kyah." They each nodded.

The deputy reached across the front seat of his rig and removed a brown paper bag, then walked toward them and handed it to Garrett. "This might help."

Garrett opened the bag slightly for Sally to get a good sniff, then he handed it to Kyah, who let Penny sniff. When she yelped, he handed it back to Deputy Sparks and they followed Garrett and the dogs up the creekside. The trail ambled to the left for about a hundred feet where the dogs stopped by a tree. They found the scent trail and took off following the stream uphill for at least a mile.

By now, Kyah's muscles were feeling challenged, and sweat beaded on his face and neck. He took his jacket off and tied it around his waist as he walked.

Garrett called back, "You feeling okay - don't want to push you too much. The dogs will do most of the work anyway."

"Thanks, I can go on, but not for too long."

The dogs doubled back and wandered into the woods, skirting the ridge and dropping into the next canyon, Penny began barking and Kyah forgot his exhaustion, and ran to her location. She looked up at him with her tongue hanging out, panting and wagging her tail. Sally stayed by Garrett and they entered an open crevice to retrieve the young woman who looked unconscious. She was cold, but she was breathing. Deputy Sparks took some preliminary photos, then called in to report that the woman was found, and that they needed an ambulance - if they could get one in there. The deputy gave them GPS coordinates from his phone. He told Kyah and Garrett to wait for the EMTs to arrive with a stretcher. Kyah swatted a hungry mosquito and said they'd be there. Then the deputy went back to his vehicle to meet the ambulance and direct the crew to the site.

Garrett came to grab Kyah's coat to cover the girl, and Kyah added a blanket roll from his pack, to put underneath. They carefully checked for trauma before slowly dragging the blanket about twelve feet into the sunshine. They took turns gently rubbing her limbs to increase circulation while they waited. She didn't wake until the dogs barked a warning of the approaching crew. Garrett and Kyah called out to them, and soon the girl was lifted onto a stretcher, and on her way to the trauma center at St. Pat's Hospital.

Kyah could see the benefit of taking EMT classes to better assess and assist. He would look into that when he got back into Missoula.

. . .

AS THEY ARRIVED BACK at their vehicles, Garrett said to Kyah, "Not bad. Your perseverance was remarkable, and that dog is amazing. You have a real future in this work."

Deputy Sparks added, "Yeah, we could use you and your dog in our Missoula County SAR K9 division if you're interested."

"I think I've died and gone to heaven – are you kidding? I think search and rescue has always been my calling. And Penny here actually rescued *me* along with several others earlier this year from the rubble of an earthquake. I'm still recovering."

"If you're free this afternoon, you could come by the department and fill out some forms."

"Okay, but I haven't got a degree – or any formal training – outside of the fact that I'm pretty skilled with ground penetrating radar." Inside he was dying of excitement – ready to tell everyone in his family the great news.

Khiergan said, "Not a problem. Just come on by. Do you happen to speak a second language?"

"Yes, Lakota, and a couple of South American dialects - but I'm not fluent."

The deputy grinned. "That's excellent!"

Garrett said, "I'm happy for you, Kyah. And count on me calling you for help in the future."

The deputy added, "That's right. We assist with operations in neighboring counties. See you at the department, Kyah."

Garrett suggested, "Got time now to grab some lunch? By that I mean fast food so we don't have to leave the dogs."

"We could do that. Or if you like lasagna, I packed a couple of frozen slabs which should be thawed by now, plus some cookies and water - in case we were out there all day."

Garrett practically laughed and said, "Great, let's do that. I brought chicken slices for the dogs. It'll be a picnic!" Kyah tried to express how much this opportunity had meant to him, how it had transformed dream into reality. The tracker seemed to understand. After they ate Garrett asked, "Need a ride to Missoula?"

"That would be great. I really need to get a car, but I don't have a job."

"You're going to find one, I'm sure of that. Hop in, I'll take you home."

## 20
# LITTLE BOY AND THE DEAD MAN

K yah was still feeling rumpled inside due to the lack of closure in his second case. L. W. felt his dismay and asked him to join Sage and herself for lunch. Kyah could smell the freshly baked bread as he sauntered to the main house. It occurred to him that it had been a long time since he sauntered anywhere. There were still things to be thankful for.

He greeted them with a grin and thanked them for their extreme kindness as they beckoned him to take a seat at their dining table. Spaghetti, green salad, and blueberry pie with ice cream shoved away a lot of the hollow ache he'd held inside.

After he took his dishes to the kitchen, Sage asked, "Any news from the deputy yet?"

"Unfortunately, no."

He and Penny had done their part to the best of their abilities. They found the trail of the missing boy, who had wandered away from his parents at a picnic area several days before. Penny was hot on his trail when she stopped cold and barked twice. Some voice inside, told Kyah to prepare for the worst. When he and Khiergan caught up to the dog, there was nothing there. Nothing but a set of tire tracks. No sign of the boy anywhere. It looked as if he had vanished. Maybe he had.

Khiergan poured a cast of the tread marks, and Kyah found and photographed a little friendship bracelet a few yards away. Kyah imagined it had fallen off when someone roughly grabbed his little hand. Deputy Sparks collected the evidence, and at that point, Kyah said the between worlds prayer for the soul of the child who may be confused or frightened. As he chanted, he reached for a rectangular silver tin inside his backpack, opened the lid and took out a braid of sweetgrass, and lit it. He waved the smoke around and raised his arms, as the sacred herbs burned into a fragrant, slightly sweet smoke.

He said, "The spirits are listening. Hey-a-ho. First, I offer this sacred smoke to Wakan Tanka, the Great Spirit who is One. Behold us on this sacred earth. O Wakan Tanka, you are my Father and Grandfather. You are everything. You have always been. Grandfather, this is your herb, its fragrance belongs to you. Behold the good child before you. He may be lost and confused. I beg of you to cause him to move toward you, as is your will. Be merciful. Help him." He laid the braid of sweetgrass on a large stone. "Our Grandmother and Mother, you are sacred. Every step upon you should be taken as a prayer. It is from you that our bodies come. Take pity on this boy and his parents. They wish to be one with all things. Like us, they serve the good of all Your peoples, the four-leggeds, the two-leggeds, the green things and the wings of the air. Help him." Turning his feet to the West, he said, "I now beseech the four directions to help him. First, to you, O winged power from where the sun goes down. Send your servants, ancient and sacred - the Thunder Beings, who come to us in the terrifying storm. Help this boy." He turned to each of the other three directions, beseeching aid for the lost child. Finally, Kyah announced "Hetchetu alo. It is finished."

Without knowing what else to say, Khiergan said, "Amen."


IT WAS ONLY a few days before Kyah's phone rang again. It was Khiergan asking him to meet up to find a missing bow hunter. Bow season had started the first Saturday in September, and it would continue into October. His wife had reported the man missing after he

173

didn't return, or call. Kyah and the Deputy found the hunter's truck parked off an old logging road west of Stevensville. They briefly searched the truck, but saw no clue as to what happened. Kyah did find an old baseball cap in the truck, and gave it to Penny to sniff, then gave her the order, "Search." She ran around the truck, chose a direction and took off. She was out of sight in an instant. They followed her for almost three miles before they found a hunting stand. The young hunter was slumped in the grass about fifty yards away. He apparently had been cleaning a deer, when a bullet tore into his chest. The carcass was gone, but the gut pile remained – buzzing with flies.

Khiergan suggested, "Rifle season starts in October, so maybe he was shot by an early poacher." He photographed the scene from every angle, and the body's position in relation to the stand. "This should help the investigation. I think he was shot from a distance – can't find any traces of another person – except that the deer is gone. You see any tracks, Kyah?"

"I think there's a boot impression by the tree under the stand. Looks quite a bit larger than this guy's foot."

"Good eye." While Deputy Sparks put up crime scene tape, Kyah kneeled beside the man, ignoring the smell of decomposition. He started saying a Baha'i Prayer for the Departed.

*"O my God! O Thou forgiver of sins, bestower of gifts, dispeller of afflictions!*

*Verily, I beseech Thee to forgive the sins of such as have abandoned the physical garment and have ascended to the spiritual world.*

*O my Lord! Purify them from trespasses, dispel their sorrows, and change their darkness into light. Cause them to enter the garden of happiness, cleanse them with the most pure water, and grant them to behold*
*Thy splendors on the loftiest mount."*

When he arose, Khiergan put a hand on his shoulder and said, "It's really nice of you to do that sort of thing. I think people need to know someone cares. I'll call the coroner and meet him where we parked. Be back as soon as I can."

Kyah sat with Penny, calmly rubbing her head as she looked up at him. "Why can't we get a simple case of healthy missing people in the forest, girl?" He ran two fingers between her eyes and down her nose, wondering if he had made the wrong career choice. In that moment, he remembered the joy of finding people alive after the earthquake, and helping them get medical care – and locating the bodies of some who were less lucky – so their families could grieve. "I guess I need to realize we are still doing a good thing by bringing closure where we can, girl.

Penny woofed, signaling Khiergan's return with the coroner and his staff. A tech began taking photographs, while the deputy began collecting evidence, starting with some of the blood that had drained into the ground, and the coroner began his initial inspection of the body.

At that point Kyah asked, "Are we going to head back now?"

"Not quite yet." The deputy spoke up nearby, "Say, did I tell you I got an update on the little boy on the way to work?"

Kyah turned. "No, what happened?"

"I think your prayers helped. The little guy was dropped off at the campground, where his family was waiting, in case he somehow found his way back.

"What? That's amazing, is he okay?"

"Seems like. Apparently, he was confused and quiet, but was unharmed. A maroon SUV just dropped him off on the road, and left. At this point we have no idea why the guy in the car changed his mind. We hope to know more later."

Kyah grinned and nodded. "Really appreciate hearing that, Deputy."

"And I really appreciate how quickly Penny found *this* guy."

When the deputy dropped Kyah and Penny off at Sage's, he said "We'll talk again soon."

KYAH COULDN'T WAIT to tell Sage and L. W. who were thrilled by the good news. Then

Sage suggested, "Tomorrow we should look into getting you a driver's license and a car of your own. Seems like it's time. You'll need a paying job for insurance, gas and upkeep. Maybe at the university, or Burger King if you like. But I'm writing a book, and could use some help collating and organizing the notes, if you're interested?"

Kyah's face lit into a smile.

"But tonight, you and Penny can sleep in peace."

## 21

# FORBIDDEN CAVE

Secora and Destiny had discussed returning to the cave to take a more detailed and leisurely look around the site. Something about Tanya wasn't sitting well with either of them. They wondered if her ex was the one to blame, or not. Tanya had aroused suspicions during their visit which led them to think something might still be going on at the property near Wapiti, Wyoming. The women speculated that perhaps Tanya might have a better offer waiting in the wings.

Secora said, "Who knows? Maybe it's a plan to develop the land around the cave into a casino complex."

Destiny prompted, "With a hotel?"

"Yeah, and a truck stop and diner. That's not so far-fetched. There's already a resort and guest ranches near the Four Bears trail head."

Destiny added, "If she was hoping to sell land to a developer, she surely wouldn't want it deemed a historic place, and therefore worthless to a commercial buyer.

Secora laughed and said, "True, not easy to develop an attraction with the US Forest Service, a geologist, a paleontologist, and a paleobotanist rooting through the dig site."

Destiny paused, then said, "If Tanya wants to sell this land, she'd better hurry."

"So, there's a ticking clock - the deal's off if they can't do it right away."

"And she wouldn't be particularly pleased if we found more than tracks in that cave, would she."

"She could try to say the whole thing was a hoax. Try to hide the evidence before she sells the land." They decided to leave early Saturday, and answer their nagging questions.

THE WOMEN WERE ACCOMPANIED by their husbands and Kyah who brought Penny. They decided to drive west from Cody which took only six hours, rather than opting to take the scenic route through Yellowstone, to Wapiti on Route 14. They worried that traffic could get backed up along the way. Kyah, who now had his learner's permit, was driving the pickup under Gideon's watchful eye. As they passed the extensive Buffalo Bill Reservoir on the North fork of the Shoshone River, Jimmy said, "That's where we'll be hanging out, while you two ladies are doing your cave exploration."

Kyah piped up, "Wish I'd brought a fishing pole."

Gideon said, "You don't have one, Nephew. Lucky for you, I brought an extra."

"You're the best, Uncle!"

Secora said. "First, we'll see if we are going to need you guys for our protection on this explore."

Destiny added, "We still don't know what exactly, Tanya is hiding."

"Or, how far she is willing to go," added Secora.

Gideon said, "Of course. The safety of our pregnant ladies *is* our primary focus."

Jimmy popped open a bag of chips. "That *is* food for thought. Anyone else want some food for their stomachs?" Soon the crunching was unanimous, even Penny got a couple of small chips that Kyah hoped wouldn't cut the inside of her mouth.

When they pulled into the trailhead parking lot, there were no other vehicles there. Gideon smiled, "Looks like the coast is clear. You're good to go."

Destiny stared at Jimmy and raised her eyebrows. "I don't like the idea of you being too far away... just in case. Remember I'm due in less than three weeks."

He chuckled and kissed her on the cheek. "What if we drop you off for an hour, get some fish, then pick you up and cook some lunch?"

Secora mused, "Sounds like a pipe dream, but sure."

Destiny asked, "Do you think it will take us an hour?"

"Maybe not for data collection, but including the hike to the cave for two pregnant ladies – yes I think an hour."

Gideon handed Secora her daypack before turning the vehicle around. In it Secora had packed water, a camera, flashlights and head lamps. There were also containers for samples and of course her first aid kit. She put on her leather jacket and hefted the pack. They waved goodbye to the men, as they left.

Destiny said, "I hope we're ready for this."

"No sweat."

The narrow trail led them past jagged rocks and brush. When they stopped for a breather, Secora puffed. "Thank God we're getting close. Not as fun as it used to be."

Destiny panted. "I have to pee."

"This is as good a place as any to rest – we're about halfway there."

A few minutes later they arrived at the cave entrance. Secora photographed the exterior of the mouth and the surrounding cliffs, on a mission to document everything this time.

When they walked inside the cave they noticed the temperature had dropped almost twenty degrees. Destiny said, "Still hot, but BETTER."

"Let's put on these headlamps. I'm not taking chances this time."

They walked to the place where Secora had taken samples, but the ground was all torn up – like someone had taken a pick-axe to everything. Secora got out her camera and took pictures of the destruction. "What a crime! Darn, looks like they tried to destroy all of the tracks as well."

"That's not great."

"It isn't, but look here, I found another set, three human footprints near the back of this grotto."

Secora picked up her russet leather backpack and moved forward. Destiny touched the back wall and said, "Hey, are these charcoal marks?"

Secora turned. "Looks like they are. Please take pictures, and I'll get a little scraping... perhaps we can get a date off that."

Destiny whispered, "What is that sound?"

Secora hesitated while she sealed the sample. "I think it sounds like motorcycles."

She'd barely finished the words, when a deafening boom made them cover their ears and drop to the ground. The thin exterior light vanished and dust forcefully clogged their nostrils.

"Destiny, breathe through your shirt."

"Did someone blow the entrance up?"

Secora answered through muffled layers of shirt. "It would seem so. Darn it! No warning."

Destiny muffled, "Someone seriously wants to get rid of this cave."

"Or us. For the life of me I can't think why."

"Guess they knew we wouldn't quit."

"But why is that important?"

The women were quiet with their thoughts for a few minutes – contemplating the finality of their situation. At last, Destiny said. "What can we do? I'm not getting a signal on my cell."

Secora looked downcast in the light of her head lamp. "Me neither. Hopefully the guys heard the blast."

Secora reached back for the wall and the tips of her fingers felt an opening. She reached in farther, then withdrew a Maglite from the pack. "Destiny, I think there's another chamber. I don't see any light, but... I think the crawl space might only be twenty-four inches high, and it seems to be fairly short before a compartment opens up. Think we can squeeze through?"

Destiny shook her head. "Hell no. I'm claustrophobic... *and* eight months pregnant. No way." After consideration she added. "Well technically, I guess we are already in hell." After a moment, she sighed. "Okay, I think we should try."

"It's better than staying here, so... here goes." Secora was on her hands and knees. "This would be tough even if we weren't pregnant."

Destiny suggested, "Try rolling on your back first, might be easier to squirm through."

"But how am I going to move that way?"

"Just stiffen your legs and I'll push you through the first part, until you can move your arms. If that doesn't work, I'll pull you back out by your feet."

"Do you have any idea how unappealing that suggestion sounds?"

"Have you got something better?"

After a big sigh she reclined on her back and tried to wriggle through, while Destiny pushed her boots. Destiny suddenly burst into laughter. Secora said, "What? Oh no, don't... say it..."

"I'm going to say it. One more push and you'll be out of the canal! How does it feel to be reborn?"

"Don't make me laugh or I'll get stuck, or worse, I'll pee!"

That only made Destiny laugh harder until she started choking from the dust in her

throat.

Luckily, the stricture was only two and a half to three feet long. Secora's head lamp allowed her to look up, and her gaze fixed on a fluttering fringe of bats, a smallish family of about thirty clinging to the ceiling above her head.

Destiny gave another shove and Secora could feel her jacket slide on something greasy. As she skated on her back through a large pile of guano, it released a particularly strong odor.

She could hear Destiny's muffled voice as she shoved the daypack through the opening. "Are you all the way through? How is it?"

"It feels *crappy*! How will I ever get this jacket clean?"

Destiny laughed again and Secora heard her wriggle into the 'canal.' She reached her arms into the gap and had to turn her head up and out of the way to get the furthest reach. Once she felt Destiny's shoulders she pulled hard against her friend's shirt and arms. After two tugs, Destiny had entered the chamber and encountered the stinking mass for herself. She said, "Dang, wish I was wearing my sweatshirt. This blouse is ruined!"

It was impossible to ignore the condition of their clothing, but there really wasn't much they could do about it. Using their headlamps, they gazed around and Secora estimated the chamber to be about thirty feet long and nearly twenty feet wide. When they moved, they realized the atmosphere was stagnant and smelly, but not dusty. There was no sound, no light – more importantly, there was no air flow. Secora felt closed in, scared – and trapped. When she could speak, she said, "Those bat guys may need a new way out of here after today."

"No kidding."

The women began to move along the walls, exploring the chamber, hoping to find some path to fresh air. It was then Destiny found cave art. She said, "I think there are drawings on this wall. Oh look, here's something that looks like Santa and his reindeer."

Secora waddled over and squinted, "I do see an arc of running deer, but instead of Santa,

I think we have a hunter holding an outstretched spear rather than reins. And over here..." as she took a step, she felt something crunch under her boot and bent down to look more closely at the earth, "I think these are fragments of bones and charcoal"

Destiny said, "What? Could that be the remains of megafauna? I mean that would be classic, wouldn't it?"

Secora took out her pen and carefully swirled it into the dust. She took out a plastic bag and marker out of her leather jacket to capture and mark two samples. "I'm almost sure I have charcoal bits from what once was a fire pit."

"S-u-r-e, you do."

"No, really. I can't wait to get out of here and look at some of this stuff through a microscope."

"We need to get out of here, PERIOD."

They kept moving along the wall to their right, until they saw and felt what seemed like a patch of old dry fence posts. Secora dug her nails into one of them. "Don't think these could get any dryer unless they were dust. Maybe this was a door or gate at one time?"

The women moved the posts to the side.

Destiny commented, "These are so light, almost like balsa wood."

When all of the posts were removed, a small tunnel was revealed which may once have opened up to an alternative exit. Now it was blocked by slide rocks and gravel.

"Do you smell that?"

"It smells fresher but I still don't see any light."

"Maybe the rockslide is thinner somewhere?"

Secora took a stone and slowly started to dig the hill of rock and dirt. "I know this is hopeless, but our children need us to try."

A moment later Destiny worked determinedly beside her. She grabbed one of the balsa poles and started ramming at individual rocks, pressing them back one by one. Secora tossed her rock and did the same. Finally, a rock gave way to a shard of light and a taste of fresh air.

Destiny tried to sound cheery. "We're making some headway."

Secora mumbled, "Yeah, if we don't manage to start another land-slide. But, I can't do more without a rest."

The women lay back panting, and Secora took out two bottles of water. They sipped in silence.

## 2 2

# PANIC

Kyah giggled and said, "Penny is acting crazy in the water. Maybe she hasn't seen anything like this before." The dog was trying to follow the lure, each time someone cast out.

Jimmy said, "Son, if you don't catch her, we aren't going to catch anything either."

Kyah abandoned his pole, trading it for a leash. "Penny, here to me." The dog swung her head back towards the shore, and hesitated for a second before she responded to the command. Bounding through the water and shaking like a hurricane once back on shore, she trotted to Kyah and put her wet face into his hands. Just then her ears picked up when Gideon hooked a large trout.

Ten minutes later, Kyah noticed a pair of dirt bikes moving up the road. He watched them wend their way past the parking lot at the trail-head, then seeing no threat, took Penny to the shoreline to watch Jimmy land a lake trout.

Gideon took pity on the boy and said, "Let me take Penny while you cast a line or two."

After several casts, Kyah was able to catch a perch near the shore. Gideon watched him put the fish out of its grief and place it on the stringer, when they all shuddered at the sound of a vast explosion. At first, they didn't know where it had come from, and searched the panorama of dry wrinkled hills. Their eyes focused in on a cloud of dust, rock, and dirt and realized it came from the direction Destiny and Secora had been headed.

Gideon yelled, "Kyah, throw your pole and the fish in the pickup – we're leaving."

Jimmy yelled, "How in the heck did that happen! We never saw any cars, trucks or anything did we?"

Once he and Penny were inside, Kyah explained that he'd seen two dirt bikes, but they'd passed the turnoff to the parking lot, and driven on up the road.

Gideon's tires were kicking up clouds of dust as he sped toward the trail head. At the parking lot, they jumped from the truck, and Gideon grabbed his 30.06 rifle, before they scrambled up the trail.

Kyah returned to the truck to grab a sweatshirt, then rushed back up the trail behind the others. Penny was already in the lead. The path was tough, they stumbled on rocks protruding through the gravel and sagebrush, entangling their boots and hindering climbing progress.

Heart pounding, Kyah now stood near a fresh landslide where once the mouth of a cave must have been.

Jimmy was puffing hard when he reached Gideon and Kyah. "Oh Grandfather, please, no." He fell to his knees.

Kyah ran to him saying, "Take it easy, we'll figure this out – just breathe and control your heart." Seeing no response, Kyah continued, "We have Penny... please calm yourself. We need you. Your *son* needs you."

Jimmy's eyes now turned to look at the boy, and he nodded.

Kyah showed the dog Destiny's sweatshirt. She sniffed it, then barked her understanding. "Penny, find Secora and Destiny."

She ran from side to side of the landslide, pawing and sniffing here or there, then ran around the lower side of the hill, to the right, and disappeared.

The men waited for a while, not knowing what to do then something odd happened with

Gideon. Instinctively, Jimmy noticed and understood. He came over, helped Gideon sit down, and waited.

Kyah looked stricken and asked, "What's going on?"

"It's okay, son, he's receiving a communication from a thunder being.

GIDEON THOUGHT, *Welcome, White Feather, daughter of Wakinyan Tanka.*

He saw through her eyes that she was soaring far above the crinkled dry canyons. When he looked closer he saw two people sitting with rifles across their knees as if waiting for their prey to show themselves down the hill. Next, he noticed movement in a rockslide near what might have been a rear entrance in the cave outcrop. A dog racing over to the slide caught the thunderbird's attention and she dipped in Penny's direction.

Gideon thought, *no please - not the dog, we need the dog.*

*I am hungry*

*I beg you to find other game, my sister.*

The bird eased up, but now they were close enough to see a small stream of bats flying out through a hole in the rubble. Penny arrived. It looked as if she was barking, then she dug with furious purpose. She even used her paws and her teeth to move rocks away from the hole she was working on.

After the bats were clear, they were followed by arms, and then the body of Destiny who struggled to scramble through sliding gravel. As soon as she was clear, Secora began to emerge.

Unexpected noises came from the rocks above the hill. Gideon noticed as the bird turned her head that the assailants were firing in their direction – or were they going for the dog? The thunderbird powered into an evasive arc and flapped higher and higher. The link was broken.

Gideon roused and picked up his rifle. "We must hurry! The dog has found a place for them to escape, but they're taking fire from two guys with rifles."

Jimmy and Kyah were already in motion. They sprinted to the best of their abilities through the ankle breaking terrain. There wasn't even a deer path to follow, just scree rock skirting the cave-bearing outcrop. After several moments, which seemed like forever, Gideon heard bullets pinging as they ricocheted off rocks with his own ears. He cautioned the others to stay down and out of the killer's sights.

When he could see the assailants clearly through his own scope, Gideon took a shot, then another. One of the men dropped his rifle, the other scrambled up to where he had parked a dirt bike. Soon the engine ground to life and Gideon imagined he would soon be history.

Once Gideon saw the injured man crumple to the rocks, he and the others began to quickly cover the ground between them. Now the injured assailant was attempting to crawl behind a large rock.

As they neared the two women, Gideon and Jimmy veered toward them. It became obvious that Destiny had been shot in the forearm and seemed to be in shock. Jimmy wrapped her in a big hug. Secora had already applied a gauze bandage, and Gideon watched her stand up to dust herself off. Kyah and Penny never stopped. They ran directly to where the assailant fell.

After a round of enthusiastic hugs and murmurs of gratitude, Secora said she was concerned the stress of the entire day might send Destiny, who was three weeks from her due date, into premature labor. Jimmy looked worried, but continued to hold and comfort Destiny. Suddenly Gideon noticed Penny was whining. She let out a yelp, and Kyah hollered back. "The guy's not dead. Can you bring Secora's first aid kit?"

When Gideon and Jimmy arrived, they tried to staunch the bleeding, it was apparent he would require emergency care. Kyah said he'd already called 911 for an ambulance and a sheriff to meet them at the trailhead. While Jimmy and Gideon awkwardly transported the injured man, Kyah volunteered to take the abandoned dirt bike down the road, around the cave area, and to the lot.

Secora and Destiny started to scrabble their way around the cliff rocks then down to the trail head. Slowly, Gideon and Jimmy dragged the injured man to the parking lot. When they arrived, Secora began assessing his condition, which wasn't good. Jimmy and Gideon collapsed in exhaustion on a park bench – no energy left in their eyes.

Finally, Secora said, "For a while it felt like we were in Clarice Paul's hunting party – ready to be picked off one by one."

Gideon shook his head and let out an extended sigh, until Kyah zoomed up to them jabbering excitedly about how the other man had completely disappeared. "The other dirt bike is lying clear off of the trail – like it just fell there. No sign of the guy or his rifle, and I couldn't find any tracks."

Everyone was quiet for a moment, then Gideon said without emotion, "White Feather *did* mention that she was hungry."

Everyone looked like they were grossed out, but nobody said anything. The deputies arrived and started taking photographs and statements. One of them climbed up to the road to photograph the other bike, and retrieve it so they could look for evidence of its owner. He returned with the bike, looking puzzled. "All I found was this giant white eagle feather."

The other deputy was on the hillside looking for brass casings or other evidence that might identify the gunmen.

But everyone's attention was drawn to the ambulance as it arrived and parked. The crew checked the gunman's injury, and loaded him into the aid car, communicating to the emergency room the extent of his injury.

Gideon hardly noticed that Secora and Destiny were being checked out by the other EMT, while an IV was started and the assailant was settled inside. The technician who examined the ladies strongly suggested they follow the ambulance to Cody Regional Health Emergency Department. Then the crew closed the doors and took off.

Kyah picked Penny up and squeezed into the truck with the others. Destiny seemed to be breathing irregularly. Jimmy said to Gideon, "Step on it, please!"

The dirt road seemed extra bumpy and ragged. The tires could not grip well if he drove over 30 mph. The ambulance could go faster because of its tonnage, but Gideon did his best to catch up when they hit the paved road, and he flew past the lake.

That evening they made arrangements to stay overnight because Destiny was still under observation. By three a.m., Jimmy called from her bedside and announced he was a father. Everyone wanted to come, but Jimmy said they should wait until around 9:00 in the morning. The maternity nurse was worried about the baby's lungs since he was three weeks premature. Jimmy headed off their worries by saying, "Don't worry too much, he is breathing on his own. The pediatrician wanted the nurse to observe both mother and child overnight." Jimmy, of course, remained with his family.

TWO DAYS LATER, around 9:00 in the morning, Gideon and the others arrived to greet the new parents. Forty-five minutes later Destiny's release papers were signed.

She said, "I am SOOO hungry, hope there's a diner, or a truck stop nearby that serves big breakfasts."

There was a surprise waiting for them at the desk. Jimmy and Destiny were presented with an infant car seat by the grinning neonatal staff. The giggling nurse said, "Junior is going to need a safe ride home." They were all amazed by such a gift, and Gideon made a sizeable donation to the Maternity Department.

The next thought on everyone's mind was where would everyone sit? They could barely fit inside, before the car seat.

Kyah volunteered to ride in the bed of the truck with Penny. There was a canopy with a sliding window to the cab for communication if needed. "Don't hit any bumps," he laughed.

"Right!" Secora teased.

They laid out Gideon's emergency sleeping bags in the bed, gave them water and food, then closed the canopy to begin the trek home with a tiny preemie they were trying to keep warm. With morning traffic, it took seven and a half hours. After dropping a very bruised and stiff Kyah off with Penny, the others drove to Destiny's house and stayed up watching over the child who had been named, *Apawi*, meaning *the star around which the earth revolves*, and his mom. Although they were all thoroughly exhausted after the day-long journey, there would be little sleep today at Destiny's house. During the night, Destiny asked, "Jimmy, can you get Apawi? Even if the place was on fire... I couldn't get up again?"

He moaned, "Sure, I'll get him, you need sleep."

Destiny sighed, "Thanks, Babe."

By the next morning no one was moving. Muffled snores and occasional cries from the child were all Gideon heard.

THAT AFTERNOON, Secora and Gideon were able to crawl away from Destiny's house and go to work. Secora needed to handle departmental business until Destiny was ready to return. The boss and the baby wouldn't come into the office for *at least* another five weeks, about the time of her own due date.

Gideon kissed Secora as he dropped her off, then drove on to the office. Secora thought wryly, *bet he gets a nap there.*

IT WAS LATER that night before Secora and Gideon even cared to think about the attack at the cave, and the injured assailant. Gideon called the sheriff's department the next day and found out the injured man had not survived. Before he died, the man mumbled something unintelligible about a woman, but they had no leads on the other guy except that a bloody hoody had turned up - found by a hiker up on Wapiti Ridge.

## 23

# SUSPICION

Secora woke, stretched, and got up to grab a cup of coffee. Gideon had already made a pot before he left for work. She took a sip, then felt cramping in her back and wondered if it was a labor pain, but it seemed to ease up and she finished breakfast. She packed a sandwich and a couple of bottles of iced tea, then walked to the door to leave for work, when the phone rang.

It was a call from the Wyoming State Archaeologist, who effused his gratitude to her for turning over all of the evidence and photos she and Destiny had collected. He confirmed that he had been in the middle of another project at the time.

Secora said, "We might never have discovered the good stuff, if it weren't for all the drama."

"We're really happy you and Dr. Hawkins managed to survive, and bring more of this prehistoric site to life. We've already notified the newspaper and the evening news about this find."

"Great, that will make it difficult for someone to sweep the site under a rug now. I'll follow your progress."

"Early examinations of the bone and ash suggested that they may include evidence of a glyptodont, a gigantic armadillo-like creature the size of a Volkswagen." He thought it would be extremely rare to find one roaming so far to the north, and assured her there would be no commercial construction on the property surrounding the trail and the cliff outcrop. The state was in the process of purchasing the land as a prehistoric monument site. There was even a chance that they would be able to carefully tunnel a new opening, to further their exploration with the help of a group of students from their university. She smiled at the outcome.

THE ANTEROOM WAS dark when she got to the office. There was no secretary and no guard, but there was a note on the door. Secora pulled the piece of tape free and opened the page assuming it would be a memo letting her know the secretary called in sick. Instead, it read: *hope your cave hunting days are over – they had better be!* To herself she said, "Won't you be surprised?"

After she'd settled at her desk and changed the date on the calendar, she took a sip of her tea. Secora was still grinning when Tarkio entered and hugged her unexpectedly. "Boss, it's so good to have you back - on several levels. I'm so happy you and Dr. Hawkins are safe now. Did you know my wife, Anida, is helping her with the baby so she can get some rest?" He hesitated. "Also, I am tired of doing your classes. I know that doesn't sound great... but..."

"No, I completely understand, Tarkio. Even for a few days, that was a lot to ask on top of your other classes and seminars. I am s.o.o.o.o grateful. But I have to tell you, my biggest worry is that when my baby comes, I'll need to call on you and Bill again."

"Probably by then, we will have recovered and be better prepared. After all, it was only a few days." He made a weak attempt at laughter.

"Probably," she said distractedly. "By the way, did you see anyone in the office before I got here?"

"No, I was concentrating on some notes. Sorry."

Bill's head popped in. "I thought I'd heard signs of life. Great that you're back, Dr. James. This place really isn't the same without you."

"I missed you guys, too. But believe me the trip was no picnic."

Her attention returned to the desk when the phone rang. Secora was surprised to hear Tanya's voice.

Tarkio and Bill took the opportunity to move on down the hall toward their office.

Tanya was calling for Destiny to thank her for convincing the University of Wyoming and the National Park Service to purchase her property and declare it a monument. She was currently in contract negotiations with their representatives.

Secora thought her voice seemed normal, as if she was oblivious to either of the two attacks, or the intimidating messages, the creepy cab nobody called for, and the disruptive class incident - and pretty much anything else. Secora shrugged as she hung up the phone, confused. *If not Tanya and her ex – who would be invested enough in shutting the cave survey down, and trying to scare us off?*

While she was cogitating, she turned on her computer and went into her emails. She was still getting notifications about cryptid sightings from fans who were amazed by the story of the scimitar cat that was making the rounds. There were two new queries today.

A student from her megafauna class was floating a stretch of the Clark Fork outside of Missoula, near Milltown when she noticed an exposed cutbank caused by a drop in the water level. People were scrambling on the embankment, collecting fossils like crazy. This student wondered if the university should check the site out before the fossils were gone forever.

Secora forwarded this email to Tarkio and Bill. It wasn't long before she heard them stirring down the hall.

The second email concerned the exposure of skeletal remains of a gigantic sea creature in the sediments of the Bearpaw shale formation along the Marias River, north of Great Falls. The woman who sent that email thought the bones might have belonged to a mosasaur.

Secora remembered that a variety of smaller marine fossils, and some dinosaur fragments, had been recovered from the silt and clay deposits of the Western Interior Seaway, other times simply called the Bearpaw Sea. Over millions of years, seawater had advanced and retreated across the region, covering much of the land from the Arctic to the Gulf of Mexico during the mid to late Cretaceous.

But even more astonishing, was the fact this person saw a humongous solitary wolf-like creature watching her when she looked up from the skeleton. It terrified her. As soon as she was able to move, she fled. She went on to say she thought she could take Secora back to that spot if she was interested.

Of course, that caught Secora's attention, yet she sat back wondering if either or both of these tidbits might be ploys to get her out of town - into a vulnerable position. She closed her computer realizing she couldn't afford any risk at this stage of pregnancy; besides, she was still tied to the office, doing her best to fill in for Destiny during her maternity leave.

Her Graduate teaching assistants were already overbooked, and she was feeling bad about sending them the river fossil email. *Great. Guess I should call them off*, she thought, and decided to go have a talk with them about her suspicion – perhaps tell them to forget it.

She'd pass it along to one of the invertebrate paleo students. *Probably more up their alley anyway.* She waddled down the hall and when she got to the office door and looked in - they were gone. Looking down at the floor tile, she sighed. *What am I worried about? Probably nothing. I'll text them.*

After trying their phones and leaving each student a message, she shrugged and dug into a threatening stack of paperwork, still wishing she could be sure who was responsible for the harassment.

*Was it all Tanya? Or is there something else I'm missing? And, who is Tanya anyway?*

Acting on a hunch, Secora looked up Robert Greenwood's obit. Even though the body never made it back from South America, there should have been an obituary in the Missoulian.

She wondered *when was that, oh right*. As she looked for the date, she recalled the situation. There it was, the Robert Greenwood obituary. Secora's eyes brightened when she saw Tanya's Lambert's maiden name, Greenwood, listed under the survivors. On the spur of the moment, she decided to type her memories of Robert's passing, to help bring Tanya closure.

*My adrenaline was screaming, as I raced down the trail to the canyon beneath the Gueros' Cliff City. A dozen of us ran from the cliff to where we thought the sounds came from, but all we saw was freshly broken trees and torn earth. My breath was roaring in and out as I hollered, for my father and Gideon. "Where are you?"*

*Finally, I saw my dad on the ground looking shaken, and Gideon who was partly hidden by a bush, holding his bleeding arm. His sleeve was soaked, and he looked like he was in shock. Dad stood up and turned toward the crowd, mumbling, 'It happened so fast, couldn't stop it.' He shook his head. 'Secora, they looked like giant hippo-sized guinea pigs. Didn't see if they had horns on their faces. Weirdest...' His voice trailed off as I put my arm around him. 'I swear Dad, everything down here except for a caiman, looks like a giant guinea pig to you.' Recovering a little, he said, 'Yeah, that's probably why you like it here so much.'*

*Kyah and Jane helped Gideon up. Your father's body lay trampled six feet away. There was nothing any of us could do to help him.*

*Gideon explained, 'I think he was trying to kill me. His gunfire probably stampeded the animals.'*

*While Kyah and Jane took the men back to the village, I spotted several clear tracks on the far side of the valley. I thought they looked way too big for a tapir. Some of the tracks had three toes, and oddly, I noticed three prints that appeared to be made by combat boots. I tried to remember what kind of boots Bob had been wearing. At that point, Azalea arrived and began screaming. She asked, 'Why didn't Bob follow Sage and Gideon to safety? Why did he wait so long?' She was still in shock when she notified the university of his loss.*

*I tried to calm her. I tried to tell her that he was already shooting, perhaps at Gideon. The shots probably caused the animals to run, then he had to make his stand. I'm sure the charging beasts were on him instantaneously."*

*In the end, Azalea chose to believe Bob had died protecting the others. Sage and Gideon's version began with going on the excursion* at Bob's request. They rambled through the lush vegetation for a few minutes before they noticed large, chewing-gum-colored bodies in the brush. The men tried to leave quietly, until Bob, who was in the lead, pulled his pistol and fired. He hit Gideon who was trying to jump out of the way of the large oncoming beasts. My dad gave Gideon a shove and they both fell into the thicket.

Dad told us, 'The university will probably send a courier for the body. We should let people here know in case soldiers find their way into the canyon, or a helicopter shows up.'

Two hours later the mystery about what they would do with his body was resolved. A black helicopter flew in—terrifying the Gueros. Many cried out or fell to the ground in fear. It hovered up at eye-level with their city courtyard. A ladder line was dropped, and three plain-clothed individuals slid down. They proceeded to load the remains, such as they were, into a bag. After they were back on board, the chopper veered away from the village.

It seemed awfully quick for a chopper to arrive from Montana to pick up the body. So many questions assailed my mind. It felt like I was in a daze. Gideon came over and said, 'Crazy about what happened to Bob.' I looked up at him. 'Sorry, Gideon, do you mean his death or the recovery of his remains?'

In the end we don't know what happened to his corpse. We are so sorry for your loss, and wish there had been a better outcome.

SHE SIGNED the letter and sealed it in an envelope. She'd let the secretary post it in the outgoing mail.

## 24

# RIVER FOSSILS

L ater that morning, as she signed the request she had been working on, Secora again wondered about the two emails.

"Dr. James? Dr. James?"

She wheeled around a bit startled. A young freckle-faced boy said, "My friend Becca Travers is sick and won't be in your class today."

"Excuse me, which class? I don't call roll, sorry."

"Montana Archaeology."

"Is Becca's illness serious?"

"Yes and no, it's the flu. I just got over it."

Are you sure *you* are well enough to be in class?"

"Still have a bit of a cough."

An explosive demonstration of which, caused Secora to answer, "Okay then, we have a textbook in that class. Maybe you should take another day off too. Both of you should stay home and move ahead with reading up to chapter five in the book. Then quiz each other about the salient point in each paragraph. That way you'll both be prepared for the test I'm giving on Friday." She smiled as the boy captured that thought.

"Oh, okay, Dr. James, thanks. See you Friday."

She scratched her head and returned to the stack of papers, when she noticed the secretary was just setting her purse and coat down on her desk.

"Really sorry to be so late, Dr. James. It took longer than usual to get the baby ready for daycare."

"It's fine Martha, breathe, it's not a big deal. Get settled in, I'll be working on requests. She turned back and added, "I'm expecting a visit in a couple of minutes from the head of the Psychology department, oh and there's a letter to mail if you don't mind."

"Ok, thanks for the heads up. I'll do that and send the visitor in when he arrives."

BY THE TIME Tarkio and Bill reached the river scene, there was only one individual digging in the soil. Deputy Khiergan pulled up, and as he got out of the car, he said, "Good morning, boys."

"Good morning, sir, sorry to get you out so early."

"I like being out and about – beats desk work."

Tarkio sidled over. "The email we got said that fossils had been exposed in that cutbank across the river and fossil hunters were mobbing the place. But we've only seen this one person."

"Maybe the fossils ran out?"

"Maybe, or maybe there were none to begin with. Either way, Bill and I were wondering how we were going to get across to the other side to take a look. We really didn't think that through."

"Guess it's a good thing I brought a raft."

"What, really?" Bill grinned. "That is so cool."

"Yeah. Why don't you help me inflate it?"

"Sure. Do you have one of those electric pumps?"

As Khiergan opened the trunk, and said, "Yup, let's get started."

After they crossed the water and cordoned off the area, they posted a two-sided 'crime scene, do not trespass' sign.

The person who had been hanging around the site wore jeans and a hoodie, and had a huge backpack apparently in anticipation of holding masses of collected fossils. The individual had moved back from the river and watched the men pull near the shore. Then losing interest, the person wandered off upriver without speaking to them. Tarkio followed for a little way, but couldn't really get a good description. Then, Bill hollered, "Any luck?"

A woman's voice answered without turning toward them, "Mmm, not yet. Who are you guys?"

Khiergan responded, "I am Deputy Sparks, can I get your name?"

"I'm no one – just a curious student."

Bill had already squatted down and was brushing soil from something he'd picked up. Rising, he showed it to Tarkio. "Take a look at this. What do you think?"

Tarkio carefully ran his finger across the slab of shale and looked back at Bill, then both of them looked over to the disappearing woman.

Tarkio yelled, "Hey, did you pick up anything... can I see what you've got in that bag?"

The girl took off running. Yelling as she ran, "It's mine. I'm keeping it."

Khiergan asked, "What's going on?"

Tarkio said, "Something's off about this."

Bill added, "Yeah, this type of shale doesn't belong here. Kinda looks like these fossils were planted for some reason."

Khiergan said, "Maybe I should go after her. Funny, she ran off on this side of the river where there are no cars, just a deer path along the water until you get to town."

Bill said, "Maybe she was salting these in the dirt."

Tarkio added, "It might have been bait to lure us in for a dangerous reason. Good thing you came with us."

Khiergan left in pursuit. Tarkio said, "I'm calling Secora." He looked at Bill and said, "It's going to voicemail." He started to leave a message, when she called back. Tarkio put it on speaker so Bill could participate.

"Hello? Tarkio, is that you and Bill?"

"Yes, we're at the site on the river, but something feels weird."

"Hey if you find anything off – at all - get out of there IMME-DIATELY."

"Okay, got it. There was someone here, Deputy Khiergan is

chasing after her. I'll text him that we need to leave. He has to take us back to the other side in his raft. After that, we'll be history's mystery – as in outta here!"

"Let me know when you are safely on your way. I wanted to talk to you earlier... I had a hunch this might be a setup."

Bill responded, "I think you're right, Dr. James. These look like small marine fossils... in, I'm guessing, Bearpaw Shale."

"That confirms the danger, *get away*!"

"Okay, here comes Khiergan, we'll see you back at the ranch – so to speak."

When he reached the boys, he told them that she was too fast and had given him the slip.


AFTER THINKING FOR A MOMENT, Secora called Treasuremont Realty and asked if Jeannie could find out who currently owned the property at that GPS location on the Clark Fork River. She couldn't wait for the results, because someone else walked into the office. "Thanks Jeannie, gotta go. I'll check back later, or better still - text me if you can, thanks."

Fifteen minutes later she was still speaking with the FCO about the Psychology Department budget when Tarkio and Bill walked past her office. They saw she was busy, but waved inside her doorway to let her know they were safely back.

She raised a hand, interrupting the man. To the boys, she said loudly, "Let me know the details soon. Thanks, I'm so glad you're safe."

# LOOK OUT!

Gideon and Secora had been showing a listed property in the Plains area. Now, in the fading sunset, the client waved goodbye and left. With a strange look on her face, Secora turned to Gideon and said, "Think my water just broke." They hurried back to the truck and down an access road on the way to the highway that led to Missoula.

It had seemed like a good idea for them to go on this outing together, to get Secora away from her stresses and worries. Although it was evening and they were miles away from the hospital, she was beginning to feel excited about becoming a mom. But things turned ugly on the access road when they had a blowout in the right rear tire. It was tough to retain control of the vehicle on the old, cracked pavement. Gideon sounded frantic, "These are new tires. Something is off."

As he pulled over, and turned off the engine, he noticed it was now pitch dark outside. The moon had yet to rise. Then he noticed a roaring engine and headlights closing in on them quickly, from behind. A shot rang out.

"Get out Secora. We have to leave the truck. *Now*." He dashed over to open the door and led her off into the darkened brush toward an obscured ravine to get out of the path of the lights.

"Oh my God," moaned Secora.

Behind them, they heard the truck leave the road and follow them to the ravine's edge, then three doors of a pickup opened and slammed.

Gideon's eyes strained to focus as he jogged along a deer path that wandered to the top of the gully. He dialed Kyah and quietly let him know they needed help ASAP. "Bring Penny."

WHEN KYAH RECEIVED THE CALL, a muffled voice gave coordinates for a rescue. As the caller hung up, he realized it was his uncle who was in dire need and his blood ran cold. Penny was watching him with concern while Kyah put a call into the sheriff's department where he gave the information to the clerk. A deputy was on his way. Next, he called his friend Garrett Mackay, fed Penny, got dressed, and grabbed his day pack adding a banana and a cup of yesterday's cold coffee as he raced out the door. After depositing the gear and Penny in the car, he hesitated, shook his head, and ran back in to grab his rifle and set it on the passenger seat.

WHOEVER WAS behind them kept firing shots in their general direction. Gideon and Secora were dodging bullets, moving from bush to bush, running for their lives. She was hurting with regular contractions and he was panicked. Hiding behind the tumbleweeds wouldn't be good enough. Eventually, they would catch up. Gideon tried to get her to climb a small hill out of desperation. It was the only thing he could think of, perhaps there were places to hide up there. Suddenly, the thought of a pack of dogs treeing a mountain lion came to his mind. When the cat ran out of rocks to climb, it sometimes climbed a tree on the top – nowhere else to go. Giving the dogs and the hunters an easy target in the end.

He turned to check on Secora's progress, and noticed she had stopped about ten feet back. He tried to encourage her but she didn't look good. She was doubled over and when she looked up her lips were blue.

"Honey, we can't stop here. At the very least we need to reach those rocks about fifty feet away. Maybe we could hide from those wild bullets. She moaned in response, "Can't move... contraction...."

"Let me try to carry you."

Lightning danced across the road, thunder rumbled, and she growled, "No... Can't believe this is happening here. Please go, Gideon, one of us should live."

At a complete loss, Gideon knelt beside her and made sure she focused on her breathing.

He was sure she already was, but he didn't know how else to help. To make things even more uncomfortable, the rain began to pour from the skies. In some ways it seemed refreshing but it was cold. Worse, Gideon could no longer hear how close their pursuers were.

He began to quietly chant. "He-a-hey, hey-a- hey. Grandfather, I offer up everything to you. You are the Source...You are the end. We thank you for all you have given us. We thank you for this child. We will care for it as long as we can, then ask that You take him tenderly into Your care when the time comes."

Suddenly, Gideon thought he heard something else. *Heyoka, the nestling is coming. So am I.*

"I have to push... it hurts."

"Concentrate...focus."

"O.K.A.Y.Y.Y."

He thought he heard another gunshot and bent lower as lightning flashed several times, pirouetting with the ground. Thunder roared and rumbled. It was then Gideon heard and felt the presence of White Feather.

*A predator is very close to you. That one is mine to take.*

Gideon's heart sank at the thought a killer was already so close, and because of the impending loss of life. *Thank you, great protector.* To Secora he said, "White Feather says there are only two attackers left."

Secora screamed as she pushed with all her strength. *"Ahhh..."* Set her jaw and pushed again. Gideon caught Steve on his way into the world, protecting his head and tiny body from the dirt and scratchy sagebrush debris, and the cold rain. It must have been a shock for the newly entered being because he cried out - daring the rain or anything else to stop his entrance.

"Grandfather thank you for the birth of this precious child."

Secora added weakly, "Thank you, Source of all beings. Welcome, Steve."

Gideon held his breath as he heard the approach of running boots.


KYAH HAD DRIVEN past Gideon's truck, noticing the flat tire. Determinedly, he moved the car smoothly forward, like water – dodging rocks, brush and other obstacles, following the GPS signal from his uncle's Satfon – away from the road. There was a ring of dawn-light edging up from the horizon, and he could see a backlit hill in the distance. *Uncle would head for cover,* he thought. He proceeded carefully, though he could see almost nothing. Suddenly, the rain poured in a stream. Kyah turned on the wipers and soon saw another truck, dark, looming about 30 yards ahead. If he continued to drive forward, he would be an easy target in deadly territory. There was no way to tell what was ahead. Penny looked intently out the window. She knew something was off.

"Girl, I can't make it to my uncle in time. Will you help me? Penny's eyes never left the shadowed earth when she barked. Kyah gave the command "Search for Uncle," and opened the car door. The dog evaporated into the rainy gloom. Grabbing his pack and rifle, Kyah quietly closed the car door, and tried to follow. He had progressed nearly 500 hundred yards toward the hill when he heard the siren of the Deputy's car.

"Thank you, God," escaped from Kyah's lips. Then he heard two voices only fifteen feet to his left saying: "Are you kidding!" They weren't voices he knew.

"How'd they find us?"

Kyah bellowed. "Drop your weapons and hit the ground!" The men complied and Kyah called the deputies to apprehend the suspects, whom they cuffed and took back to the squad car.

SECORA SHIVERED. "We have to keep the baby warm."

"I know." Gideon cuddled Steve inside his coat.

"I love you Gideon."

"I know." His tears joined the rain.

There was sudden movement right beside them and Secora yelped despite herself. Fear faded slightly, as Penny sniffed Gideon's face. She barked twice, signaling Kyah as to her whereabouts. The sound of two sirens could be heard - way too close. Secora asked, "What if they don't stop and run over us?"

How could Gideon respond? He put his arms around her, and together, the three of them made the best of their circumstances. Penny left and soon returned with another dog and two men. The storm along with the backlight of dawn pretty well obliterated their flashlights, so Garrett nearly stumbled over them. Once he caught his breath he patched in to the ambulance crew, and fed him the information about the birth and current status of the small family.

It was tough for Gideon to reach up because his cold wet clothing clung to his skin, and bound his limbs to him, but somehow, he grabbed Kyah's other hand and thanked him. Kyah bent down and hugged his uncle, while Garrett continued to monitor Secora.

**Steve was** still crying but paramedics who just arrived seemed to be tending his every need. Secora and Gideon were still mumbling prayers. Within fifteen minutes they were all on the way to Community Hospital, shivering from the ordeal.

It took time to get them checked in at the maternity center, and Secora was feeling frozen. She shivered so hard she wondered if her clacking teeth might break. She knew part of that was the adrenaline. Gideon was also shivering, and tried to smile though he looked drained. Their soggy clothing was eventually traded for scrubs, and they were given heated blankets. After another few minutes, the shivers became intermittent. Secora delivered the placenta and the couple was moved to an observation room while the neonatal nurses looked after brave little Steve.

Kyah called Gideon to update him about the two assailants who were captured. They had been questioned about the purpose of the attack and whether there were others involved. They mentioned that a fellow by the name of Robert Greenwood had a daughter who had hired them to "make sure Secora was punished" for the death of her poor father... who would get no other justice.

Kyah continued, "The Missoula Police arrested Tanya Lambert for conspiracy to commit murder, but they never found the third guy. Don't suppose you know what might have happened to him?"

Gideon took a deep breath before answering. "Maybe."

"Just... maybe?" Kyah laughed, and they continued to talk for almost half an hour. He said he wouldn't be coming into the hospital because Penny and Sally had managed to get bad chills from the outing. They both needed to be rubbed dry, and get some rest. "Garrett is already asleep in the second bedroom, and I'm afraid I can feel a cold coming on."

Gideon advised, "I hear that! My wife is making me use one of her Zicam swabs. I'll bring you one... oops, no, don't have a car."

Kyah laughed, "Never mind. She's already bought boxes for me, Tarkio, and Bill. I'm covered. Don't you have insurance that covers towing? Give them a call."

Gideon sneezed a couple of times. "Thanks for everything, Kyah, I'll do that."

# CELEBRATE 129

S ecora woke from a deep sleep, remembering she had been given something to help her rest. She saw Gideon crumpled in a big chair, still snoozing. At least she hoped it was Gideon. The figure was all covered in blankets. Then she remembered Steve was with the nurses, and pressed the buzzer. It seemed like forever, but at last a man came in with the baby wrapped in a tight little cocoon.

"Here you go mamma. He is doing just fine."

As she received the child, she noticed her breasts were leaking milk, and asked, "Can I feed him?"

"It will be another few hours before we can be sure the sedative has broken down and is completely out of your system. But, don't worry, we are making sure he is fed until then." As he left, he added, "I'll have someone show you how to use the breast pump in a few minutes."

Gideon was rousing. He came to take Steve from Secora – eyes glued to the new spirit. There was a knock on the door, then Destiny, L.W., and Sage entered. For the time being, Jimmy stayed with little Apawi out in the waiting room. Sage and L.W. were in awe of the newborn and the desperate situation of his birth. Secora could tell Destiny was grinning beneath her mask as she held Steve. Everyone wore masks, gowns, and gloves to protect the little one.

L. W. hugged her daughter. "So grateful you are okay. But be careful, your immune system has been severely challenged."

"Right, can you get some more Zicam swabs for Gideon and me, as a preventative?"

"Sure, I'll check with your nurse first, to see if it would be safe for your baby."

"Thanks for thinking of that, Mom." They held each other as they hadn't in a dozen years. Neither wanted to be the first to break away, but Sage came over to get his chance to hug his weary daughter. L. W. said to Sage, "Okay, your turn, but it's my turn with little Stevie." Secora felt refreshed and renewed by their love.

Her parents and Destiny said brief goodbyes, so the next group of visitors could get a chance. Aparu and Kantun entered with Jane and Iris. Aparu gave Secora a doll made from brightly painted corn husks, and Kantun had a beautiful little painted bowl for Steve. Iris flounced onto the bed with her sister, while Jane offered Steve to Kantun and Aparu. Jimmy, who had been in the waiting room with his infant son, Apawi, traded off with Destiny and joined them for his turn to meet Steve, and offer a greeting prayer.

Finally, it was Mitch and Jeannie's turn to meet Steve. They brought Alai and Monta in to congratulate the new parents. Monta couldn't take her eyes off her brother. "I'm a big sister now." Alai had her sit next to her, while Mitch placed the baby in her arms. She began to sing a little song to her brother, with words that no one recognized.

Alai suggested, "Perhaps it's a tune she remembers from her birth mother – or Auntie Teresa."

Jeannie told Secora they had set the date for the family gathering six days from today. Mitch boasted, "We've invited *everybody!*"

Gideon winced and Secora laughed. Within six hours after all their wonderful guests left, the new family was back in their home, sleeping.


A KNOCK on the door eventually woke Secora. Too tired to dress, she decided to answer it in her nightgown. "Who is it?"

"My name is Salwa Ahern. I am one of your students and I came to bring a present for your child."

"Could you please leave it by the door? I don't have enough energy for a visit today. Perhaps tomorrow would be better, Salwa."

"I have already waited a long time. Too many months."

"Months? What do you mean? I didn't have any summer classes. Perhaps you have me confused with someone else."

"No. I know that you had something to do with the death of my brother."

Secora couldn't think of anyone she had killed – this summer or any other. "I am at a loss, why do you think that?" She took a moment to peek out the den window, and noticed the back corner of a white pickup with a dented tailgate. Adrenaline caused her heart to pound.

"Why don't you come out and face me?"

"Perhaps I will. What was your brother's name?"

"Mosa. You killed him in a *cave* in the Ennedi, then made up a story blaming an imaginary beast. I am here to avenge my brother. I am your death, *cave monster*."

Steve started crying, and as Secora left for the crib, six shots pierced the front door, then a seventh shot seemed final.


GIDEON HAD HEARD part of the discussion and became alarmed. Quietly he grabbed his rifle and slipped out the back door. When the woman fired through the door, he yelled "No," and shot the attacker in the arm which held the pistol. As he took away the gun, Gideon screamed, "Secora, Secora please be alright? SECORA..."

The splintered door slowly swung open, though Secora didn't show herself, at first.

"Yes, Love." A moment later she came out when she heard Gideon talking to the police on his phone.

Secora knelt beside the woman. "I have a towel to cover your wound." After a moment she added, "You're wrong in your assumption. We all cared about your sweet brother, and we grieved his loss. I think the funeral was recorded, maybe we can show it to you. That cat killed him in the daylight. Unusual in so many ways. It must have been his time. I guess you didn't stay to see the pictures of the animal. I didn't lie."

Sirens could be heard down the block and soon the police pulled in, followed by the ambulance which pulled up right in front of the steps. Gideon moved to his wife's side. "You, okay?"

Secora, felt overwhelmed. The tears flowed while she rested her head on his shoulder. "Thank you, Love."

As the woman was cuffed in front, because of the injury, she looked remorseful and said, "Perhaps I had it wrong. If so, may Allah forgive me."

Secora responded, "Allah is merciful to all. The hard part is forgiving ourselves. Mosa was a good man. It's easy to see why you miss him so much. When you're alone, things can become twisted in your mind. For what it may be worth, I forgive you Salwa. I can't speak for my husband, however... well... he has to fix the door." She tried to smile. "This is a lot. God be with you."

Their statements were taken, and then they were left in silence. Steve had cried himself back to sleep. As they looked at him in the crib, Secora whispered, "Thanks son, for getting me to move out of the way just in time."

Gideon smiled, "I guess he was born in a sacred manner. Can't wait to see who he becomes."

"Thank God Alai took Monta to Mom and Dad's house for a few days."

"That will give me time to get the door fixed."


FOR THE SAKES of the new moms, Jeannie decided to have this gathering of friends and family at Sage and L.W.'s place on the hill, rather than take the usual climb up the mountain. From here, they still had a great view of the area. It turned out that it was probably the only home far enough out of town, where a large teratorn might be welcome, but Gideon doubted she would come. Secora scolded, "Are you kidding? Wouldn't White Feather honor your 'nestling'?"

As if in answer, the gigantic teratorn circled lower and lower, totally awing the crowd. Gideon squinted and saw there was something in her beak.

White Feather landed on Sage's roof, so close that a few people were blown back by the force of her lancing wings. She raised her red feathered crest as she turned her head toward the 'nestling' then dropped the offering – a large dead fish, probably some sort of lake trout. Gideon bowed, picked it up and gave it to Sage to take to the house, while poor little Steve desperately tried to get his eyes to focus on the gigantic blurry being in front of him. Gideon heard in his head *Hetchetu yelo, so be it.*

The End

www.ingramcontent.com/pod-product-compliance
Lightning Source LLC
Chambersburg PA
CBHW061142170626
46809CB00003B/956